Love Walked In

Also by Sarah Chamberlain

The Slowest Burn

Love Walked In

A Novel

SARAH CHAMBERLAIN

ST. MARTIN'S GRIFFIN
NEW YORK

This is a work of fiction. All of the characters, organizations, and events portrayed in this novel are either products of the author's imagination or are used fictitiously.

First published in the United States by St. Martin's Griffin, an imprint of St. Martin's Publishing Group

EU Representative: Macmillan Publishers Ireland Ltd, 1st Floor, The Liffey Trust Centre, 117–126 Sheriff Street Upper, Dublin 1, D01 YC43

LOVE WALKED IN. Copyright © 2025 by Sarah Chamberlain. All rights reserved. Printed in the United States of America. For information, address St. Martin's Publishing Group, 120 Broadway, New York, NY 10271.

www.stmartins.com

Library of Congress Cataloging-in-Publication Data

Names: Chamberlain, Sarah, 1987– author
Title: Love walked in : a novel / Sarah Chamberlain.
Description: First edition. | New York : St. Martin's Griffin, 2025.
Identifiers: LCCN 2025007534 | ISBN 9781250894748 (trade paperback) | ISBN 9781250894755 (ebook)
Subjects: LCGFT: Romance fiction | Novels
Classification: LCC PS3603.H3368 L68 2025 | DDC 813/.6—dc23/eng/20250321
LC record available at https://lccn.loc.gov/2025007534

The publisher of this book does not authorize the use or reproduction of any part of this book in any manner for the purpose of training artificial intelligence technologies or systems. The publisher of this book expressly reserves this book from the Text and Data Mining exception in accordance with Article 4(3) of the European Union Digital Single Market Directive 2019/790.

Our books may be purchased in bulk for specialty retail/wholesale, literacy, corporate/premium, educational, and subscription box use. Please contact MacmillanSpecialMarkets@macmillan.com.

First Edition: 2025

10 9 8 7 6 5 4 3 2 1

For every single friend I've made in the UK over the last eighteen years.

Home is where I want to be, and I know I'm already there.

A newspaper man I knew, who was stationed in London during the war, says tourists go to England with preconceived notions, so they always find exactly what they're looking for. I told him I'd go looking for the England of English literature, and he said:

"Then it's there."

—Helene Hanff, *84, Charing Cross Road*

Love Walked In

CHAPTER ONE

Mari

As soon as I saw you, I knew a grand adventure was about to happen.

I looked up at the gray stone facade of Ross & Co. and shifted the straps of my overloaded camping backpack, a smile forming on my lips as I remembered Winnie-the-Pooh's immortal words.

This was my first time in England, but it felt familiar to me just the same. This place had lived between the covers of so many books I'd devoured from practically the moment I'd learned to read, a world I could escape into whenever I'd needed, on good days and bad.

To my kid self, England was Pooh, Paddington, Mary Poppins, and as I got older, it was Dorothea Brooke and Bridget Jones and the heroines of dozens of Regency romance novels.

And London? London was the beating heart of it all, the capital of the world, full of possibility.

Now I squinted through the city's drizzle. Speaking of English novels, Ross & Co.'s facade gave strong *Rebecca* vibes. Gothic turrets and extravagant medieval-style carvings on the front of the building made me think of a rambling great house like Manderley, not a humble independent bookstore. There were *gargoyles,* for God's sake.

This late afternoon in early January wouldn't have been out of place in a Gothic novel, either. Dark coats and pale faces flowed past me on the sidewalk, phones pressed to ears or gripped tight in hands. Heads down, brows furrowed, mouths closed.

> *The cold winter wind had brought with it clouds so somber, and a rain so penetrating, that further outdoor exercise was now out of the question.*

I shivered. It was one thing to read Charlotte Brontë's description of British weather, another to experience it for myself. For a split second I missed the bright colors of Orchard House Books, the closest thing I had to a home. The little store in Loch Gordon, California, had warm yellow walls and deep-blue trim, neon-pink camellia bushes blooming by the front door, and a store cat, a fat orange tabby named Emperor Norton, who was probably snoozing in the sunny patch on the front porch right about now. Best of all, it had Suzanne, my purple-haired mentor and my favorite person. She'd taught me most of what I knew about bookselling, and after I turned Ross & Co. around, she was going to retire and turn over Orchard House to me.

But Suzanne was the reason I was here in London at all. Ross & Co. looked warm, too, the tall front windows glowing gold in the twilight, and I had almost two decades of experience working in bookstores and an MBA. I was going to give this beautiful old building a bright new future, and I needed to stop imagining myself inside a book. Go see what I was up against.

I tried to push the feeling of missing Orchard House away, the same way I pushed away any emotion that wasn't helpful. Away with the fear that I could mess this up, away with the suspicion that I just might be in over my head. Sure, this place was twice the size of anywhere I'd worked before, and decades older. But a bookstore was a bookstore, right? I'd helped four other stores become more profitable in the last four years, what was another one?

I readjusted the load on my back, about to cross the street.

"Excuse me," a British woman said, almost knocking into me. She said it in a snotty tone that sounded a lot more like *Fuck you*.

"Sorry about that!" I called after her, trying to balance out her bad energy. But she had a point. I needed to be inside that building with the Ross family, figuring out how to get their store back on track.

When I opened the wooden double doors, a blast of dry heat greeted me. My hairline exploded with sweat as I unzipped all my layers as fast as I could and tugged my T-shirt away from my chest. There was central heating, and then there was stepping into an oven.

Once I was a little more comfortable, I could take the place in. Straight ahead of me was a spiraling staircase, burgundy-carpeted steps leading down to what must have been a basement and up to more floors. A wooden counter to my left held a computer monitor that looked over a decade old, no one behind it. I leaned over the counter and saw an old-fashioned wooden desk chair, a battered gray laptop, and an open sketchbook full of delicate pen-and-ink drawings: a black cat pouncing on a dragging piece of string, a girl winding up to kick a soccer ball, another girl wrapped around a cello almost as big as her. The pen was uncapped so it looked like whoever was drawing had just stepped away for a second.

Figuring the artist would come back soon, I meandered around the space. In the center of the main room was a round table piled with books, with a sign on top saying "Mr. Ross Recommends." A personal touch, how nice. But I didn't recognize any of the titles. Mr. Ross seemed to have a thing for polar exploration, Trollope, and biographies of famous artists. It was an interesting collection, but not the most up-to-date.

I wandered through each room on the ground floor, trailing my fingers over the old tobacco-colored wood of the shelves. The air was a little stale, but I could still smell the enticing aroma of books, the vanilla-y sweetness of aging paper. The old-fashioned light bulbs gave everything a golden tint that LEDs couldn't match. My fingertips revealed that everything needed to be dusted, but I could feel that someone had loved these nooks and crannies once, even if the selection on the shelves was like the recommendations table in the entrance—it really needed to be culled and reorganized.

I smiled a little to myself. I wanted to revive this place, nurture it the way my mom had rescued dying plants and brought them back to life with warmth and water and attention. Suzanne had told me once that books actually needed human touch to stay intact, needed to have their spines bent and their pages turned.

Speaking of human touch—where was everybody?

I saw a few people with old wooden carts stocked with books, but if they were employees, they didn't act like it—they didn't even look up as I moved past them. There was being distracted, and then there was slacking on the job, and this felt a lot more like the second one.

When I arrived in the empty Natural Science section, I stopped and just listened.

Ross & Co. was hushed, and not in the focused, everyone-is-contemplating-good-books way. It was quiet the way a graveyard was quiet. I climbed up to the next floor, looking from side to side, seeking any sign of life. Finally, in the Lifestyle section I saw an older woman in a hooded black parka quietly standing and reading an enormous cookbook. But she put the book back, then slowly shuffled toward me and then past me down the stairs, not saying a word.

For a second, I wished for some of Suzanne's sage to burn. There was a seriously bad vibe lingering among the tables and shelves, of long-term illness and decline. I thought of what she'd told me for years: that the beating heart of a bookstore wasn't the books, it was the people who sold and bought them. Without people, the books were just stacked piles of nothing, gathering dust.

Maybe the shop needed a test. I always liked visiting my old friends, anyway. Something about holding a copy of a favorite book, running my fingers over the spine, flicking through to a familiar scene, grounded me in a place. Nothing made me happier or more at peace than

Francie Nolan reading a library book and eating broken peppermints on her fire escape, or the three Fossil sisters escaping to the English countryside to camp out together. I trotted back down the stairs to see if the doodler was back behind the front counter.

My feet slowed, stopped, as I took in the man who'd made the little drawings. Silver threaded through his messy black hair, and the bookstore's warm light glinted off the lenses of his browline glasses. The long fingers of one hand cradled his cheek as the other hand moved across the notebook, but the resting pose was deceptive. His eyes were totally focused, his mouth pursed in concentration.

He was handsome in a starving-artist kind of way, quiet and intense . . . but as I looked, I realized with a pang that the emphasis was on the "starving." His oval face was too drawn, his olive skin sallow, and the shadows under his eyes deep and dark, like his last full night's sleep had been a very long time ago.

My first urge was to tell him gently to head home, eat a hot meal, and go to bed early, that tomorrow was another day.

But that wasn't my job right now. My job was to see what I could do to get this place back on track, then make suggestions to the three Rosses I was supposed to meet later today.

"Hi," I said cheerfully as I walked up to the artist. "Can you help me?"

He froze, then looked up at me, his eyes narrowed suspiciously as he capped his pen. "Possibly," he said in what sounded like a fancy accent, the same way the woman on the street had said "Excuse me."

"Snooty" was not a vibe I liked in customer service. It

didn't help that he was wearing a black button-up shirt that made him look like a hipster undertaker. My eyes zeroed in on the top button. Who buttoned the top button of their shirt when they weren't wearing a tie? It was the fussiest thing I'd ever seen.

I waited, propping up my bright smile on sticks, for him to say something else. A welcome to the store, even an apology for not noticing me before.

Nothing.

The smile was on the verge of falling off my face, but I wanted to give him the benefit of the doubt. "I'm looking for something," I said, emphasizing my uncertainty, giving him room to step in and, you know, *help*.

He stood, and now I was looking up at him. But that wasn't saying much for his height, given that I was only five foot three. "Aren't we all?" he sighed as he stretched out his narrow back.

Yeah, I wasn't looking for a philosophical answer, here. "It's called *This Wallflower Breaks Hearts* by Beatrice Dashwood."

"Is that a bodice ripper?" he asked skeptically.

Oh, for crying out loud. Reading romance had given me so much joy over the past decade that I had no time for people's crusty old ideas about the genre. I mean, Americans were still making references to Fabio, and he hadn't been on a cover for thirty years. My smile turned into a grimace for a second before I forced out a cheerful "That's not the term we use for romance novels nowadays, given that it's pretty sexist and rapey, but yes, it is."

His shoulders straightened. "Well, we don't stock *romance novels*."

I stared at him in disbelief. "Why not?"

He folded his arms. Behind his glasses, his eyes were almond-shaped and a brown color as flat as his voice. He was the dismal January afternoon in human form. "We're not that kind of shop."

I hadn't been dismissed so callously since my last girlfriend had dumped me seven years ago. My hands clenched on the straps of my backpack. "Then you're missing a trick," I said, trying to keep warmth in my voice, anger out. "Romance is the biggest-selling genre in publishing, and it's only getting more profitable. Haven't you seen the news about social media driving demand?"

He shrugged. "We don't pay much attention to fads, and romance novels aren't what our customers want, anyway."

No wonder Judith Ross had asked Suzanne if I could come help for a few months, if this was the employees' attitude to selling books. "But it's a chicken-or-egg problem. As long as you don't stock romance novels, romance readers won't come to your store."

He shook his head and said slowly, like I was a kid, "We serve a different clientele."

I dramatically looked from left to right. "Your clientele is definitely different. Are invisible shoppers a thing in England?"

"Miss," he said, like the honorific was rotten in his mouth, "I don't know what you want, but you're clearly not going to find it here."

I could feel fire building in my chest, waiting for me to breathe it at this pain in the ass, but I wasn't going to win friends with vinegar. "Look," I said tightly, "the bookstore I work at in California has a whole case of romance novels, and we're not exactly bringing down the town's tone, so maybe it's something you should consider. Even a shelf to start with might help?"

All of a sudden, his mouth gaped and his eyes widened. "Wait, you're American."

My eyebrows shot up at his appalled face. "It took you this long to notice my accent?"

"And you work at a bookshop in California." He closed his eyes like I'd stabbed him. "Your name's not Mari Cole, is it?"

"Sorry to be the bearer of bad news," I said, a little bemused at his discomfort.

He buried his face in his hands and groaned something that sounded like "Fuck my life." Then he dropped his hands and said flatly, "I'm Leo Ross, the general manager. I would say I've been expecting you except . . ."

"You weren't," I finished for him. But he wasn't what I had expected, either. This hipster mortician dickhead was Leo Ross? The manager of the whole store, and one of the owners? The one I was meant to work closely with for the next ninety days of my one wild and precious life? Disappointment cramped my stomach. It was like I'd been promised a bowl of ice cream and served soggy broccoli instead.

Obviously I wasn't going to be friends with him.

But I'd only been in London for three hours. I had to make the best of it, despite the jet lag starting to play a loud drum solo in my skull. I forced one more smile and said, "Maybe we got off on the wrong foot?" *No maybe about it.* "It's nice to meet you, Leo." *Lie.* "Could you tell me what I'm supposed to be doing for the next three months?"

He was quiet for a second, and I hoped against hope that

he'd tell me that the last five minutes had been a gruesome nightmare from the pit of my insecurities. But he shook his head. "I'll take you up to the office, and Judith can tell you what she was thinking."

Judith, his step-grandmother and Suzanne's friend. Not him. *He* didn't want me here.

I ignored the shrinking feeling in my chest, the urge to curl up in a ball so I'd inconvenience him as little as possible. Instead I put on my biggest smile and swept my arm grandly. "Lead the way, Your Highness."

CHAPTER TWO

Leo

How embarrassing that Mari had caught me scribbling in my notebook instead of working. Though drawing was the only refuge I had from the pig's breakfast I'd made of my life. I ended most days face down on my mattress in my childhood bedroom, which I was back living in at the age of thirty-one because my wife had left me for someone else. I'd be utterly drained, my stomach in angry knots from too much caffeine, not enough food, and the knowledge that I had to keep returning to the shop day after day, be reminded again and again and again that my grandfather was gone and I was lost.

Mari's warmth, her cheer . . . it was borderline offensive, made more so by the fact that if I'd met her two years ago, before Becca left and Alexander died, I might have liked it. Might have shook her hand hello, asked her about her reading and life in California and what she was looking forward to in London.

Instead, I silently led her up the spiraling oak staircase that made the spine of the shop, climbing up two floors and then ducking around a corner into the Religion section, then left around the last bookcase full of Buddhist and Hindu texts to the khaki-colored metal door with "Employees Only" on it. As I punched the code into the mechanical lock, I snuck another look at the woman who was supposed to be our best chance to keep Ross & Co. open.

She was going to freeze to death, wearing those clothes.

First of all, the Converse would be an utter disaster. I had a pair of canvas high-tops deep in the back of my closet, plain black instead of her purple with rainbow (*rainbow!*) laces, and I knew they were only good in an English summer, on a day when it wasn't raining. They'd be sopping wet in a second, beyond saving in a minute. On the other hand, her iridescent silver puffer jacket was meant for trekking to the North Pole, not going in and out of heated shops and suffering London's drizzle. She was already showing the effects of our temperamental thermostat, her round, pale cheeks flushed, a delicate sweat on her hairline.

As if she sensed my thoughts, she took off her rucksack, enormous jacket, and the ocean-blue jumper underneath, revealing a brilliant yellow daffodil with a saffron heart unfurling up her forearm, and a short-sleeved forest green T-shirt that stretched across her... My eyes snapped up to her face, and my cheeks warmed.

It was the colors that made me notice her, I told myself.

The blues and greens and yellows of her. Not her curves, not her peaches-and-cream skin. I hadn't looked at anyone like that in eons.

Now I saw her hazel eyes glance around, and for a moment, she looked uncertain, shy, a new girl on the first day of school. An effect that was amplified by the long chestnut-brown braid that dangled over her shoulder, flickering with bronze and copper.

I could tug it, not too hard, just enough to make her forget her nervousness.

I pressed 5 instead of 8, mumbled "Stupid" under my breath as I punched the Clear button. Where the ever-loving fuck had *that* thought come from? Nowhere mature and sensible, that was certain. Mari blinked and gave me that toothy grin again, a reminder that she was here because I hadn't had anything resembling confidence in donkey's years.

"Everything OK?" she asked lightly.

Now I remembered I had bigger problems than one can-do American and successfully unlocked the door. "Fine, thank you."

I hadn't had any ideas for how to improve our sales, let alone good ones, in what felt like eons. So when Judith had told me six weeks ago about her old friend Suzanne and Suzanne's protégée Mari, who was something of a bookshop whisperer, I had absent-mindedly agreed that an outsider might have fresh ideas for how to turn the shop around.

I marched up the last staircase, this one lined with pictures of the three generations of Rosses who'd run the shop. Great-Grandfather Leopold in a three-piece suit and fedora in front of Rosenbaum Buchhandlung on

Friedrichstrasse in Berlin, before he'd seen the writing on the wall when Hitler seized power. He'd moved his shop and his family to London, changing our name to Ross in the process. Then Alexander at the height of his powers in the rust-toned 1970s, thick black hair and sideburns, arms folded and grinning widely in front of a display of signed bestsellers. I didn't touch the frame like I usually did when I was alone. I couldn't be seen to have that kind of silly superstition.

Then me two years ago, aged twenty-nine, smiling and a little distracted, unburdened even though I was carrying an armful of art books, totally unaware of the hurricane of loss about to rip me apart.

"In here," I said to Mari, who was sizing up the photographs.

"You guys have a real history," she said wonderingly. "I've never been to a family-run store that's lasted this long." She pointed at the picture of Leopold. "He founded the store in Germany, what, ninety years ago?"

"One hundred," I said. "The anniversary's this year, actually."

She glowed in the dim light of the staircase. "That's *incredible*. You know that's incredible, right? You definitely should do something to celebrate."

For a moment, I wanted to bask in the warmth of her compliment. Leopold had restarted the business from scratch after he fled Germany, been interned as an enemy alien on the Isle of Man at the start of the war, and still managed to create a British bookselling institution. But then I sighed. Mari wasn't wrong, but the thought of celebrating when the life force had gone out of the shop and out of me made me want to lie on the floor. "Possibly. Come on, my father gets impatient."

When we walked into the office, my father immediately stood up from my chair and said loudly, "What kept you? I have better places to be, you know."

"We know very well, David," Judith said from the chair beside the desk. "But you own a share of this place the same as we do, so why don't you greet our American guest politely?" She stood slowly, the grimace on her face telling me that her arthritis was particularly vicious today. "Welcome," she said, reaching for Mari's hand while she leaned on her stick with the other. "I'm Judith Ross. Suzanne has sung your praises for so long, I feel I know you already."

"Suzanne exaggerates, but I'll take it," Mari said warmly as she put her things down and shook hands. "She tells great stories from when you two were at Oxford together."

"We got into a lot of trouble back then, yes. Usually at her instigation," Judith said dryly.

"Oh, I find that impossible to believe."

Mari winked and they smiled at each other, a delightful little conspiracy already forming between them, and no, I did not feel a twinge of jealousy at being on the outside of it. Judith hadn't said a word to me about her life before Alexander until he'd died, and even then it was only vague glimpses of parties and debates and endless piles of books for her politics, philosophy, and economics degree. But how much curiosity had I actually expressed?

"I'm David," my father said impatiently. "I own a share of the shop, but I'm normally running my own political communications firm, so I won't be very helpful. You'd best address your concerns to Judith and Leo."

"But you're part of the history of the shop, too, right? Leo was telling me you're celebrating your hundredth anniversary this year," Mari said, smiling bravely.

"Yes, yes, we're very old and prestigious, and we're also on our way out," my father said. "I don't know why we keep going, when we know bookshops are fighting over the scraps Amazon is dropping from the table." He made a show of checking his watch.

Mari held her hand up. "May I explain?" she asked, and I marveled at her daring. When Judith nodded, Mari put her hand in her pocket and said, keeping the same calm and easy tone, "I started working officially at Orchard House Books when I was fourteen years old, and I became the store manager four years ago. I have a bachelor's in English literature with high honors from Huntington College and I studied for my MBA at Sonoma State at night while working at the store. In the past four years my initiatives have increased Orchard House's revenue by eight percent year on year, and I helped four other California bookstores come up with similar ideas. Long story short, I know a fair amount about this business." She looked my father in the eye. "Yes, Amazon is really, really good at piling them high and selling them cheap, metaphorically speaking. When they entered the market, it was like when deep-sea trawlers started vacuuming up the ocean. All the fish, from the sharks down to the minnows, got outcompeted on sheer volume." She turned to Judith and to me. "But stores like yours can play a different role."

"What are we if not a business?" I asked, a little exasperated.

"You can be a refuge."

I stared at her smiling face like she'd spoken Martian.

"Refuge" wasn't a word Alexander ever used in relation to the shop. "A what now?"

Judith gestured. "Tell us more, Mari."

"The problem with Amazon is that it's purely transactional," she began. "We've ended up in this terrible alienated place where everyone's an individual consumer, and we've forgotten how to *be* with other people. But indie bookstores can be community hubs, the place people come to buy a book and linger for a while, talk, maybe buy a cup of coffee as well as more books than they planned to. And we can do stuff for our neighbors. We run storytelling hours for little kids, we collect used books for our nearest food bank to give away, and we run a big book festival every May to raise money for this amazing free creative writing workshop for local teenagers. We're a business, but we try to be a force for good, too."

"Sounds to me like you'd rather run a charity," my father sneered. I didn't like his tone, but I still agreed with him.

"Seriously?" Mari snapped. "OK, let me put it in blunt terms. You need repeat customers. You need *customers*, period. And right this second, I can see why you don't have any. You have apathetic employees, out-of-date stock, and shelves covered in dust." She shook her hands emphatically. "It feels *dead* down there."

Judith gasped slightly, and I swallowed hard, again and again, my eyes finding my shoes so Mari wouldn't see my hurt.

Mari's face was suddenly stricken, and she clapped her hand over her mouth. "I'm so sorry. That was a thoughtless thing to say. I know you guys lost someone recently."

Judith shook her head. "Thank you for your apology,

Mari. And yes, we miss Alexander dearly. But we have to carry on without him, don't we?" She stared at me, but I could only bring myself to nod.

"I know you love this place," Mari said gently. "The way I see it, my job is to help you remember exactly why, and to figure out how we can get other people to love it too."

"That sounds good to me," Judith said. "David? Leo?"

My father shook his head, a grimace twisting his face. "My father loved it, but he shared that with Leo. Not me." He grabbed his coat and his briefcase. "This place could close tomorrow, as far as I'm concerned. I wouldn't mourn it." He stalked past Mari, not responding to her "Nice to meet you," and the office door slammed shut behind him.

"Wow, tell us how you really feel," Mari muttered at the closed door. She turned around and looked at us. "Do you two want to sell, or close? Because you don't need me for that. I'm in the business of keeping stores open, not shutting them down."

"No," I said, the denial coming from deep inside me, the place where missing my grandfather hurt the most. "Never."

Mari nodded. "Well, that's something. What about you, Judith?"

Judith reached for my hand and squeezed it. "I want whatever Leo wants." A burst of affection filled me, and I squeezed back.

"And can David decide anything unilaterally?" Mari asked.

"No," I answered. "Alexander left him forty-five percent of the store, and the same to me. Judith holds ten percent."

"My widow's portion," Judith said wryly.

Mari rubbed her eyes. "Wow, old-school, OK. Even though David hates this place?"

Judith shook her head. "I suppose Alexander hoped he'd return to the shop if he knew he had a say in its future."

"So much for hope," I muttered. Dad and Alexander were both too bullish to make for an easy reconciliation. It was simply easier to go along with what Alexander wanted, because he had almost always been right.

"All right, well, now I know I need to be working with the two of you," Mari said with forced cheer.

But Judith shook her head. "I'm not involved in the day-to-day operations of the shop." She held up her stick. "I'm afraid my arthritis can't handle all the standing and the up-and-down stairs. But I trust you and Leo will work together for the good of the business."

I folded my lips together at that bit of emotional manipulation. I knew that Mari wasn't just a young, bright-eyed bookseller. She was our Han Solo, the brash heroine swaggering in to save the day. I knew we needed someone like her. I just wished with everything I had that we didn't need *her*. My nerves were already on edge from her color and energy and confidence and she'd only been here for twenty bloody minutes.

"Of course we will," Mari said, a hint of a question in her tone. She raised her chestnut eyebrows at me, and I couldn't help but take her skeptical expression in. She had a long, full nose and a mouth that was borderline too large. A mouth made for smiling, whether joyfully or mockingly. Her hazel eyes danced with specks of forest green and rich deep brown, and I thought for a moment of a wood nymph out of a Pre-Raphaelite painting. That's what she would look like with her hair down, sweetly chaotic and not a little bit sensual.

I just barely resisted the urge to smack myself across the face. It had been forever since I'd been touched, let alone attempted to have sex with anyone, and there was no reason for me to lose any sense of self-discipline now. "Certainly," I said to Judith.

Mari rubbed her eyes again. "This is going to be a fun challenge, but it's going to have to wait until tomorrow. I've been awake for twenty-four hours, and I feel like someone's been pushing my Off button for the past twenty minutes." Her wide mouth stretched in an enormous yawn.

"Oh, of course," Judith instantly said. "Why didn't you tell us sooner? You must be exhausted from the journey."

Mari's smile was strained. "No problem. But if you could point me in the general direction of where I'm staying?"

"Leo can show you," Judith said, gesturing to me. "You're just upstairs in the garret." She smiled. "It's where the family lived when they first moved to London from Berlin. I hope you find it comfortable."

"I'm easy," Mari said. "As long as it has somewhere I can be horizontal and unconscious, I'll be happy." She shouldered her rucksack, grabbed her puffer and jumper, and raised her chin at me. "After you."

As we climbed up the last narrow flight of stairs, Mari's massive pack bumping against the walls, hurt and fear snarled up inside me. She'd pressed on the bruise that wouldn't heal, the feeling that I'd left the shop to crumble. But I couldn't bear to touch what Alexander had left behind. My grandfather had been gone for eight months, but I felt his warm, charismatic spirit in the walls, on the shelves, on every step of the staircase.

I couldn't let her change things. I wouldn't.

CHAPTER THREE

Leo

"Where are you going?" Mum asked, her voice still soft with sleep.

I sighed with my hand on the brass doorknob of our front door. I thought I'd successfully crept down the stairs from my bedroom in my stocking feet so as not to wake anyone up, but my luck continued to be abysmal. "I'm off to meet Vinay," I said, keeping my voice down so I wouldn't wake my father or the girls.

She glanced at the grandfather clock in the hallway. "At half six?"

"It's the only time we're both free." It had also been the time that Vinay had informed me I couldn't possibly be busy. I'd been making excuse after excuse for six months, pleading tiredness, distraction, busyness. Never saying the real reason, that I didn't want him to see how every day for the last year had felt like pushing a massive boulder uphill.

Mum nodded eagerly. "I'm glad. I'm glad you're seeing him. You should ask him and his wife round for Shabbos again. He always makes things livelier."

I grimaced. My misery didn't love company. My misery wanted to be curled up in a corner, facing a wall. "Sure, I'll ask him." I turned back to the door, hoping and praying she wouldn't ask what I knew she wanted to know most.

"Have you eaten?"

Of course she couldn't resist. *"Mum,"* I groaned.

She put her hands up. "I know I shouldn't ask, I'm sorry, but you look haggard."

She thought I hadn't looked in a mirror lately? Hadn't seen how knackered I was? "I'm *fine*," I snapped. "We're meeting at a caff, there'll be food there."

"All right. But I'm your mum, and I worry." She reached into her dressing gown pockets, took out a glossy red-and-green apple and a protein bar. "Just take these with you to eat on the way? Please?"

I couldn't repress a sigh at the sight of the emergency rations. I'd spent enough time in hospital as a small child because of food, and I didn't like being treated like a patient again. But I reached out and took them anyway, to see my mother's face relax, her shoulders drop. "Thanks, Mum." I bent down and pressed a kiss to her cheek. "I'll be back after dinner. Don't wait for me."

And I tried to eat on the walk to the Tube, I did. I managed one big bite of the apple and half of the protein bar before my stomach cramped. I shoved the bar in the outside pocket of my backpack and left the apple where the local squirrels could find it.

Half an hour later, I was sat across a table from my best friend, nursing a milky coffee while he waited for his veggie fry-up. Thankfully he'd only given me raised eyebrows when I hadn't ordered food.

"What have you been up to?" he asked, leaning forward a little.

I felt my shoulders go up an inch. "The usual. The shop, home, shop again."

"Sounds thrilling." He paused, then said, "Sonali and I saw Bex . . ."

"No," I said automatically.

Vinay sighed. "She didn't bloody evaporate when you split up. She's the same as she ever was, except she . . ."

I couldn't hear it. I couldn't hear how well she was doing without me, I would *scream*. "What part of 'no' did you not understand?" A surge of frustration twisted in my chest as I remembered Mari's frank assessment of the state of the shop. "Why is everyone suddenly acting like they know best and I don't?"

"Because you look like week-old shit? So forgive me if I think you're a bit of a walking disaster."

I had nothing useful to say in response to that, so I put my head on my arms and groaned instead. "I've forgotten what it's like to sleep through the night. And I don't want food."

He nodded. "I know. You were always like this during exams, a ball of stress. But that lasted a week or two. It's been months, Leo." He hesitated, his mouth moving silently, before he said, "You know you can talk about things with me?" He played with a sugar packet, staring at it instead of making eye contact. "I know we were a foursome, Sonali and I and you and Bex, but I thought you'd still be my friend after it all ended. The breakup was what you both wanted, wasn't it?"

If you could say Becca begging me to let her go because she had fallen in love with someone else was mutual. I'd been a rubbish husband in every way that counted, and the least I could do was let her be happy.

But if I had to explain to my friend exactly how I'd been to blame for my marriage ending, there wouldn't be a hole deep or dark enough for me to crawl into.

I stared into my coffee as the server delivered Vinay's breakfast, and he ate a forkful of beans and hash brown before he said, "I actually wanted to chat to you about something for work."

I blinked. "What about work?" He'd worked for a commercial real estate firm for years, but he'd always waved away any polite questions about what he did, saying that it was too boring to talk about when there was football and telly and books.

"My bosses are looking for buildings to turn into flats," he said now. "Particularly for wealthy students coming from abroad. One of the higher-ups went for a walk around Bloomsbury and saw Ross and Co. Was talking about what good bones it had."

I half choked on my drink. "They want to buy the building? Tell them they can fuck right off."

Vinay put his hands up and shook his head. "No, listen, listen. I'm just meant to see how you're all feeling. Now I know about you, so it's fine. I'll just tell them no. David and Judith are on the same page, yeah?"

All at once I was grateful my father wasn't here for this conversation. But he couldn't do anything about it on his own with his 45 percent share, and Judith said she was with me. "As good as," I lied. "And we have an American consultant who's just arrived; she's going to help us turn things around, come back from the losses on the Covent Garden shop."

His eyebrows rose. "A consultant? One of those suited types? I'm surprised you can afford one, or that they'd work with just one bookshop, as prestigious as Ross and Co. is."

I snorted involuntarily. Mari, with her wild chestnut hair, worn jeans, and floral tattoos, was about as far from a "suited" type as we could have gotten. "Not quite. Mari's more of a . . . bookshop whisperer, I suppose. Wanders around, observes things, makes suggestions." More like constructive criticisms, but Vinay didn't need to know that.

Now Vinay's smile brightened. "Mari, hmm? Is she pretty?"

Involuntarily I remembered hair that shone with auburn lights, deep hazel eyes, a smile that promised mischief. I shook my head at myself. "She's temporary. Going back to America in April."

Of course he saw right through that. "So yes, she's pretty."

"She's . . . cheerful," I conceded. "But mouthy. Confident, to the point of arrogance, the way that Americans all seem to be."

He whistled as I took another sip of my coffee. "Mouthy and arrogant? You sound like you're about to complain about her being overpaid, oversexed, and over here."

My spit take sprayed brown droplets everywhere. "Fuck, don't *say* things like that."

"Wasn't that the phrase, though, back in the day?" His smile fell away, and he leaned forward. "If keeping the shop's what you really want, that's what you should do. Even if it means dealing with an obnoxious American." He tilted his head. "But if you might want to do something else, you'd tell me, right?"

I blinked at him. "What else would I want to do?"

He rested his chin on his hand. "You're still drawing, yeah? I think you'd be shit hot at art college."

I winced a little as he hit the bull's-eye. Art college had been sixteen-year-old me's idle dream, before Alexander had sat me down and explained that I could always make art as a hobby, but that if I really wanted to secure the future of the shop, I'd go to uni and read something useful like accounting instead. Which is exactly what I'd done.

"Even if I wanted to do that, I'm far too old to study again," I said now. Any dreams I had, of traveling the world, of going to art college, were just that, fantasies, insubstantial and meaningless. My cause now was to preserve what Alexander had left me.

Vinay glared at me. "Mate, you're *thirty-one*. You're not decrepit, unless something happened to send human life expectancy back to the Stone Age."

I knew I was only thirty-one, but I'd been working in the shop for half my life, already been married and divorced. Every morning when I looked in the mirror, I found new gray strands in my hair. "Fine, but I'm still not selling."

Vinay checked his watch. "I knew you wouldn't want to, but I had to ask. And now I can tell my boss I did."

He stood up, reached over and patted my cheek lightly. "Next time you take a day off, text me, yeah? I'd like to think we're not boring old men who can only talk about our jobs."

I wanted to object to being called "boring," but instead I smiled wanly. No wonder Judith had wanted to call in bright and chirpy Mari. Who'd want to buy books from me?

CHAPTER FOUR

Mari

Jet lag. Such a boring name for something so totally evil. I'd blinked awake in the depths of the night like I'd had eight hours' sleep, but it was only three fifteen. I'd paged through the sixty-year-old copy of *The Bibliophile's Guide to London* I'd found by deep-diving on eBay, five pages of which were dedicated to the wonders of Ross & Co., the brilliant double act of Leopold and Alexander curating their Aladdin's cave of literary treasures. I'd trailed my fingers over the illustrations of the store as it was, packed floor to ceiling with the latest books and wall to wall with eager customers. I'd thought maybe I could bring a little bit of that energy back to this tired place.

I'd collapsed back into sleep, the book on my chest,

only to wake up what felt like thirty minutes later, sweaty and strung out. A hangover without the party.

I took the pillow, wrapped it around my head, and groaned into it. Sleep-deprived was not how I wanted to start my first full day at Ross & Co. It didn't help that the mattress was thin enough that I could feel the slats of the bed frame digging into my back, and that a chill lingered in the air, like the walls weren't as much of a barrier to the winter outside as they should be.

I shoved the pillow off my head and inhaled deeply, feeding my tired brain oxygen. I wasn't feeling great right now, but a hot shower and a steaming cup of coffee loaded with sugar would make everything better.

When I was clean and dressed, and feeling a little more ready to take on Ross & Co., I boiled water for instant coffee and looked at my phone.

Shit, I had a voice note from Walker.

Warily, I pressed Play. His surfer's drawl told me he'd missed making my oat hazelnut latte for the last few days, and how much he'd liked the last book in the Daevabad trilogy, and he asked if I could recommend him more things like that. After a long pause, he'd also said he'd missed me last night, describing in vivid detail exactly what sexy things he wanted to do to me when I came back from England.

I sighed and pinched the bridge of my nose, then typed a quick text telling him about Katherine Arden's trilogy set in medieval Russia, but I didn't mention anything else he'd said, the dirty talk or the missing me.

This was why I'd tried not to mess around with people who lived in my small town. When I was feeling fidgety, I usually drove over to Napa and picked up a tourist for a quick oxytocin boost. But I'd had a little bit of a thing for Walker in high school, and when his longtime girlfriend had moved to New York without him and he'd asked if I wanted to hang sometimes, I couldn't resist his bright green eyes and easy smile. We'd been fuckbuddies for the last six months, but now I hoped he would take the hint that I didn't want anything else from him. My life was better if I kept both my feet on the ground, my expectations of relationships low. The last time I'd pinned my hopes on someone, she'd treated me so badly I *still* felt embarrassed at my own stupidity.

Now I closed Walker's messages and checked the time: seven thirty. The shop opened at nine, so this was a good moment to wander around the store before anyone else got here.

Once I'd braided my hair and twisted it into my usual bun at the nape of my neck, I stepped out of the attic, and the damp, cold air instantly sank its teeth into my bare skin. I dove back into the room and grabbed the bright blue sweater I'd worn yesterday and the hibiscus-pink scarf Suzanne had knit for my Chanukah present one year. Now I looked like an Easter egg, but at least I was warm. First order of business—figure out where the thermostat was. I sipped the black coffee I'd laced with three spoonfuls of sugar to make it not taste like burnt sadness, still wincing at the acrid flavor. Second order of business—buy oat milk.

After I'd found the thermostat on a random wall in the science section and converted my idea of room temperature from Fahrenheit to Celsius, I sat down on the single wooden chair in one corner and submerged myself in the silence of the store before opening, sending out positive thoughts into the empty space. Imagined hearing cheerful voices here again, books sliding off the shelves into eager hands, paper bags opening to hold purchases. For a split second Leo Ross's weary face, his pursed mouth, his stiff movements popped into my head. I couldn't help but compare the man now to the candid photograph of him on the upstairs wall, with his armful of art books and his mouth turned up in a smile. It had been a shy smile, tentative, but it still lit him up. What would it have been like to work with that Leo?

Grief wasn't strange to me, and obviously he missed his grandfather a lot. I would have to be a little more careful to get him on my side, help him see what needed to change about this place. Maybe I could put that smile back on his face again.

I heard the scrape of a metal gate lifting and jogged downstairs to the main floor to investigate. By the time I reached the bottom of the steps, the wood-and-glass doors had opened, and a tall blond man was closing them, his black wool back turned to me.

"Hi," I said, and the man jumped sky-high. He pressed his hand to his heart as he turned around.

"Fuck me," he yelped. "Gave me a start."

He wasn't the only one. His accent was different from Leo's, rounder and less crisp, but if it weren't for the twenty-first-century clothes, he'd look like he'd stepped out of a Renaissance painting. His nose was long, his mouth was wide, sensual, his short blond hair full of sunlight.

I'd never believed in the cliché about time stopping when you meet someone, but if I'd spilled my coffee and the drops floated in midair, I wouldn't have been surprised. The man's cornflower-blue eyes were wide as he stared at me, equally stunned.

He was beautiful, but more than that, he was *familiar*. Orchard House had always had some British tourists come through the door on their daytrips to wine country, but it was pointless to rack my brain. I knew I'd have remembered this man. I'd never bought into Suzanne's astrology charts and colorful array of crystals, but I was having a feeling I could only describe as *eerie*.

"I *know* you," he said through my thoughts, his high forehead furrowed.

I blinked. So I wasn't the only one wondering if there'd been a wrinkle in time. "I don't think so," I said, my voice a little shaky.

We stood there, staring at each other. It was absurd. Of course we'd never met before. I clapped to break the spell and said warmly, "But we can absolutely fix that. I'm Mari."

He shook his head hard. "Of course. The American who's here to help. I'm Graham, the nonfiction buyer." Suddenly, he giggled a little to himself.

"What?" I said, confused.

"Honestly, I only had the one pint last night. I shouldn't be seeing things." He stared at me intently. "Are you *certain* you've never been here before?"

I shook my head. "Never been out of the US, and I have the brand-spanking-new passport to prove it."

"That's so *strange*. But anyway, Leo messaged me last night and said I should keep an eye on you. Show you the way we do things."

I repressed a groan. Because I obviously wasn't trusted to wander around on my own.

"Come on, then," Graham said. "I need my coffee first."

I followed him across the main floor as he threw on light switches, then unlocked another "Employees Only" door. Inside was a lousy excuse for a break room—a metal table with two folding chairs sitting catty-corner to each other, a gray love seat that looked like it belonged to an office lobby in 1991, and a short counter with a microwave, a sink, and an electric teakettle. The air smelled vaguely like tomato soup and the same instant coffee I was struggling to drink.

"So, Graham, how long have you been working at Ross and Co.?" I asked as he filled the teakettle with water.

He leaned back against the counter. "Two and a half years? I started when I was in my last year of uni and I've been here ever since."

"What made you decide you wanted to work here?" I told myself I needed to learn about him to understand how he fit into the store, but the sense that I knew him from somewhere was still itching away, and maybe if I scratched it, this would all make sense.

He rubbed the back of his neck shyly. "Honestly? I was here most days anyway, because my girlfriend at the time worked here. I just wanted more chances to snog her. But Leo's grandad, Alexander, found out I was reading history and politics at UCL and insisted that they needed my expertise." He shrugged. "The relationship didn't work out, but I really liked being here. The first year was really lovely. I learned a lot from Alexander about all the publishers, what people from the different unis liked. I liked being surrounded by all these books. And I like having more time for my own stuff. I'm in the middle of my PhD and I have a bit of space for research and writing when I'm not here." He chuckled a little. "Besides, where's a better home for a swot like me than a bookshop?"

I couldn't help smiling at him, laughing too. His warmth made it impossible to resist. "You said your first year working here was lovely. What changed?"

The teakettle boiled, and Graham turned away from me, the smile sliding off his face. "Alexander, Leo's granddad, died eight months ago. It was a shock."

I swallowed hard. I knew something about shocking deaths. I pushed the image of my mom in her hospice bed away. "It was sudden?" I asked, keeping my voice even.

"Yeah," Graham answered, then his voice faltered for a moment. "I mean, he was in his eighties, it wasn't like he was young. But he acted years younger than he was. He was vital, I suppose. Dynamic. The lifeblood of the place. And then he had a heart attack one night, and he was gone."

"What's been going on since then?"

His mouth twisted. "Not much, as you've probably noticed. Leo's a good egg, but since Alexander died, he's just been sitting still. Doesn't want us to touch anything." He sighed. "He and the old man were thick as thieves, and I think he's a bit lost without him. We all are."

Which would explain the tension and stress written all over Leo's body. "So how many people actually work here?"

"We had to cut back on staff when the other shop closed—the Rosses lost a lot of money when that went." He opened his hand. "Right now we have Izzy, Jonathan, Sayeeda, and Neil, each coming in three days a week to sell books," he said, tapping his fingers while he named them. "Catriona and I are here five days a week. I handle all the science and social science buying, she buys all the fiction and children's books. And Leo is here every day, it feels like, handling everything else—art, cookery, sport, you name it."

The nonexistent romance section niggled at my brain. "It'd be good to meet Catriona, if she's coming in today. The fiction section definitely needs some love."

"Grammie, where are you?" a grumpy Scottish voice called now. "We have a shop to open."

Graham groaned. "Yes, she's in today. *Unfortunately*."

A six-foot-tall woman shoved the employee door open and glared at us both. Her frizzy strawberry-red curls were half-contained in a bun, the other half flying every which way. I could see her waving a sword and leading an army of burly men with blue-painted faces.

"You must be Catriona?" I tried.

"I am, yes." Her sharp accent gave a new meaning to "businesslike." "And you're Mari, the new girl who's come to turn the shop around. Best of luck with that. Now, if you could stop flirting, Grammie, we have work to do."

Before my eyes Graham's body language transformed, became rakish, borderline louche. "You know me, sweetheart," he said with a toothy smile totally unlike the one he'd given me, his accent suddenly stronger. "Can't help myself, now can I?"

"Someday soon, *sweetheart*, you won't be able to play the cheeky chappie and charm your way out of work," she replied coolly.

He shrugged. "But I'm so good at it, and you make work about as appealing as a soup made out of haggis and Irn-Bru."

She sniffed disdainfully and walked out the door

without responding, but the acrimony and not-funny teasing lingered in the atmosphere. The charming grin had fallen off Graham's face the second she'd turned her back.

"Am I right in thinking that's the relationship that didn't work out?" I asked carefully.

"Well spotted," he said, shuffling his feet like a contrite teenager.

"I'm guessing it wasn't that . . . amicable?"

He stared into his coffee mug. "As amicable as it could be when one person got a lot of attention just walking down the road, and the other person was so jealous she wouldn't listen when I . . ." He shook his head and said bitterly, "When *he* tried to reason with her."

Graham's voice was light, but it was a paper-thin cover—his shoulders were hunched, his eyes downcast. It was a weird feeling, to feel sorry for someone for being too pretty for his own good. But lost love wasn't my business, Ross & Co. was. "I guess that's a compliment to the store, that you're both still working here in spite of that," I said thoughtfully.

"I suppose. Or just a comment on how stubborn we both are. What about you, then? Pining for someone back home?"

I rubbed the back of my neck, thinking fleetingly of Walker's puppy-dog eyes. "Nope. Not the pining kind." More the love-them-and-leave-them kind. I didn't let myself catch feelings for anyone, but I needed the occasional human-assisted orgasm just like everybody else.

"Lucky you." His lady-killer smile came back online, and I grinned back. But some lingering sense of weirdness made me ask directly, "Was that smile just a reflex, or do you actually want to flirt with me?"

He sized me up for a moment. "No," he said wonderingly. "I don't. You're fit and all, but it just . . ."

"Feels wrong?" I filled in.

He nodded, and the weirdness surged back full force for a second. Then he took a big sip of his coffee and asked, "Now that we're definitely just going to be mates, can I give you the full tour, new girl?"

I pushed away the sense of déjà vu and followed him.

CHAPTER FIVE

Mari

We walked through some of the rooms I'd seen before, but Graham colored things in for me and told me more about the history of the shop. He pointed out the framed and labeled photographs hanging on the walls of the sections of famous novelists, historians, travel writers, most of them with Alexander shaking their hands. In one picture, an older Alexander was clearly telling a story to John le Carré while holding a skinny black-haired boy on his lap. The little boy was leaning into Alexander's chest, and I felt a pang at the security, the sweet trust that the camera had captured. But I thought I recognized the thick glasses and the beginnings of high cheekbones. "Is that . . ."

"Leo, yeah," Graham said. "This place was his nursery.

Alexander liked having him around, teaching him little things."

For a split second, I remembered my mother's arms around me when I was that age. That sense of trust and safety, gone. I'd had nearly two decades to live with that loss, and those hugs had been few and far between anyway. But Leo had lost that sense of safety so recently.

"And now we get to go to the best part of the shop," Graham said, and I slotted that thought away for later.

He led me all the way back down the staircase, into the basement I hadn't explored. "Catriona and I have our differences, but I can't deny that she's brilliant at selling books," he said. "Lovely taste in music, too."

I stopped to listen. It was Billie Holiday, asking softly if she was blue. The melody twined around me like a friendly cat, reminding me so much of Orchard House on a rainy day, Suzanne playing crackly old records on her hi-fi, that I was . . . choking up?

No, I couldn't be homesick. I was having an adventure, there wasn't any room to be homesick. I guessed I was feeling tender after seeing the picture of little Leo and Alexander.

We followed the notes through cluttered rooms that got smaller and smaller, until we arrived at a doorway that said "Gallery" over it in worn gold lettering. When we passed through, it was like we'd walked into someone's living room. The music floated from what looked like an ancient record player, a dinged-up wicker box next to it full of sleeves.

There were two squashy chintz armchairs, a little worn and cat-scratched, sitting around a big coffee table, a scattering of classic novels calling to me to pick them up and sit in one of the chairs for a spell. If I squinted, I could tell that this section had the same under-stocking problem as the rest of the store, but someone had taken the time to make a virtue of the empty space, to turn it into a kind of salon.

Catriona glanced up from behind a register, which sat on top of what looked like a Victorian teacher's desk decorated with white Christmas lights. "Ah," she said, a small smile on her face. "I see you found my hideaway."

I turned in a circle, taking in the cozy space. "It's beautiful," I marveled. "You've done an amazing job."

Her ears turned pink. "It's no bother," she said a little shyly. "It was sitting empty when I first got here and Alexander said I could try to do something with it."

"I mean, you totally have, it's incredible. How much did it cost?"

"Basically nothing."

"Nothing?" I blurted, astonished.

"Never doubt a Scot's ability to squeeze a pound until it screams for mercy," Graham said with a grin.

Catriona rolled her eyes. "And never doubt a Cockney's ability to fall back on regional stereotypes. It's all Facebook Marketplace," she explained. "The furniture, the record player, all of it was going to the tip before I rescued it. You'd be amazed at the things old posh people in North and West London want rid of. I fix up what needs fixed up, cover up what can't be fixed, and there you have it."

I observed Catriona with new appreciation. Behind her sharp tongue and no-nonsense attitude was someone who got a lot of fulfillment from making things nice for other people. It was like finding a gleaming geode inside a forbidding piece of rock. "Damn, you're talented," I said, meaning the praise.

She didn't respond, just smiled and looked down. Maybe that was enough compliments for today, before I killed her with sheer embarrassment. "So you remember how it was before Alexander's death?" I asked.

"Of course I do," she said bluntly. She paused for a second. "It was a really good place," she said more gently, "when Alexander ran it. He was a big personality, but he had a way with customers, to make them feel welcome and to encourage them to buy books they might not have bought otherwise." She sighed. "I suppose you could say he gave this place heart."

Clearly those days were over, and everyone had lost that heart. "How did Leo feel about everything you did here?"

"I suppose he was a bit skeptical at first, but he was really happy with the result."

The wheels were turning in my brain. "OK," I tried, "then why isn't the rest of the shop like this? It's warm, it's welcoming, it would make people want to stick around."

Catriona shook her head. "We were talking about it, but it was right before Bex . . ."

"Cat," Graham said sharply.

Flickering expressions and turned-down mouths telegraphed silent messages back and forth between the exes, and after a few seconds, Catriona rolled her eyes. "Before it all went wrong," she finished.

"Now it's too much like change for Leo," Graham said with his hands open.

Catriona nodded in agreement. "He's got so much else on his plate. I don't want to push him."

It seemed like Leo Ross was both the master key and the unbreakable lock, too. "It's time for honesty," I said, putting my hands in my pockets and trying to sound both warm and businesslike.

Catriona snorted, but I continued firmly. "Judith brought me here to give an outsider's perspective on what's wrong with the store. I have some thoughts already, but I want to hear from you."

The two of them looked at each other for a long time, until Graham finally said quietly, "We're doing the best we can, but after Alexander died, it's like we all got untethered. It's not what it was."

"It started before that, Grammie," Catriona said. She looked at me and folded her arms. "Alexander had very strong ideas about what he wanted on the shelves. And he was slow to return books that had been gathering dust for ages."

That would explain the piles sitting in front of the shelves. If you only had a certain amount of space, you had to return older books to the publisher regularly to make room for new ones. "Are you behind on your invoices to publishers, too?"

They both nodded. "Seems so. Leo's been meaner with our buying budgets," Catriona said. "But you'll need to chat to him to get the full picture."

"I'll do that. Is Leo equally slow to do returns?"

Graham rubbed the back of his neck. "Yeah. It's like . . ." He paused, sighed. "Like he wants to leave things as Alexander had them. I understand he's hurting, but I know it's not a good thing, either."

I exhaled. No wonder Judith had wanted to bring me over. I knew the Rosses were unhappy, but they obviously needed an outside person who wasn't emotionally tied up with this place.

I leaned forward, making eye contact with the two booksellers. "Look, I think we can put this place back on track." I patted one of the shelves. "It has good bones. But we need to think about what Ross and Co. could be, not what it was."

A pause while they took my words in. But instead of nods, I got an uncertain look from Graham and a downright skeptical one from Catriona.

"You make it sound so straightforward," she said, implying that it was as straightforward as a hill full of switchbacks. "And I know Americans have all this can-do attitude, but don't be surprised if Leo's allergic to it." Suddenly Catriona sat up in her chair, and Graham straightened where he'd been slouching against the shelves.

"Good morning," Leo said behind me. "What am I allergic to?"

I turned around and casually shoved my hands in my back pockets. "Good morning," I non-answered.

He squinted suspiciously at each of us in turn, and my muscles tensed in preparation for having a more serious discussion right off the bat. But he only said, "We open in fifteen minutes. I take it everything's ready, if you're chatting down here?"

A stupid part of my heart felt sad at how he looked even more tired than he did yesterday, like sleep was something he'd loved and lost a long time ago. But the patronizing way he said "chatting" made me want to stick pins in a little Leo-shaped doll.

He turned and walked out without waiting for an answer, and Catriona and Graham followed him like ducklings, me trailing behind. When we got to the main floor, Catriona turned into the fiction area while Graham gave me a wink and continued climbing upstairs. Leo paused for a second, taking what looked like a deep and necessary breath.

Why did he already look so exhausted?

"Are you OK?" I asked gently. "Something on your mind?"

His eyes snapped open and his shoulders hunched. "Nothing. And I'm perfectly all right."

His curt tone was as good as a hard shove. Clearly his state of being was none of my business, even if his words didn't match his weary expression. "Cool, cool," I said, forcing good cheer. "I'd like to help out today. Where do you want me?"

Leo's eyes narrowed as he considered me, and out of nowhere I felt the urge to squirm. I hadn't been looked at like that since my stepfather, Greg, moved away, like he wanted me to disappear but needed to think of a second-best option. I made a point of not being a burden to anyone these days, but I'd been here less than twenty-four hours and this man with a permanently furrowed forehead and prematurely graying hair had already decided I was one. I needed to show him I could be helpful. "I could look through the piles of books on the floor? Or see if there are any books you should pull from the shelves?"

"Pull?"

"For returns. Do you have boxes? I could start putting together some boxes to ship back to the publishers. It'll make more room and you can get some money back. Is there a section that you'd like me to focus on?"

His headshake was so strong it was almost funny. "No, absolutely not. I don't want you to touch any books at all. No returning anything. Just . . . watch. Shadow the others, take notes, try not to get underfoot."

So much for having worked in bookstores for fifteen years. "As you wish."

Westley had never said those three words to Buttercup with so much sarcasm. But Leo didn't even bother responding, just turned around and walked away fast, mind already on another problem.

I spent the morning moving around the shop. An hour sitting next to Graham on the second floor. Or the first floor, he explained to me, because the first floor was the ground floor in England, bizarrely. An hour with Catriona in the basement, flicking through one of Patricia Highsmith's books about Tom Ripley while Catriona served a grand total of three customers. An hour on the main registers with Leo, where I switched between studying the bookstore's database to see how long books had been sitting on the shelves and staring out the tall windows at the gray day outside. People strolled by, but only a few people stopped to look at Ross & Co., and fewer came through the doors. Idle curiosity was the lifeblood of a bookstore, what turned a day without buying a book to a purchase, what turned a trip to buy just one book into two or three.

After a sad lunch in the break room (a surprisingly expensive tuna fish sandwich from the chain place around the corner, and a good reminder that I needed to buy groceries and make my own sandwiches), I wandered up to the first floor and found an older man looking uncertain in Military History. He was wearing a beige trench coat that wouldn't have looked out of place in a spy novel, and he had a corona of white hair around a freckled bald spot. I took a step forward to help.

"Don't," Leo whispered right in my ear.

A gasp jumped out of my mouth. "Jesus." I pressed my hand over my heart and glared at him. "What the hell?" I whispered.

He hissed, "You were about to go talk to him, weren't you?"

The way he said "talk," like it was a dirty word. "It's called customer service. Look it up."

He looked over my shoulder, then his long fingers mimed zipping his lips. He pointed around the corner and beckoned.

My own mouth clamped. I hadn't done *anything* yet, and that customer was still looking lost, and now Leo wanted to dress me down for no good reason. A flash of pure cussedness made me shake my head and turn away.

He grabbed my upper arm. Hard.

My shocked eyes shifted up to his face, to his pursed lips and his determined expression behind his glasses. A wave of goose bumps rolled up my arm and across my chest. I flexed my bicep, but Leo's grip was solid for someone who looked so skinny.

He blinked, his lips parted, and in different circumstances, it might have been hot. If we weren't coworkers and Leo Ross weren't an uptight asshole.

I tugged, and he immediately let me go, his face stricken. "Sorry," he mouthed.

Fuck his apologies, especially a half-assed one. "Whatever," I mouthed back.

For a second, I saw something in his brown eyes that

looked like pain. But he shook his head once and it was gone. "Go on, then," he whispered now, tilted his chin at the old man. "Show me."

The condescending *jerk*. Indignation propelled my feet across the room to where the old man was still hovering in front of the bookcase. "Hello there, are you looking for something in particular?" I said warmly.

He turned and blinked at me. "Not really."

I waited for more words, but nothing doing. Maybe I came on a little too strong. "All right," I said, making my voice more mellow. "I'm Mari, and I'm around if you need any help."

I got a nod in response.

OK. That was fine. Some people liked to browse before they made any decisions. I moved to the other side of the room and crouched down in front of the books about Asian history. I trailed my fingers over the spines, half my brain checking whether the countries were arranged in the correct order, the other half listening to the older man shifting on his feet, sniffling, occasionally coughing. I could sense Leo's smug presence still hovering just around the corner.

Sixty seconds later, the old man hadn't moved. He wanted something, but he wasn't seeing it.

I sidled back over to him. "What do you like to read?"

He looked at me, shocked, like I'd asked which sexual position he liked.

I smiled and soldiered on. "Do you like reading about particular battles? Or about branches of the military? Army, navy, air force?"

I was about to call the conversation dead when he said, "Intelligence," his face and voice totally bland.

"Oh, spies!" I said, unable to keep the relief out of my voice. "I like reading about them, too. Ordinary people like you and me doing extraordinary things."

"Mmm," he non-answered.

It was like someone had limited him to speaking one hundred words a day, but I could work with that. "Have you read *The Confidence Men* by Margalit Fox? It's not really a spying book, more a book about breaking out of prison, like *The Great Escape*. Have you seen that?"

His brow furrowed. "Yes."

"Well, it's like that, but with Ouija boards and people pretending to lose their minds," I continued to babble, feeling more and more ridiculous with every word the man didn't respond to. "It's awesome. I think you'd love it." I leaned down and checked the shelf under *F*, but of course it wasn't there. "I'm sure we could get it for you."

"Not today, thank you," he clipped out.

His face was closed, his words coldly final, and for a second I clamped my mouth equally shut. "Oh" came out of my mouth high and tight. But I couldn't help but take one last chance. "OK, but maybe next time you visit? We should have it anyway, I can tell Leo to order a copy."

Now he wasn't nodding, or shaking his head. He was just . . . *looking* at me, simultaneously annoyed and concerned, and for the first time as an adult I felt the intensely painful urge to put myself in time-out in the corner somewhere, facing the wall.

"Well," I forced out, "I'll leave you to it."

I went back to the Asian history books, and a second later heard him leave the room and make his slow way down the stairs.

I stared blindly at the shelf, a wave of embarrassment and failure crashing through me. It wasn't just the weather that was frigid. The people here were cold, too.

"I tried to tell you," Leo said behind me, his voice weary. "But you wouldn't listen."

Hurt twisted inside my chest. He'd set me up to fail, to what, teach me a lesson? I flashed back to my eleven-year-old self, who'd misjudged the distance between two branches of the oak tree in the front yard and plunged to the ground. I'd been sitting in the dirt with tears and snot cascading down my face, holding my broken right wrist to my chest, Greg's folded arms and icy voice a shadow over me.

You won't climb that tree again in a hurry.

I couldn't paste a smile on my face right now, not with that shameful memory still coursing through me, so I stayed facing away from Leo. "Tell me what?" I said, hating the thickness in my voice that meant tears were closer than I wanted them to be.

"British people don't want to be sold to. They want to shop for their books in peace."

So no hand-selling? No learning what your regulars liked? There was no way to make a community if you *ignored* your customers.

I took a deep breath, reminding myself where I was. I was twenty-nine now, not eleven, and I didn't have to take this. "Why?" I asked as calmly as I could as I turned around.

"Why what?" Leo asked impatiently.

Clearly the prince of the store wasn't used to being questioned. "Why is being friendly to customers a problem?"

He thrust long fingers into his hair. "Because this isn't

America. We don't want people in shops to be our friends. We don't want to be chatted to, and we don't want to be pushed into buying something."

"I wasn't pushing. I was just trying to help," I said, exasperation seeping into my voice.

Leo didn't say anything, just stared at me. I felt like a small child with a dirty face and hands, Greg glaring at me while my mom tried to clean me up for his parents' weekly visit. Hoping for once I'd please them, even though I'd known I never would.

"Why am I here?" I asked, unable to keep the frustration out of my voice anymore.

Leo looked at me for a long time, and I studied him too, this rigid man impossible to reconcile with the one smiling in the photograph on the wall. For a second, I saw a flicker of an emotion besides exhaustion on his face.

I wasn't sure anger was an improvement, though.

"I don't know yet," he said finally. "So stay away from the customers, please."

Well, wasn't that the dumbest sentence I'd ever heard. "Fine. You're the boss." Or what passed for one around here.

I went back down to the basement, where Catriona was clipping pictures out of a pile of old magazines. I sat in one of the comfy chairs and took my phone out.

"Defeated already?" Catriona asked absent-mindedly.

Now was not the time to show weakness. I forced a smile and said, "Down, but not out." If Leo wasn't going to let me interact with customers, I'd have to figure out some other way to fix things.

Better to ask forgiveness than permission, Suzanne's voice said in my head. Or her favorite version, *Forgiveness, permission, etc.*

I thought of the database full of books that hadn't sold and likely never would, the piles of books on the floor. The way the old man had stood staring at shelves that didn't speak to him.

Something had to change.

CHAPTER SIX

Mari

The next day, the jet lag was even worse. My skull felt too small for my brain, my joints ached like I'd been rolled through a pasta machine, and saying I felt tired was like saying that the North Pole felt cold. But all things were possible with help from ibuprofen and caffeine. I stormed through my morning routines, propelled through showering, getting dressed, and eating breakfast by Leo Ross's know-it-all face, his self-righteous voice.

I waited until Leo was holed up in his office for the morning, then I dug cardboard boxes and tape out of a storage closet and carried them up to the history section. Last night, when everyone had gone home, I'd dug into the Ross & Co. database and printed out a list of books that had been lingering on the shelves for over a year. It was way too long for the size of the shop.

He didn't want me to talk to anyone? Fine. I'd pull books and package them to send back all on my own.

I grabbed a wooden chair that looked like it belonged in a Victorian schoolroom, sat down in front of the first bookcase, and took a deep breath.

Pulling books was always a little bit sad. When we put new books on the shelf at Orchard House, they were full of possibility, just waiting for the right reader to come along and take them home. But removing them said that right reader had never come along, and now they were just heavy shapes that needed to be stacked in boxes, fit together like a depressing game of Tetris. But it still needed to get done, no matter how anybody felt.

I'd gone methodically through three cases of books and packed a whole box to send back when I heard someone shuffling behind me.

"What are you doing, mate?" Graham asked.

Time to brazen it out. "What should have been done months ago," I said, turning to look at where my new friend was pulling on his fingers, his mouth turned down.

He took in the open boxes on the floor, the empty spaces on the shelves. "Does Leo know you're doing this?"

I raised my eyebrows. "What do *you* think?"

He raised his eyebrows back. "You're a shit-stirrer, you know that?"

"Well, you have to break a few eggs to make an omelet. And am I here because Leo knows exactly what to do and is doing it?" I gestured around me. "This place deserves so much better. It's so beautiful, and it needs to be full of customers who love spending time here, and for that it needs new books on the shelves."

Graham's mouth opened, closed. "I know," he finally said, resignation in his voice.

"So that's what I'm trying to do. Are you going to help me or not?"

He glanced over his shoulder, and I thought for a second he was going to go find Leo, or flat-out tell me to stop.

"Oh, go on, then," Graham said instead, holding his hand out. I just barely kept back a sigh of relief.

I handed him the list of books. He studied the pages for ten seconds, then tapped a row of lines, all marked with the name of a publisher I'd never heard of. "It'll help to get rid of most of the Buller Press books. Alexander was mates with the director, but no one wants to buy the memoirs of backbench MPs from the 1920s. And I say that as someone who researches political history."

I grabbed one of the books he pointed at and flipped through the pages. "Drier than the desert?"

Graham smiled. "Right."

I gently put the book in a cardboard box. "What else should I be looking for?"

We pulled books companionably for a little while, me occasionally holding up a book I wasn't sure about and Graham telling me about it, but mostly only listening to the shuffle of stacks of books in cardboard boxes and the rip of packing tape.

Eventually I stood up on tiptoes and stretched for the ceiling, my back complaining about all the crouching and bending I'd been doing.

"Do you have any brothers or sisters?" Graham asked from the floor.

I glanced down. "Nope, only child. Why?"

He smiled wryly. "You remind me of my youngest brother. Tim. He's just as pigheaded as you. He knows what he wants and goes after it, fuck the consequences." He pulled out his phone and held it up to me. On his lock screen was a picture of Graham, his arms around two teenage boys. One of them had Graham's height and golden-boy complexion, but the other was several inches shorter, his shaggy hair a sandy brown instead of blond.

And now the sense of familiarity I'd had when I met Graham came back at double the strength.

"Which one's Tim?" I asked, my voice a little tight.

Graham pointed at the shorter boy. "That's him. He wants to be an actor, and he's the lead for every single play and musical going at school." He smiled indulgently. "He drives us all a bit mad when he's rehearsing, reciting things over and over again, but he's really good at it."

It had been so long since anyone besides Suzanne had looked at me with that kind of fondness, the kind that said they enjoyed being around me even if I drove them up the wall. Of course, my mom had looked at me that way sometimes when I was little, when my stepfather wasn't around demanding her attention. But that was twenty years ago now.

What would it have been like, to have a sibling, someone who loved me unconditionally? If Greg had been able to have kids, and I'd had a little half brother or sister?

Maybe I would have had an ally.

I sensed that Graham was waiting for me to say something and bit my lip. It didn't help to let myself dwell on the past. Instead I thought about what was possible and I made it happen. "He looks like a fun kid," I said warmly.

"But I don't think it's a bad thing to want to be the best you can be. Just means he's got ambition."

Graham snorted a little as he put his phone away. "You've clearly not been in England long enough. 'Ambition' is a bad word here."

I opened my mouth to comment on the utter stupidity of that.

"*You*," Leo Ross snarled from the doorway, and my hands flailed. Graham and I both winced as the book I'd been holding landed cover up, pages splayed open and bent.

I inhaled, recovering my composure, and turned to face Leo, who was breathing so hard I was sure I could see steam coming out of his nose like a cartoon bull's.

"Yes, Leo?" I asked, my tone innocent. "What can I do for you?"

He took a step forward into the room. "I *knew* you were up to something," he said, jabbing his finger at me. "I knew it from the second you looked at me like butter wouldn't melt."

Was it twisted that I thought rage suited him? His eyes were amber, his cheeks flushed, and his spine was ramrod straight, giving him an extra inch of height.

"What the fuck do you think you're doing?" he said, his tone on the edge of exploding.

Yes, I was definitely a little twisted and absolutely not in the mood to back down. I smiled at him oh-so-sweetly and said, "Did you know that if books aren't selling, you can send them back to the publisher? Which then makes room for other books that people might buy?"

"I do know about returning books for credit, thank you," he bit out.

"Then why aren't you *doing it*?"

Leo ignored my question and knelt down on the floor, pulling out the Buller Press books Graham and I had boxed up. "You can't send these back. They're important."

"Why are they important?" I asked, like Leo was a small child having a tantrum.

He clamped his mouth shut, stacking the books into some kind of order.

"I get it, your grandfather loved them," I said, trying to keep my voice gentle. "He was friends with the publisher, Graham told me. But you can't just keep things the same because you miss somebody. I don't think that's what he would have wanted."

Graham groaned quietly and put his face into his hands. "Now you've gone and done it."

I'd never seen someone stand up so fast. "You arrogant, presumptuous . . ." Leo shouted, his face bright red and his hands opening and closing.

A big hand grabbed my forearm, and I grunted as Graham shoved me behind him. "Don't finish that sentence, mate," he told Leo.

Leo threw up his hands. "Oh, on *her* side now, are you? Bloody typical!"

With Graham's and my height difference I could barely *see* Leo. "What is your *problem*?" I yelled at him over Graham's shoulder. "Honestly, Leo. Would you have let me do this if I had asked nicely?"

He didn't immediately blurt *no,* and internally I kicked myself. Instead he yelled back, "I don't know! I honestly don't know what I would have done." He let out a sound halfway between a sigh and a growl. "But that's not the point! The point is that this isn't your shop, it's my family's.

We've been running it for a century, it's our legacy. You can't just come in all blithe and oblivious and do whatever the fuck you like."

I stepped out from behind Graham. "Sure, I can't do what I want, but when I ask you if *you* want me to do something, if I can *help*, you dismiss me." My exasperation was building, and building, and I finally snapped, "Would it kill you to make up your mind?"

He looked like I had slapped him. I almost expected him to put his hand on his cheek, to see a red mark there. Then the shock faded, leaving behind his usual tired, closed expression. "Just . . . stop what you're doing. Put the books back. We'll talk about this later."

Oh, he wasn't going to get to dismiss me that easily. I was so fucking tired of being Alice in Wonderland, being told that everything I knew about selling books was wrong and that I wasn't worth listening to. "What is the point, Leo? What is the point of this store's existence? As far as I can tell, it's a mausoleum for your grandfather's hopes and dreams, not a functioning business." I took a deep breath. "You'd rather live in the past than save this place."

Now Leo's brown eyes became a tundra in the depths of winter, icy and hard, and I fought the instinct to take cover. I was braver than I'd been as a child, when my stepfather's anger had made me put my arms over my head.

"Oh, just *fuck off*, Mari," Leo said, his voice a frozen knife in my chest.

The dismissiveness, the contempt. It *hurt*. My throat contracted, my sinuses suddenly felt hot and tight. But I couldn't let him win. The last word had to be mine. "Sounds fun," I said cheerfully, my voice only shaking a little. "Maybe later."

Then my feet carried me out of the room, down the main stairs, across the entrance hall to the wooden double doors. I had my hand on one to push it open when I heard someone skid to a stop behind me.

"Don't go," Graham said. "He'll calm down in a minute."

I gulped once, twice, but my voice still came out thin and teary. "I don't think it's going to take just a minute to calm down after you tell someone to 'fuck off.'"

A big hand reached out and squeezed my upper arm. "He needs time. Please, Mari. If you leave us now, it'll all be for nothing."

I tried to marshal up some kind words, something that would show Graham I was my usual can-do self. But Leo's anger had emptied me all out of platitudes. I had really messed things up out of sheer stubbornness, and I needed time and space to figure out what to do next. "I'm not leaving for good," I said, stating the simple truth. "Even if I wanted to, I can't afford to change my flights. I just need to get away for a second." Away from Ross & Co., away from Leo Ross, away from my stupid mistake.

Graham stuck his head out the door and looked up at the sky, his brow furrowing. "But it's freezing. And with those clouds, it's going to snow any minute."

I shivered as a strong, icy wind whirled across the sidewalk, scattering fragments of dead leaves; my joints ached and my head throbbed. But going upstairs for my silver parka wasn't worth the possibility of another blast of Leo's contempt. "I'll walk fast. Back soon."

"Don't get lost!" Graham called after me as I walked up the street.

A tiny part of my brain replied, *Too late.*

CHAPTER SEVEN

Leo

Sounds fun, maybe later. Why were Mari's insouciant words playing on repeat in my head as I stood on a Tube train heading north, like a particularly obnoxious jingle?

She had left the shop after saying them, though. And for a moment, her mouth had trembled, like her expression of bravado hadn't been earthquake-proof. That if I had said any more harsh words, she would have crumbled.

And I had been harsh. No wonder she'd gotten away from me as quickly as she could.

Something about those empty spaces on the shelves, the books Alexander had loved stacked unwanted in boxes, had reminded me too much of the empty space inside me. I knew that Mari was fundamentally right, that there would always be new books to replace the old and we needed to make room for them. But I didn't have anything to fill the gaping holes in my future, so I found myself looking backward instead, clinging to sepia-toned images of my teenage self sitting in a big leather chair next to Alexander in Tony Buller's office, wrapped in their tobacco smoke and feeling utterly safe.

Maybe I should have told her that story, instead of telling her to fuck off. Though honestly, there was no "maybe" about it. Graham had made that abundantly clear when he'd come back from following Mari.

She'd gone out without a coat in January, just to get away from me.

Now another refrain started as I left Hampstead Station, my steps on the pavement leading toward home beating out *What have I done, what have I done,* accompanying thoughts of Mari's slumped shoulders, her hazel eyes muddy with defeat.

Once I'd unlocked and opened the front door, I could smell something savory and herbal and rich wafting up the stairs from the kitchen, and my stomach cramped hard. I couldn't bear the thought of trying to eat in front of my mum right now. Maybe I'd slip down much later tonight, warm up leftovers in the microwave when hunger finally got the better of me.

I leaned against the wall and carefully pulled off my boots. If my luck were good, I could sneak down the front hallway and up the stairs to my room.

I froze when a figure appeared at the top of the kitchen stairs, then relaxed when I saw who it was. My younger sister walked toward me, tangling the fingers of one hand on the drawstring of her bright red Arsenal hoodie, her eyes totally focused on her phone.

"Soph," I whispered.

I held my arms open when she looked up, and she ran up to me, grinning. "Oof," I exhaled as she wrapped her wiry arms around me tightly.

"You always give the best hugs," my little sister said into my chest.

I relaxed for what felt like the first time today, simple affection like a balm. "You make it easy." Her long black hair left a damp spot on my chest from her post-football shower. "Good practice today?"

She smiled up at me. "Really good. We worked on set pieces and I scored on a corner kick."

I squeezed her shoulders, pride stretching my mouth into a full-on grin. "Well done." I looked behind her for her twin. "No Gabs?"

"String quartet rehearsal tonight." She sighed. "I'm glad she's out, to be honest. I've been hearing bloody Schubert in my sleep."

I nodded in sympathy. Gabi was a Level 8 musician who we suspected would have taken her cello to bed with her like her teddy if there were any possibility of playing while she slept. "What about homework, then?"

Her thick, dark eyebrows shot up. "You think they haven't already asked?"

I shook my head ruefully. "Sorry, ignore me." I knew I wasn't an ordinary older sibling; fifteen years was far too wide a gap. But it wasn't my job to be a third parent. My job was to be fun, even though it felt like someone had drained the fun out of me in the last year.

"Are you all right?" she asked, her forehead wrinkled. "Did something happen at the shop?"

How had it come to this, that I was the one who caused

all the concern? She was the teenage girl and I was the thirty-one-year-old. I should have everything figured out, not be floating in nothingness. My hand found the back of my neck and massaged the tight muscles there. But I didn't want to overburden her. "There's someone new working there. She tried to do something to help the shop without asking me first and it made me really angry."

Soph thought for a moment. "But was she actually helping?"

I sighed as she hit the bull's-eye. "Yes. I didn't like it, but yes."

I got a very teenage eye roll in response. "Then it sounds like you need to make it easier for her to ask."

"You're absolutely right." I tilted my chin toward her phone. "Show me something silly?"

She flicked through the video app she and Gabi loved. "Oh yeah," she said with a smile. "This one."

We had thirty seconds of joy as a Siberian husky dog threw a screaming tantrum at being made to get out of its owner's bed. "Thanks," I exhaled when it ended. "I needed that." Needed that burst of uncomplicated happiness.

Sophie jogged up a few steps toward her room, then turned around. "Can we go see Arsenal Women soon?" The question spilled out like she'd been holding it back for ages. "Because Dad keeps saying he'll take me, but he forgets the way he does about anything that isn't work, and we haven't gone in so long. They're playing at the Emirates more now, so we won't have to go all the way to Borehamwood."

I scrubbed my fingers through my hair, feeling a wave of regret that she even had to ask me to take her to the football, that I hadn't organized it and made it happen already. "Of course; we'll go soon."

She paused. "Promise?"

The single soft word reached into my rib cage and twisted, another reminder that I was dropping every single ball I was trying to juggle.

"Never mind," she said before I could answer. She came back down the steps and gave me another huge hug. "I love you no matter what."

I sighed, soaking in that affection while feeling like she should be giving it to someone who deserved it. "I love you, too." I held her away from me. "I'll look up the fixtures tonight and make a plan, all right?"

She nodded, but her face was more kind than eager.

As I followed Soph up the stairs, I resolved that I would be the grown-up tomorrow. I'd find Mari, apologize, actually listen to her ideas.

"Mari's off today."

I blinked at Graham, who was conspicuously looking at the register screen instead of at my face. "What?" I said brilliantly.

He glared at me as he picked up his phone and held it out. "She messaged this morning. Said she's not feeling well."

I squinted at his message chain with Mari. Clearly they'd been getting on like a house on fire if it was so long after only meeting two days ago.

Hi friend, I read. *I think I caught a bug on the plane. I'm feeling pretty bad and I don't want to give anyone else my germs, so just text or send a carrier pigeon if you need anything.*

I checked the timestamp. She'd last been seen on the app at just before 5 A.M. What had she been doing awake that early? "Has anyone looked in on her?"

"What, to make sure she's really ill?" he scoffed.

I replayed the memory of yesterday, this time muting my anger. I remembered the redness of her cheeks, the hoarseness of her voice. The way she'd been pressing her fingers to her temples like they pained her, how she'd been rubbing her arms like she was cold even though the heating was blasting away. "No. I believe her."

"Maybe you need to give her some space," Graham said neutrally. "Let her decide when she wants to talk to you again."

I rubbed my face, chagrined. "I suppose." So I had to wait to apologize to Mari, but there was something I could do right now. "I'm really sorry for what I said yesterday, when you defended her."

Graham nodded. "Thanks." He paused, then said, his voice a little awed, "I've never met anyone else like her. Have you?"

I shook my head in answer, ignoring the thin needle of jealousy in my chest at his tone. "I'm going to write returns notifications to some of the publishers," I said now. "Would you please help me pack more books when those are approved?"

His face relaxed into a smile. "Course I'll help. You only have to ask, you know that."

As I worked on my laptop in a quiet corner of the first floor, snowflakes fluttered and drifted outside the shop windows. A few bundled-up figures braved the whitening pavements, but I was fairly certain we wouldn't earn enough today to have made it worth putting the lights and heating on.

At least it was pretty.

"Hello? Anyone here?" an elderly man's voice called from the other side of the floor.

"Just a moment," I called. I cursed Jonathan's too-long tea breaks as I jogged through the rooms to the nonfiction till.

I almost tripped when I caught sight of a dingy beige trench coat I hadn't expected to see back so soon. Normally Mr. Gissing would come in twice a week to browse the history section and very occasionally buy a paperback. Alexander had always said he looked like he'd escaped from a spy novel, with his nondescript clothes, thick 1970s glasses, and general air of furtiveness.

I rounded the counter and woke up the register. "Mr. Gissing, hello."

"Hello, Leo," he said, his voice a degree warmer than usual. "Everything all right?"

Another surprise. He hadn't ever used my name before, or asked about my well-being. "Fine, thank you," I answered in the way he expected. Was he about to initiate an entire conversation? I wasn't sure I could cope with that level of unexpected familiarity.

He put his hands on the counter and leaned toward me. "Now, I've borrowed *The Confidence Men* from the library and started to read it, and it's absolutely terrific. Have you read it?"

The Confidence Men? Wasn't that the book Mari had been trying to push on him? "Er, no, I haven't."

He smiled, showing teeth that hadn't seen the best of NHS dentistry. "It's fascinating," he said, waving his hands in a positively un-British way. "I hadn't realized that there were POWs in Turkey during the Great War, let alone that they'd tried to escape. That clever young American woman makes good recommendations." He glanced around. "Is she about, so I can ask for more?"

I tried very hard not to gape at his enthusiasm. Mari hadn't driven him away. She'd been right. It'd just... taken time. I barely resisted the urge to bang my head on the counter. I'd given her so much grief for being impatient and bullish, but I'd been just as heedless and stubborn, dismissing her ideas without even giving them a second's chance.

"Mari's off ill, I'm afraid," I said finally.

Mr. Gissing's shoulders slumped a little. "Oh, well, just my luck."

I hastened to reassure him. "She's working here until spring, so once she's recovered, I'm sure she can make more suggestions." And for the first time, the thought of Mari running around the shop for the next few months didn't fill me with dread.

Optimism. It was a strange feeling.

"I'd like that," he said quietly. He looked down at his hands, covered in liver spots and greenish-blue veins. "I wanted a chance to think about it, you know. I wasn't expecting anyone to be like that with me." He shook his head. "I'm used to being invisible, these days. But I couldn't get what she'd said out of my head, about ordinary people doing extraordinary things." A sigh. "Made me miss being young, I suppose. That kind of energy, that sense that I could just do anything. But being old doesn't mean I can't enjoy things. Try to get the most out of life."

I stood there, blinking at him. It was like I'd been hibernating, and someone had shone a torch into my burrow.

When was the last time I'd genuinely enjoyed, well, anything?

"Are you giving the books away now?" he asked peevishly. "Because I have places to be."

Ah, there was the Mr. Gissing I was more familiar with. "Sorry," I said, shaking my head as I took a paperback from him and scanned it. "That's ten ninety-nine."

He handed over crumpled-up bills and coins and I put the book in a paper bag with his receipt.

As he turned to leave I found myself asking curiously, "Did you want me to tell her all that?"

He sniffed. "Certainly not. No need to get all soppy about it."

I repressed a smile as he walked away. Once he'd climbed down the stairs, I found myself looking up the stairs toward the garret and worrying.

Maybe she was just sleeping. But Mari had been so chatty before; total silence from her didn't make sense.

Telling her she'd been right about Mr. Gissing might cheer her up. I could check on her at the same time, just to shut up the small part of my brain repeating that something was terribly wrong.

I went to my office to find and put on a spare mask from pandemic times, then climbed up the stairs quietly to the very top, tapped on the door to the garret.

No answer.

I tapped again, a little louder this time.

Was that a groan? The urgent voice in my head started to panic. I turned my tap into a proper knock. "Mari?"

"Go away," I finally heard Mari's voice say faintly. It sounded much hoarser than yesterday, like she'd been swallowing sand.

"Mari, it's Leo," I said loudly.

"Yeah, I know, that's why I told you to go away." She coughed explosively.

No chance, not after hearing that horrible sound. I tried to smile. "I have some good news. It's about Mr. Gissing."

A moment of quiet. "Who the heck is Mr. Gissing?"

"The old man who dresses like he works for MI6. He's reading *The Confidence Men* and loves it, and now he wants more recommendations from you, once you're better."

"Well, that's just peachy," she said, her tone a little warmer. "I'm more than happy to talk to him." She paused. "If you'll allow me to."

I rested my forehead against the door. I knew I deserved that. I was about to apologize when I heard a horrific sound, retching and coughing combined into one. "What was that?"

"Nothing," she finally said breathlessly.

This was getting absurd. "You sound really ill."

She coughed and laughed bitterly at the same time. "A-plus for observation! Now, go the fuck away."

"Sounds fun, maybe later," I immediately replied, and was rewarded by a snort. I couldn't hold back a small smile. "But you really do sound awful," I said more seriously.

"Like *you* care. You never wanted me around."

I bumped my forehead against the wood. She may have been acting like a stroppy teenager, but how much confidence had I actually given her? My self-hate took on a new serrated edge as I realized, not much at all. "Mari, I really am sorry I said those awful things to you. You didn't deserve them. And I'm sorry I haven't been listening to you and taking you seriously. But I do care that you're ill, and I need you to let me in and make sure you're all right."

"Or what?" the smartarse said.

Of course Mari Cole was the worst patient in the history of medicine. "Or I'll..." *Think, Leo, think*... "Or I'll use the master key and let myself in," I said quickly, my whole body jerking with surprise as I said it.

"You wouldn't dare," she said, outrage and astonishment blending together in her voice.

In for a penny, I supposed. I took a deep breath. "Try me."

After some top swearing and a rummaging noise, the door opened. "There," she said through a surgical mask. "Happy now?"

"Fucking hell," I blurted. No, I wasn't happy at all. Her skin was as pale as blancmange except for two dots of bright color high on her cheeks. Her long hair was flat and lank in a ponytail, her usual upright posture crumpled. She was wearing red flannel pajama bottoms and a gray sweatshirt that said HUNTINGTON COLLEGE on it in forest-green letters, and had one of Judith's crocheted afghans wrapped around her shoulders. Fluffy green slippers shaped like frogs completed the cozy outfit, but the fingers that held the afghan around her were white to the tips, not pink. My fingers twitched with the urge to press my hand to her forehead, to tug her into me and warm her up.

I walked in and closed the garret door behind me instead. A heavy chill sat in the air, and I internally cursed the single-glazed windows.

"You know you could get sick, too," she said, the fight mostly out of her voice.

"I don't care," I said flatly, knowing in my bones it was true. "On a scale of one to ten, how ill do you feel right now? Honestly?"

She thought for a long moment, then held up seven fingers.

"Right," I said, worry a stone in my stomach. "Can I touch your forehead?"

Another pause. If she could still be this stubborn, she clearly wasn't at death's door. "I appreciate you asking first," she said quietly. "Go ahead."

As I'd suspected, she could have started a fire, her skin was so hot. "I need to go get the first aid kit to check the exact number, but you absolutely have a temperature."

She feebly grabbed my wrist before I could take my hand away. "Keep it there for a second, please. Your hand is cool, it feels good."

Something inside me shifted. I had done something right for her, and it was . . . satisfying. It made me want to look after her even more. "All right," I said. "Just say when you're ready."

CHAPTER EIGHT

Mari

I'd never asked someone to touch me except in very particular circumstances, ones where I felt powerful or at least equal. But when every joint in my body ached and my internal thermostat couldn't decide whether I was sledding in Antarctica or hiking across the Sahara, Leo's cool skin on mine was sweet relief. "Thank you," I sighed.

For a second we stood there, my hand pressed to his.

"About yesterday," he said, his voice shaking a little.

My head was throbbing and my whole body was one big ache, and unhappiness still simmered in the pit of my stomach. "Can it wait?"

His face fell. "Of course, I just wanted to say . . ."

I pulled away from his gentle touch, despite my urge to

keep him there for the next week. "Please don't," I forced out. "I can't have it out with you right now."

"All right, not right now. I'll be back in a moment with a thermometer." He paused. "Are you going to lock the door behind me?"

I rolled my eyes at the hint of snarkiness in his voice. "Oh ye of no faith whatsoever," I said. Though what had I done to earn his trust? The bare minimum. Maybe not even that. It took two to tango, after all. "I won't lock up behind you, I promise."

Leo left and came back a minute later with a plastic case with a green cross on it. I was used to first aid kits being red, but I learned something new every day in this place. He pulled out a plastic wand and hovered it in front of my forehead until it beeped. "Thirty-eight point three," he said, squinting at it. "That's definitely a fever. I'm going to call the NHS helpline and see if you might need to go to hospital."

I shook my head, then cringed at the pain. "I can't afford to go to the hospital." Suzanne paid for my health insurance, but I had insisted she get me the basic package because I never got sick. Until now.

Leo glared at me. "We have the National Health Service here. Going to hospital is free because medical treatment shouldn't depend on whether you're in work or not."

I snorted. "I don't disagree with you. I'm just not used to other places being humane."

He shook his head, then put away the first aid kit, and I climbed back into bed, tugging the covers up over me as he settled on the love seat and took out his phone. "Is your full name just Mari Cole?" he asked. "They might ask, for their records. I need to know your birthdate, too."

I recited my birthdate, then hesitated. "I'm Marilyn Gardner Cole legally, but if you call me Marilyn, I won't answer."

He cocked his head. "Why not? It's a nice name. Old-fashioned."

Because my step-grandmother and namesake had made it blatantly obvious she thought I was nothing but a burden on her saintly only son. "It never felt like it fit me." I tilted my chin toward him. "Is Leo short for anything?"

"Not legally. I'm Leo Nathaniel on my birth certificate." His eyes crinkled. "But Alexander wanted me to be Leopold, after his father. My mother refused to saddle me with that, so they compromised."

I let out a laugh of disbelief. "Oh my God. *Leopold*. Seriously?" It was a name made out of muttonchops and starched collars, not one meant for the twenty-first century.

He trailed long fingers through his hair, and I had a flash of understanding why some women were into silver foxes. "Not a word of a lie. One of the few times my grandfather didn't get his way."

While Leo pressed some buttons on his phone, I curled up in a ball and stared into space, trying not to think about how much my body hurt right now. I looked back on my childhood and was grateful I'd never been this sick when Greg was in charge of me. Goodness knows it had been bad enough when I'd gotten my period. I'd had to ask for advice from my Spanish teacher and buy all my own pads and tampons.

But I was so tired now, and it sounded so nice to have someone else competent take care of things for once. Still, something in me kicked against it being *Leo*, the man who made Eeyore look like a cockeyed optimist. "Why are you doing this? I'm your least favorite person right now."

Leo looked up from his phone. "Because you need someone."

I cringed away from the words. I didn't need anybody. I *couldn't* need anybody, because they'd all leave me in the end. But I was so tired, and so sick, and some old childish part of my brain cried out at the thought of being left alone.

He said shyly, "Unless you want me to get someone else? Graham?"

Warm, friendly, *easy* Graham would be the logical choice, not this tight-mouthed ball of grumpiness. Not that he looked grumpy right now, more determined, and that determination made me feel like nothing else bad would happen to me. He wouldn't allow it. "No," I said, finally letting myself give in. "I'll let you do it. You owe me, anyway."

"How generous of you." After a few seconds I heard the robotic voice of a phone menu, then tinny hold music. "All right, I'm in the queue. Now, what have you been doing to look after yourself?"

I shrugged. "I thought I could just wait it out."

He looked like he was resisting the urge to slap his forehead. "I won't tell you what a terrible idea that was. You could have an infection. You could get pneumonia and then you'd really have to go to hospital."

I studied the strain in his eyes. He was genuinely anxious about me getting sick. Like he'd been where I was and had hated every second of it, too. I guessed someone as skinny as him could catch whatever was going around way too easily. I hoped he'd had someone to look after him, the way he was looking after me.

"We should get you some chicken soup, no matter what," he said firmly. "Judith always has a batch in her freezer, it's the best thing in the world when I'm ill."

I shook my head. "No, no. I'm pescatarian, so no chicken, thanks."

He blinked for a second. "All right, we can find you vegetable soup. I didn't know that about you." He paused, then said quietly, "I don't know much of anything about you, besides what's on your CV." A click came from his phone, a distant voice saying "Hello?" and he put his phone to his ear.

As he spoke to the nurse, his wondering words repeated in my brain. I'd never been one of nature's oversharers, at first because no one was super interested in what I had to say, and then because time spent talking about myself meant time not spent listening to what customers wanted or what Suzanne envisioned for Orchard House. It was just easier not to confide in anyone.

But this was the first time I'd felt less than fine with that. That I'd felt like I might want to remove a layer of armor. Just one.

I pushed away the unhelpful guilt, and when he'd hung up the phone, I said, "You don't have to do any of this. I can take care of myself."

"Mari," he sighed. "You know you need this. Stop fighting me."

Healthy Mari would have happily argued back just to show him he wasn't the boss of me, but I honestly didn't have the energy to keep telling him no. "What did the nurse say?" I asked.

"That you most likely have the flu and will just have to, as you said, wait it out." He put his hand up at the beginning of my "I told you so." "But she said you should have lots of fluids, and medicine to help with the symptoms." He walked across the room and stuck his head into the fridge in the corner of the kitchenette, then stepped into the bathroom.

"I have ibuprofen already," I called weakly.

He stuck his head out of the bathroom. "That's good, but I'm going to get you Lemsip. It has paracetamol in it."

I blinked at him. "I don't know what those two words mean."

"They'll make you feel better, I promise." He went to the front door, then turned around like he'd forgotten something. "Why don't you eat meat?"

I loaded up the short, sanitized version of the story. "My step-grandparents had a farm just outside town. I liked the chicks and the piglets too much to eat the grown-up versions." I left out that they'd told me repeatedly that I was a baby for crying about dead animals, that this was the way the world worked. That they'd made me sit at the table in front of a cold plate of food long after dinner was over.

I was waiting for a nod, or a platitude, before the conversation moved on. Instead Leo said quietly, "I don't like eating red meat. The texture's just . . ." He shuddered audibly. "Took my parents years to understand that, and I spent a lot of time pushing it around my plate before my mother gave in."

Out of nowhere, I had the urge to . . . thank him. I'd been sincere with him, and he hadn't pushed it away, or treated it like information he'd use against me later. I'd had this outline of Leo in my head, harsh lines and sharp edges, but why couldn't I try to fill it in with some color?

It didn't have to mean we'd be close, or that we'd go nuts and end up in bed together. It'd be good for the store, to understand the man a little better, and for him to understand me.

"I hear you," I said. "I had to learn to cook when I was twelve because my stepfather didn't believe in pescatarianism."

Leo's eyebrows went up. "You learned how to cook when you were twelve? What did you make?"

I shook my head at his astonishment. "I mean, we're not talking Michelin-starred tasting menus here. I figured out how to make a tofu stir-fry and mix vegetables and canned tuna into pasta. Not rocket surgery." I shrugged. "I've always been able to look after myself. I had to."

"My sisters are a lot like you," he said thoughtfully. "Self-contained. Always wanting to do everything themselves."

Leo's revelation grabbed my attention. I was so used to thinking of him as the crown prince that it hadn't even occurred to me there might be Ross princesses. "You have sisters?"

His eyes were suddenly warm, fond, and all of a sudden I wanted to get closer to him, feel that warmth in my bones. "I do," he said. "Gabi and Sophie. They're twins."

"I didn't know that," I said lamely. Because I didn't know much about Leo, either, besides what was on his résumé. "But wait, why aren't they helping out at the shop if it's such a family concern?" *Helping you*, I didn't say.

"They're only sixteen," Leo said.

"But—"

He held up his hand. "I know, you and I have both worked in bookshops since we were children. But it's not the same for them. Gabi's a brilliant cellist, and Sophie can't imagine life without playing football." He rubbed the back of his neck. "I can't deprive them of what gives them so much joy." He paused. "More than that, I won't."

I studied his firm expression, putting the pieces together. How tense and exhausted he was all the time, but also how he sat drawing in his sketchbook whenever he had a second.

His joy hadn't disappeared, but it was weak, flickering, starved of oxygen.

What would he be like if he could do what he really wanted? If his eyes had spark and his mouth curled up more?

It was only when Leo turned to the door that I realized we'd been staring at each other for a solid fifteen seconds. "I should go get your medicine," he said, sounding distracted. "I'll buy soup and fruit juice, too. Anything else?"

"Nope," I said automatically, not wanting to tip the scales back to owing him again. But when he opened the door, I found myself blurting, "Leo?"

He turned. "Yeah?"

An emotion I hadn't acknowledged in years surged up inside me. I knew I would always end up on my own, but just for today, I didn't *want* to be. I pulled my blankets around me, warmth and courage. "When you come back, will you stay for a little bit?" I asked, unable to keep the plaintiveness out of my voice.

His eyes softened. "Yes. I'll stay."

CHAPTER NINE

Leo

Once I got back from my errands and made sure Mari had drunk some Lemsip before she fell asleep again, I messaged Graham and Catriona that I'd be upstairs for a little while, then settled on the gray velvet love seat with my laptop, tugging another of Judith's afghans over my lap for warmth.

After I'd handled my emails, I paused. My eyes hunted for the touches of Mari while she dozed. A few tubes and pots of lotion and makeup on top of the chest of drawers, a small, colorful pile of laundry on a chair in the corner, a clean plate and mug drying in the dish rack.

It'd make sense that she traveled lightly, if she was used to going from bookshop to bookshop. It was a lightness I'd never had, I realized. The thought of simply picking up and leaving just with what I could carry on my back was as strange as thinking about spontaneous teleportation.

But now I saw a battered hardback on the nightstand next to Mari, the cover a yellow like summer sunshine. I picked it up like I was a burglar and it was a ruby in a bank vault, then found myself smiling at the familiar wide-eyed bear in his floppy hat.

I sat back down and opened *A Bear Called Paddington*, looking for the beginning as familiar and sweet as marmalade sandwiches, Mr. and Mrs. Brown meeting the stowaway bear on the railway platform. As I turned the first pages, I saw a flash of blue scribble on the front matter. Curiosity flickered, and I turned back and found a note:

For my sweet baby girl, Mari, on her tenth birthday. May you be as brave and adventurous as little Paddington. Love, Mama.

The date was just under twenty years ago.

Tender affection radiated off the page, but it was a too-bright splash of color on a darker picture: Mari shying away, Mari fighting any hint of care, Mari curled up tight under the covers like she was used to being her own comfort.

I've always been able to look after myself. I had to.

My heart twisted in sympathy. Were she and her mother estranged now? A lot could happen in twenty years. But then would she have kept the little book at all?

Had her mother disappeared?

Or died?

She hadn't mentioned a father either, just a stepfather who sounded like a right bastard.

It was like the light in the room had shifted, and what

looked like an easy kind of living transformed into absence. Into loneliness.

I turned the page and a small picture slipped out of the middle of the book.

A woman with long wavy hair the color of chestnuts looked at the camera, laughing, her eyes Mari's striking hazel. She was kneeling on the ground wearing dirt-covered dungarees and garden gloves, surrounded by brilliant scarlet tulips.

But the coloring was where the resemblance between Mari and her mum ended. Mari's features were softly pretty, welcoming, in a way. It almost hurt to look at the woman in the picture with her model-like planes and edges, while I could have studied Mari for hours, captured the weather shifts in her expressive face.

It was aesthetic appreciation, I told myself, shaking my head hard. I was noticing her colors and expressions because I wanted to draw her from across the room, not because I wanted to get closer to her.

A strangled gasp, and my head snapped up from the photograph. Mari sat up quickly, clutching at her chest, and I could hear the rattle when she coughed. She threw herself out of bed and ran into the toilet, slamming the door, and I heard her coughing, gagging, retching. I put the picture back in the book and the book aside, moved to the door and listened closely, holding back until I heard a heavy sound like a body hitting a floor.

When I opened the door, Mari was in the fetal position in front of the toilet, moaning softly. Without thinking I went on my knees next to her.

"I'm fine," she gasped.

I would have laughed if I hadn't been so afraid. "Right,

enough of that," I said, trying to channel Judith's warm, businesslike voice as I tugged her upright. "Back to bed with you."

I pulled her up until she was standing, shivering. Her mouth opened, and I waited for her to put on her brave face, to joke. But then everything crumpled, and she suddenly pressed her face into my shoulder.

"I feel so bad," she sobbed. "I'm so cold, and I hurt, and I want it to stop. Please make it stop."

Her voice . . . it was curled up on itself the way she'd been in bed, small and pained. An electric surge of something I'd never felt before went through me, like I wanted to wrap myself around her, keep the world at bay, make her warm and safe. But she wouldn't welcome that. Instead I hummed and chafed her back briskly until she lifted her head. Tears trickled down her cheeks. Without thinking my thumb went to rub one away.

"I know . . ." *Darling* had tried to get past my lips, but I shoved it back. "I know," I said hoarsely. "I'm so sorry. But more fluids, more sleep, and I promise you'll feel better. All right?"

Her hand came up and pressed against mine and she closed her eyes for a moment. "All right," she said softly, and I felt a wild urge to press my lips to her forehead. Instead I got her a glass of water so she could rinse her mouth and rehydrate, then shut myself in the bathroom so she could change into fresh pajamas. When I came out, she was curled up on her side in bed, and I bustled around making her a fresh Lemsip. Even with the blankets, I could see the shivers pass through her.

If she were mine, I'd climb into the bed, curl up around her so she could absorb my body heat.

What? There were so many things wrong with that thought I didn't know where to begin. Starting with her being mine, because what woman in her right mind would want me?

Instead of making an idiot of myself, I offered her the little hardback. "You like Paddington?"

She hesitated, her eyes flickering between the book and me. I kept my face innocent, and she took it from me, running her hand over the cover before putting it back on the nightstand. "I do." She smiled a little. "I actually love a lot of books set here. I think there was a little part of my brain when I got off the plane that expected to walk into a storybook, not passport control at Heathrow."

I snorted. "The writer hasn't been born who could make passport control charming or romantic. But which books?"

She extended her fingers and tapped them one by one. "*Mary Poppins*, of course. Noel Streatfeild's books, like *Ballet Shoes*. I read my copies of them so often they fell apart. Adult books, too: *David Copperfield*, *Mrs Dalloway*, *White Teeth*, *Bridget Jones's Diary*, *One Day*."

I found myself smiling, remembering summer afternoons and sunlit chapters in the grass on the Heath, rainy Sundays in an armchair, alternating pages with sips of steaming tea. "I love all of those. There are some less famous London books you should read, too. *Small Island* and *The British Museum Is Falling Down* and *The Morning Gift*." I tilted my head. "You really should read *The Morning Gift*, actually. You remind me a lot of the heroine."

"Is she a pain in the ass?"

"Ha. I was going to say she's plucky."

"Thanks. Though I don't feel super plucky right this second."

"You know Dickens lived not far from here? We..." I swallowed, not wanting to be presumptuous. "You can visit his house and see where he set his books."

She'd either missed or was ignoring my slipup. "I'd like that. Plus, a lot of the historical romances I love are set here." She raised her eyebrows. "Though I know you don't approve of those."

"I don't mind," I protested. "You can read whatever you like. I just don't see the point of rehashing Jane Austen plots over and over again."

"Have you actually *read* one?"

I clamped my mouth shut.

"That's what I thought." Then the tease in her voice disappeared. "But what's actually going on with the shop, Leo? Why won't you tell me what's happening?"

God, thinking of it made me feel as ill and tired as Mari looked. "It's a rubbish bedtime story," I hedged. "It should wait until you feel better."

She snorted. "Think of it this way: I'm too tired to do anything but listen, for once." Her tone changed, went softer. "I just want to understand. Start at the beginning. How did you get here?"

Maybe telling her the story would make my load the smallest bit lighter. "Alexander died eight months ago from a heart attack, but he wasn't quite himself for a long time before that," I began quietly. "He was a little vague. Detached. Quicker to shout when something wasn't the way he wanted it." I rubbed my face. "Judith had told me a week before he died that she was trying to persuade him to go in for a consultation with someone who specialized in dementia."

Mari's eyes were intent, and I continued, "He also decided all of a sudden to open another branch of Ross and Co., in a shopfront in Covent Garden. The rent was very high, but we'd get tons of foot traffic, he said, much more than we got here." I sighed. "So I went along with it. But it didn't work. We were too close to competitors, didn't have enough to differentiate us. It was a white elephant, a bottomless pit for money."

Mari studied me. "You thought it was a bad idea from the beginning."

A bitter laugh escaped my mouth. "I did. Taking on so much debt when business was static was foolhardy. But Alexander had always known what he was talking about before, so I wasn't brave enough to say anything."

She nodded. "Classic copilot syndrome." She paused. "I haven't heard of another Ross and Co., so I guess that shop is gone?"

I nodded. "Even Alexander couldn't deny that the shop wasn't earning enough to pay the rent. So we got out of the lease, at great expense." I looked down at my hands. "And then he died. And I've just felt . . . so lost ever since. Like I don't trust myself at all."

"I'm so sorry, Leo."

I looked up at her. "What for? It happened long before you arrived."

She said softly, "No, I'm saying that I feel for you. It sounds like things have been really tough for a long time, and you've been hurting. I'm sorry I made it worse."

I felt my shoulders slump. She didn't know the half of

it. But still, letting Mari see some of my shame, and getting kindness in return? Despite the snow falling outside, I felt the smallest bit warmer.

"Mari, I'm sorry, too. I said such cruel things, and you didn't deserve them in the slightest."

"I kind of did, though," she said with a sigh. "I was going about things the way I usually do. Which was dumb, because every bookstore is different, every bookstore owner is different. I needed to be in listening mode, not doing mode."

"But you were in that mode because I've been moping around doing fuck all."

"Can we say we've both been assholes and start over?" She reached out her hand. "Shake on it?"

I told myself that the rightness I felt was to do with having someone on my side in the middle of all the chaos. Not because of the softness of her skin, or the urge I felt to kiss her hand instead of shake it. "Yes. Let's not be arseholes anymore," I said, trying to joke the awkward feelings away.

She released me and I watched her pull down her mask to take a long sip of water. The truth climbed up my chest, and I let it out, unable to hide anymore. "Maybe if I can't lead this place the way Alexander did, I should just give it up."

She tilted her head. "Do you really want to quit? Without even giving it a shot?"

I straightened at her challenge. "No. But I don't know how to *be*."

After a moment of thought, she said, "I think you might know this already, somewhere deep down, but you don't have to copy Alexander. You can be your own kind of leader, and I can help you change direction." She looked me in the eye, determination in her gaze. "I *want* to help you, Leo."

Her expression of faith—it was like a burst of light when I was fumbling around in the darkness. But I found myself asking, "Because you want to save the store?"

She studied me for a moment. "I mean, yes. I think the store can be great again, with some love and some ambition. But I also want to help because I've been where you are. I've been face down in the mud, lost and stuck, and Suzanne took the time to get me up and moving forward again."

Gratitude and curiosity collided. It was a relief to hear that I was worthy of help, that I could hold out my uncertainty to her and she'd treat it respectfully, not dismiss it or try to coddle me.

But I also felt like Mari had finally let me into the entrance hall of her life, one that had furniture and carpets and a vase of flowers on the sideboard but that led to yet more locked-up rooms. The battered copy of *Paddington* with its inscription, the passing allusions to her stepfather, how adamant she was about being called Mari, not Marilyn: they were all hints at what lay beyond.

What were the keys that would unlock those doors?

Now Mari lay back and stared at the ceiling again. "We could try channeling the Muppets," she mused.

I stared at her, bewildered. "Sorry?"

"Don't apologize. I mean putting on a show, like when they tried to save the Muppet Theater."

I laughed a little bit. "Please tell me I'm not Kermit in this scenario."

"I don't know," she said teasingly. "I could see you with a ukulele, singing 'It's Not Easy Being Green.'"

I sat back in my love seat, not sure I wanted to play along. "Pity I can't play any instruments at all and have a singing voice that makes dogs howl."

She shook her head. "No singing, no dancing. You told me that this year is the hundredth anniversary of the store. Why not put on a festival? You guys must have so much goodwill from all the writers and readers who have come through here over the years. It's a good moment to cash in any outstanding favors." She coughed, already sounding a bit less grim from the Lemsip.

"What kind of favors?" I asked.

She held up her hands. "Make a big list of every author who's ever had a tie to Alexander, or to the shop. Authors, editors, agents, other booksellers, even. You had all those big names doing talks here, back in the day. I'm sure you could convince the ones who are still alive to come support the store as it goes into a new era."

I couldn't help my incredulous laugh. "See, you find it very easy to just accost someone and ask for things, but you need to remember that I'm British."

She raised her eyebrows. "So what, you're just going to hang around politely drowning because you're scared of inconveniencing people?"

It was a very tidy summary, and I could hear how silly she found the whole concept. "Well, yes."

She snorted. "Someone needs to explain to me how you all conquered and pillaged a quarter of the world's surface, because I'm not seeing it right now."

An appreciative smile grew on my face. For a split second, I felt like the fog around me had dissipated. She could see me, and I could see her. "Those weren't my ancestors, but a good point all the same."

After a moment, Mari said, "I'm not going to harp on this, because it'll annoy you and bore me, but I'll ask you just one thing." She leaned forward and looked me hard in the eye. "If not now, when?"

The words echoed through me with a crystalline tone, a bell calling me. I had to answer it, had to see where it would lead. "I'll talk to Judith. She came to parties here back in the day, she might still have information for some of those people."

"Perfect," Mari said, and for a fleeting moment, I agreed with her that it was.

CHAPTER TEN

Mari

After six days of bed rest, my body wasn't on strike anymore, but I had about as much stamina as a ninety-year-old. I still hauled my ass out of bed, got dressed and put on a mask, and made my way down the bookstore stairs out of pure stubbornness and boredom.

Now I was trying to resist the urge to sit down on the bottom step and put my head between my knees. But what the hey, no one was looking. I plunked myself down and sighed.

As I tried to pull together the fragments of energy that were buried six feet deep, my brain returned to its new favorite fixation.

Leo's gentle hand on my back, the soft nonsense he'd

crooned when I'd sobbed into his sweater. His thumb rubbing my tearstained cheekbone.

Of course I'd had so much of other kinds of touch, been skin-to-skin with near strangers. If you'd asked me before I got to London, I'd have said I knew plenty about intimacy.

But what Leo had offered had been another thing entirely.

Something selfless.

I'd been like the remnants of a bad dinner at the bottom of a pot, scorched with fever and raw with pain, and he'd soothed me. The gentleness, the care. I'd felt... *safe*. No one had touched me like that since...

Since my mom died.

"Mari? Are you all right? Maybe you should have waited another day to come down?" the man himself asked, crouching in front of me so we were eye-to-eye.

I gaped at his serious face for a minute, then shook off the realization. No more being vulnerable. I was here and had a job to do. "Did you want me to climb out the skylight and shimmy down the drainpipe?" I joked.

"Now, that would have caused some serious issues with health and safety." He paused, the corner of his mouth crooking up. "If you had been able to climb, of course, what with the superhuman strength flu's known to give."

"You are *such* a smartass," I said, half laughing.

"Insults? Now I'm certain you're feeling better," he said without any heat. He held out a mug that I hadn't noticed. "Would a smartarse bring you a coffee with oat milk?"

My fingers flexed, but I didn't immediately reach out to take it. It wasn't the first little gift he'd given me in the last week. He'd come upstairs to check on me each day, and every visit there'd been something: homemade vegetable noodle soup from Judith, carrot-orange-ginger juice from the café around the corner, a Saturday newspaper to keep me entertained.

Leo's humor was as sharp as cactus needles, and he wasn't one of nature's optimists, but he was thoughtful, too. Maybe even sweet.

I knew from my history that I needed to keep sweet at arm's length. But who would it hurt right now to have a little taste when I was weak and exhausted?

"Maybe," I said, taking what he offered. I turned the warm cup in my hands, looking at it instead of his face. "Thanks."

"You're welcome." After a moment he continued more briskly, "I've got you set up at the main register with a comfy chair. I told Judith about our festival idea and she said she'd pop by when you were well enough with some of Alexander's mementos, see if that sparks anything for us." He looked me over. "Tell me if you need to go rest and I'll get one of the others to take your spot."

I opened my mouth, but he shook his head. "Sorry, I forgot to whom I was speaking. *Please,* could you tell me if you need to go rest? And then actually *do* it?"

He was sassing me, so why was a goofy smile spreading across my face? I guessed that after a week of tending me, he'd have my number. "Yes, Leo," I singsonged.

"Cheeky thing," he muttered.

"Insults, huh?"

He sighed dramatically. "Come on, then. I won't offend your pride by offering to help you stand up."

But he hovered as it took me two tries to get vertical,

and as I headed to my desk for the day, I felt his gaze on my back.

I settled into the cushioned chair and picked up the piece of notebook paper that said "To Do for Mari" at the top. For someone so neat, his handwriting sprawled and piled up like dirty laundry. When I decoded the scrawl, I smiled, then opened the two publishers' catalogs he'd emailed me and started marking new books for the fiction section. No Regency romance yet, I didn't want to push my luck, but I snuck in some Mhairi McFarlane and Emily Henry with the literary fiction.

Once I'd done that, I dug through my laptop's files and found all the preparations I'd made for the small book festival I'd organized with Suzanne a few years ago. We'd run events in the store and in a few other places around the Loch Gordon town square, drawing in locals but also tourists who'd come to enjoy the gorgeous May weather in the vineyards and stayed to hear from the collection of wine writers and chefs, poets and novelists we'd put together.

Now I studied the old paperwork, writing my own action list of what Ross & Co. would need. I found myself settling into the comfort of spreadsheets and schedules. When Suzanne had first tried to teach fourteen-year-old me to use Excel and Bookmanager, I'd resisted, protesting that I hated computer science at school and didn't want to have to do it in my happy place, too. But Suzanne had said firmly that dreams opened a bookstore, but systems kept it running, and I'd quickly come to appreciate the sense of certainty that came from every piece of data in its right place.

As I worked, the others stopped by to say hello and

check on me, lighting up when I told them about the idea of a festival in April. Even Catriona half smiled, though more in the aren't-you-cute way than in the that-sounds-exciting way.

I was googling authors who'd talked about Ross & Co. when a waxy brown bag dropped next to my elbow. Butter stained the paper, and I smelled sugar and cinnamon.

"Can't imagine you've eaten much lately, being ill and all," Graham said above me, leaning against the counter.

My stomach growled. "Hello to you too, and your imagination is accurate. What is this, a custard tart?" I asked as I pulled the pastry out. It was larger than the desserts I'd had at dim sum restaurants with Suzanne, and the top of the custard was caramelized in spots.

"A pastel de nata. The Portuguese bakery around the corner from my flat bakes them fresh every day." He hesitated. "I also wanted to say sorry for not coming to see you upstairs. Tim has asthma and I didn't want to risk bringing a nasty lurgy home to him."

I nodded. "Don't worry about it. Leo was checking on me, so I wasn't going too insane with boredom."

Graham's mouth curled up. "He told us. I was surprised you let him. You two didn't exactly hit it off."

I shrugged a little. "So was I. But he's grown on me some." I pulled my mask down and took a bite out of the pastry, and a wave of sweet spiced richness hit my tongue. "*Fuck*, that's delicious," I managed once I swallowed the bite. "You can give me one of those anytime."

Leo

"Pardon, I didn't mean to interrupt," I said, my voice trembling a little.

Mari looked up from the pastel de nata in her hand. "No, it's fine," she said quickly. Too quickly? She looked at Graham with raised eyebrows, and he nodded, straightened up, and wandered past me with an easy "Hiya."

What would it take to have that kind of silent communication, where the twitch of an eyebrow and a nod became sentences and paragraphs? My sisters had it, too, and it always made me feel like I was standing on the other side of a glass window.

"Are you OK?" Mari asked me, her head tilted.

No, I thought. *I'm not all right, because when I saw Graham leaning toward you and heard you moan with pleasure, I wished I could shatter that window.*

But I barely knew what to do when I got close to someone. I didn't share my smiles easily like Graham and Mari did, didn't wear my confidence like a broken-in leather jacket. Didn't have confidence in the first place. When I moved through the world, I crept instead of swaggered like the two of them did.

Then why was I jealous? Because Mari had given me that bit of quiet insight in the garret, talking about falling-apart books and daydreaming about a storybook London.

Because she'd let me hold her while she cried. Because she'd asked *me* to stay.

"Hello, grandson," Judith's warm voice said behind me, and I turned around, grateful for the interruption to my thought spiral. She was carrying a basic ivory-colored archival box under one arm, leaning hard on her stick.

"Hi, Judith," I said, bending to kiss her cheek and take the box off her at the same time.

"Good lad," she said, reaching up and patting my cheek. "And hello, Mari," she said over my shoulder. "I'm so glad to see you're feeling better. Leo was worried about you."

Mari raised her eyebrows at me. "Yeah, he's been really helpful. I appreciated him nursing me when things were really bad."

"Nursing you?" Judith said to me with a hint of a smile. "Well, isn't that sweet of him."

I could see the matchmaking cogs turning inside her head. "It wouldn't do for an employee to catch pneumonia."

"Of course it wouldn't," she said, mischief all over her narrow features. She pointed at the box. "Your mother got that out of the loft for me. Still smells like Alexander's Cafe Cremes, doesn't it?"

I put my nose closer to the cardboard. She was right, it gave off the aroma of the cigarillos that Alexander had loved to smoke for half his life. He'd quit when I was still young, but the sweet, toasted scent drifted through my early memories of him. I closed my eyes for a second, missing that feeling of being embraced, of knowing that he would make everything all right, no matter what. All I'd had to do was listen and follow.

"I'm sorry," Judith said, tight with pain, dragging me

back to the present. "I can't bear the thought of the stairs today, so could we look at these somewhere on this floor?"

"Of course," I said immediately. Some days her medicine helped more than others. I led her into the break room, Mari following behind, and placed the box on the tea-stained table. Judith pulled off the lid, revealing leather-bound photograph albums. When Mari and I lifted all six of them out, loose photographs drifted to the bottom.

Mari brushed her hand over one of the covers. "Dusty," she said. "No one's looked at these for a while, I guess?"

"No," Judith said. "I only remembered yesterday that we had them, and they're not the kind of thing that David ever wants to look at or talk about. You've seen how he can be."

I sighed. Dad had always treated Judith like an imposition. He was swift to correct anyone who used the word "stepmother," snapping back "father's wife" instead. Which was in some ways fair, because Dad had been eighteen and she'd been twenty-four when she married Alexander. Judith was nothing but cordial to Dad, but whenever he spoke to her, he still sounded like that bitterly resentful teenager.

"Bless Alexander," Judith said briskly, "he took the time to write everyone's names and the dates, so we should be able to make a timeline." She started sorting the loose photographs into piles, telling us names and contexts. "Some of them he took," she said. "Some of them I did. And here's a set of professional ones, from the fiftieth anniversary party." She handed me a gold-engraved album.

"It was the *seventies*," Mari said in wonderment, leaning in next to me. When I breathed in, I could smell a burst of ripe mango, an instant dream of white sand and turquoise water.

It was criminal, having shampoo that smelled that delicious.

Mari poked me in the shoulder. "Turn the page."

"Bossy," I muttered, hoping she hadn't noticed me blushing.

"Takes one to know one," she muttered back.

I snorted, but straightened my face at Judith's speculative look.

The photographs had a yellow-brown haze over them, like cigarillo smoke had permeated the film. I flipped through groups of white men talking to each other, recognizing Alan Sillitoe, Keith Waterhouse, Ted Hughes. Occasionally I saw my teenage father in the background, hands in the pockets of his wide-lapeled suit and expression sulky.

"Were there any authors there who *weren't* white men?" Mari asked Judith.

Judith's mouth twisted. "Yes, but only a few. It was all very much a boys' club then." She reached over and turned the pages. "Ah, here's one," she said, tapping one of the photos. "Elizabeth Jane Howard. She would have been there as Kingsley Amis's wife, even though she was an author in her own right." She chuckled a little. "She actually kept doing brilliant work long after they divorced, and she wrote her finest novels when she was well into her sixties. Something for the rest of us to remember."

I leaned in close to study the photograph. Elizabeth Jane Howard's silver hair was in a smooth chignon, a striking contrast with her cobalt-blue dress. In contrast, the young Judith wore a flowing poppy-red caftan revealing quite a bit of cleavage. Shiny dark brown hair cascaded over her shoulders, her eyeliner was coal-black and Cleopatra-thick, and her pale fingers held a cigarette in a long black holder.

"Wait, that's you," Mari said to Judith admiringly. "Damn, you were a fox back in the day. The cigarette holder is fire."

"Why, thank you," Judith said, preening a little. "Though I won't linger on it so my grandson doesn't die of embarrassment. Smoking was such a filthy habit, anyway. Everything in those days was under a haze of tobacco." She shook her head. "But I do miss that red dress. I felt so powerful when I wore it."

Mari looked again at the photograph. "Who's he?" she said, tapping the face of a very young man in the background, with dark blond hair that needed a trim and light blue eyes.

Was that a blush on Judith's cheeks? "That's Tommy Clifford. Or Cliff Thomas, as he's known these days."

Mari and I looked at each other, equally astonished. "I saw posters for his new book in the airport. He's a huge deal in thrillers here, right?" Mari asked.

"Very much so, yes," Judith said. "Writing about gangsters and spies made him a good living."

Mari tilted her head. "Do you think he'd come speak if we asked?"

Judith pursed her lips. "If you'd asked me that before recently, I would have said absolutely not. He and Alexander had a terrible falling-out shortly after that picture was taken and I haven't seen him since. He lives in a cottage near Frome, and as far as I know, he's a bit of a recluse." She thought for a moment. "But maybe enough time has passed now."

I'd heard Judith sound wistful before, but it was always

when remembering something lovely my grandfather had said or done. We'd never spoken about how blustery Alexander could become when he'd felt someone had wronged him, how some editor or salesperson could go from being a friend to persona non grata in a mere moment, the way the London weather flipped from sunshine to thunder clouds and back again.

Mari looked at me. "Where is Frome and how do we get there?"

I could see a plot forming in the swirling green of her eyes. "It's in Somerset, the West Country. We'd get a train from Paddington." But I had to be the voice of reason. "Perhaps we should get in touch with his agent, first?"

Mari ignored me and turned to Judith. "Alexander and Tommy fell out, but you didn't fall out with him, did you?"

Now Judith was blushing fully. "We've occasionally corresponded."

"So you have his address."

When Judith nodded, still blushing, I blinked at the revelation that my step-grandmother had a life that didn't involve my family, a life that might have involved longing glances, flirtation. Then Mari poked me in the shoulder. "No agent required. We can mail him a note to let him know we're coming and that if he doesn't want to meet, he can call the store and tell us."

I had to shake my head at Mari's audacity. "That's forthright of you."

She shrugged cheerfully. "We have reclusive writers in California, too. Suzanne and I realized that the best way to handle them was for contact to be opt-out, not opt-in."

Judith grinned at her, an expression I hadn't seen on

her face in forever. "I knew we did the right thing, asking you here."

For the first time since the day Mari arrived, I found myself wholeheartedly agreeing with Judith. Mari had enough courage for the both of us. I was . . . in awe of her. "I suppose we're going to Somerset, then," I said wonderingly.

"Road trip! Or train trip!" Mari said, holding up her hand for a high five, and I shook my head but slapped her hand anyway. The thrill I felt afterward was just a little chemical zing, the sense that the game was afoot. Not Mari's laughing eyes making me feel just that little bit braver.

CHAPTER ELEVEN

Leo

It had been a long time since I'd taken a train out of London, I thought as I looked for Mari in the herds of tourists milling around Paddington Station. I'd gone on so many trips to Cambridge and Oxford with Alexander, slow, rattling trains out to Buckinghamshire to visit my mother's mother at her so-called country pile. I'd run off to Edinburgh with Vinay and our other friends for a long weekend during uni, and Becca and I had taken the Eurostar to Paris for our honeymoon. My shoulders slumped a little when I remembered that trip, the feeling of my wife's hand in mine as I'd dragged her through as many art museums as she could stand, hers tugging mine to look at every single posh restaurant menu and sparkling designer window. I closed my eyes now as I remembered the absence of touch too, how far away she felt curled up in a ball on the other side of the mattress, my failure to please her in the cold, empty space.

But Becca was gone, and taking a train with Mari now would be a whole new experience. I found her in the middle of the crowd, scanning the departures board with wide eyes. She wore a soft-looking knit dress the color of pine forests, with bell-shaped sleeves, and a small green pendant on a long gold chain. She had her hair a little higher too, chestnut wisps escaping down her neck.

I was so used to seeing her in jeans and baggy jumpers that I almost didn't know who this Mari was. If we were strangers, maybe this would have been the beginning of a different story. Not two colleagues on a work trip, but a shy man who admired a clever, pretty woman, who'd gather all his courage, stammer out a compliment and a request to buy her a drink.

I shook my head hard to drive off the unwelcome thought. Too much of our story had already been written, and she was more suited to Graham, anyway. That moment with the custard tart in the bookshop had made that clear.

She turned and saw me, and I couldn't help but smile at her huge wave of greeting.

"I'm so excited!" she said as I approached. "This is a real adventure already. I'm at Paddington and I'm about to go on my first-ever train ride. I should have brought marmalade sandwiches."

"Surely you have trains in America," I said incredulously.

"Of course we have trains, in New York and Boston. Rural Northern California, not so much." She bounced on her toes. "Your place names are ridiculous, by the way. Pewsey? Weston-super-Mare? Not to mention Cockfosters. I keep seeing it on the Tube map, that's a real double entendre."

I flushed a little bit. I had no idea why the end of the Piccadilly line was called Cockfosters, and she'd probably just take the piss out of my answer, anyway. But some demon of perversion made me blurt, "Fingringhoe."

Mari froze. "You did what?"

Mortification made me stutter. "It's a village. In Essex. With a filthy name. Probably a single entendre, not double."

For a moment she just stared, and I wished for the train station floor to open and swallow me. Then she *cackled*, raucous and joyful as a magpie. "Fingringhoe! I love it! Amazing. Also, you should say crude things more often. It works for you."

Thoughts of the rude things I could say turned my bit of a flush into the full scarlet. "Err, thanks," I said brilliantly. "Tickets. We need tickets." I walked her over to the machines and pressed buttons to pay for our journey. "So you really haven't taken a train before?" I said, trying to keep myself present in the loud, overlit train station, not imagining darkness and warmth and closeness.

"Nope."

"What is that even *like*?"

"There's this newfangled contraption called the automo-bile." She held her hands palm out and swept them away from each other. "It's like a carriage, but powered by a combustion engine instead of pulled by horses."

I snorted at the impeccable piss-take. "I deserved that."

"*Yeah*, you did."

Once we'd gotten our tickets and settled on the largely empty train, I studied her face. Most of the color was back in her cheeks, though she still had shadows under her eyes. Uncertainty made me ask, "How are you feeling?"

She didn't look away from where she was checking her ruby-red lipstick in a pocket mirror. "Fine."

After hearing her say she was "fine" when she was prostrate on the bathroom floor, I knew that word was like a false wall, appearing solid to the naked eye but utterly hollow behind. I sat forward, hands folded in my lap, and waited until she'd stopped looking in the mirror.

When her eyes caught mine, her round cheeks flushed a little.

"How are you really feeling?" I asked.

She looked down, focused on closing her compact and putting it away. "I'm definitely not sick anymore," she sighed. "Can't deny I'm still pretty tired."

"Close your eyes if you like. I can wake you up when we get to Frome." I'd arranged for a minicab to pick us up at the other end and take us to Tommy Clifford's cottage.

She opened her mouth with the spark in her eyes that I now knew meant she was about to argue with me, but a huge yawn came out instead. "Not a terrible idea," she finally said.

"Sometimes I have good ideas," I couldn't help but snark.

"Idea, singular," she said playfully. "Keep trying, maybe you can get a streak going."

She leaned her temple against the window, tucked her legs under her, and closed her eyes, and I kept my own eyes down on a copy of Tommy's first book, a coming-of-age novel he'd published under his own name. Mari had speed-read the battered, yellowed paperback and passed it to me with a Mona Lisa smile, saying that I might find it enlightening. But I'd kept getting distracted and had only made it two chapters in. I tried to read instead of doing what I really wanted, which was to take out my sketchbook and draw Mari's face gone soft with sleep, the delicate strands of hair that had escaped her bun, her deep-red lips parted ever so slightly.

But it was wrong to draw her when I couldn't ask permission. It was wrong to even look at her as anything besides a colleague.

We were somewhere between Reading and Hungerford when she opened her eyes again and instantly sat up. I closed the book to ask how she was when she exclaimed, "Look! Everything is so green!" She pressed her nose to the window. "And look at the sheep! Baa."

"You don't have sheep in America, either?"

She raised her eyebrows. "Of course we have sheep. But people who don't baa when they see a sheep or moo when they see a cow fundamentally hate joy."

I chuckled at how matter-of-fact she was. "What else gives you joy, then?"

Her facial expression made me think of a doe hearing a twig snap nearby. "That's a big question."

I tried to keep my voice relaxed. "We've got over an hour until Frome, plenty of time for a big answer." All at once, I wanted a big answer. I wanted the unabridged guide to whatever Mari Cole liked.

She rested her chin on her fist and watched the countryside go by. "Hot coffee on a cold day, or iced tea on a hot one. Driving to the beach and inhaling the salt, listening to the waves. Running through the vineyards on a sunny morning. Putting a book in the hands of a customer and knowing they'll have their own little world to escape into, hopefully one that will stick with them when times are tough." She smiled at me. "And reading, of course. I wouldn't be here without it."

I smiled back, but I couldn't help but notice that everything she was describing was solitary. Of course we didn't know each other well enough for her to talk about past or present lovers, but someone as charming and pretty as her surely must have had loads of people who'd happily go running with her. Who'd love to bring her coffee and sit by her side on the beach and talk endlessly about books.

For a flickering moment, I thought about doing those things with her, though the only time I ran was to catch a bus, and I associated the beach with piercing cold and sandy picnics.

Oh, *fuck*. Did this mean I fancied her now? What a fundamentally silly thing to do.

"What about you?" she interrupted.

Now I had to pretend I hadn't had an embarrassing revelation. "My sisters. Listening to Gabs play her cello and kicking the football around with Soph. Supporting Arsenal, especially when they win. Wednesday nights with Judith—we used to have this ritual on nights Alexander played poker, where we'd take turns picking a record and sit around listening, and she'd knit or crochet while I read or drew."

Guilt rolled in my stomach as I remembered that we hadn't had a Wednesday night in months. Judith had invited me a few times after Alexander died, but I'd begged off so often with tiredness that she'd stopped.

"Drawing gives you joy in general?" Mari asked. "I saw your sketchbook the first day."

I blushed a little at the memory of being caught doodling instead of working. "Yes, always. Since I was little. Did your mum read to you?"

Mari blinked.

The words came out of me in a pained rush. "I'm sorry, I saw she wrote in your copy of *Paddington* and I was curious. Tell me to fuck off if you want."

"I think we've done enough of that to each other already," she said with a weak smile. "And yeah, every night before bed. She wanted me to love books as much as she did. Picture books and poetry when I was little, then Greek and Norse myths when I was older. But she passed away when I was ten."

The book . . . it must have been her mum's last gift. No wonder she'd carried it six thousand miles, kept it by her bed. "Fuck, Mari, I'm so sorry."

"Thank you," she said, the words bland.

I found myself pressing forward, looking for more. "Do you miss her?" Because I missed Alexander like someone had cut off my right arm.

Her lips folded in for a moment, like the words had tried to come out and she'd shoved them back. "It was a long time ago. I'm OK now."

Which wasn't quite an answer, but I could hear the finality in her tone, sense her about to slip behind another door and lock it, so I put my own feelings aside with an internal sigh. "Have you been out exploring London yet?" I asked instead.

She blinked at the change of subject. "I haven't been anywhere except to buy groceries. Been kind of busy, you know, trying not to cough my lungs up. Small stuff like that."

"Of course you've been." I exhaled. "Maybe I could show you around town a bit, when we both have time off. Is there anything in particular you'd like to see?"

Now her eyebrows went up, not that I could blame her for her skepticism. "I never thought you were the tour guide type."

"I've been a rubbish host." I put my hand up to stop her objection. "And I know you're here to work, but this is your first time in London, isn't it?"

She looked at her lap. "First time leaving California at all."

I paused. I knew Americans weren't great travelers, but that seemed unusual to me. "You've never left your state?"

"I love where I'm from. Sonoma County is the most beautiful place on earth. The mountains, the vineyards, the beaches and the forests. I love working at Orchard House too, and I never wanted to be anywhere else."

There was something a little tremulous in her words. This place wasn't just her home, it was her safety, too. "Well, I can't give you most of those things," I said, smiling to take the sting out of the negative. "But are you up for seeing something different? Maybe going to look at some art?"

"Sure," she said. "Since you're the artist, why don't you take me to your favorite place?"

Must not smile like a loon, must not smile like a loon. But she was happy again, her eyes bright, and I couldn't help it.

I was afraid I wasn't going to be able to help a lot of things, when it came to her.

CHAPTER TWELVE

Mari

When we got off the train at Frome in weather that was half mist and half drizzle, I took a deep breath of air that smelled like rain and green things, then another and another. I wished I could bottle it up and take big, deep swigs of freshness when London's smell of exhaust and grime was too much.

Once we were in the cab, Leo seemed happy to look out the window in silence as we drove out of the town and into the velvet-green countryside. I leaned my temple against the cool glass and closed my eyes. I told myself I was getting centered for the meeting with Tommy Clifford, but my mind kept circling back to the last hour.

Leo was so soft for his family, the way his every word glowed like embers when he talked about his sisters and

Judith. He made me want to listen to Gabi's cello too, to watch Sophie play soccer. And I knew Judith felt the same affection from how warmly she looked at him, how clear she'd made it to me that she was on his side no matter what.

I'd had that warmth once.

Now I closed my eyes hard as a wave of sadness went through me. It was a strange kind of travel through space and time, how Mom felt so close to me now, six thousand miles from home. The memories felt clearer, brighter. When Leo had asked if she'd read to me, all of a sudden I was back in my childhood bed with its worn pale pink comforter, soft shadows dancing on the walls from the lamp, giggling as Mom recited Shel Silverstein poems in a goofy voice, or totally rapt as she told me about Odin and Loki, Zeus and Athena.

I was remembering more and more . . . and I wanted to tell Leo what I remembered. Even if the stories had a bitter aftertaste, knowing the pain and the loneliness that had come after.

He'd been so focused sitting across from me, so intent, forearms resting on his thighs and his hands clasped as he listened. Like he wanted to absorb every word. Part of me knew that he understood more about grief than anyone I'd met before, that he knew what it was like to lose your center of gravity and be left spinning helplessly. He wouldn't cringe, wouldn't change the subject, wouldn't throw up his hands and walk away.

But I still didn't want to look back for too long. Didn't want to get trapped in the past. I wasn't helpless anymore, and I refused to be that way again.

Twenty minutes later, we arrived at what had to be

Tommy Clifford's cottage, since there hadn't been another house in sight for the last half of the drive. It was built out of stoop-shouldered red bricks, small square windows glowing warm in the gray.

"Is that roof made of real straw?" I asked.

"Thatch, yeah," Leo said as he climbed out of the car after paying the driver. "Still works as a building method after hundreds of years."

I shut the car door behind me. "Bilbo Baggins, eat your heart out."

A tall, thin man with a slight stoop to match his house opened the front door as Leo and I walked up the gravel driveway. His hair had turned stark white, but there was still plenty of it, needing a trim like it had in that picture fifty years ago.

"Tommy?" I asked, reaching out my hand.

He smiled, his aquamarine eyes wrinkling in the corners as he shook. "The charming Mari, how nice to meet you. I enjoyed your letter. Very pretty." He sized up Leo and his mouth turned down. "And you're a Ross. I'd know you from a mile away."

"Leo," he said stiffly.

Tommy rolled his eyes. "Of course, for the Holy Leopold, Father of the Ross Myth."

Leo was finding the toes of his black brogues fascinating, and I smiled as winningly as I could at Tommy. "It's a helluva drive from the station, isn't it? All those steep hills and dips. Must be a pain in the butt if it snows."

That got me a tiny smile and a head shake. "It's already a palaver in the rain. Come in out of the weather, then," he said, gesturing us into the hallway. As he shut the door behind us, he said, "Before anything else, my answer is going to be no to anything related to Alexander Ross." As he took my parka, he said, "But since you've come all this way, you can have a cup of tea with me before you get a car back to the station."

Leo and I glanced at each other, our faces both falling. "Then why did you let us come all the way here?" Leo asked for both of us, clearly trying to keep the pique out of his voice.

Tommy looked me up and down. "Curiosity, I suppose, at whoever had the audacity to write to me. And my latest book has been going a bit more slowly of late. I thought a change of pace might jog my mind." He snorted. "I can't recommend getting old."

"It's not for cowards, my boss has always said," I replied, and he chuckled.

After Tommy waved me away from the tiny kitchen while he made the tea, Leo and I settled on an overstuffed brown sofa in the living room. A fire crackled cozily in a little stove in the corner, and the straw roof seemed to do a good job at keeping the heat in. Old walnut bookcases sagged under the weight of hundreds of battered paperbacks, literary fiction, mysteries, and old-school sci-fi shuffled in with each other. I smiled at the sight of a complete collection of Georgette Heyer novels, the spines thoroughly broken. The author may have been dubious in her personal views, but I couldn't deny that she wrote a good romance. Even though Tommy didn't seem like the Regency romance type, I suspected that he was more of a dark horse than anyone knew.

"One black tea, one with milk," Tommy said as he placed a big wooden tray with two chunky white mugs in front of us. "Honey for you," he said, nudging a small jar and spoon toward me, "and sugar for the Ross heir."

"What are those?" I asked as I sweetened the steaming black tea, pointing to the golden sandwich cookies on the tray.

Tommy's eyebrows went up. "You've never had a custard cream? Finest biscuit ever made. *He* knows." He gestured to my partner in crime, who'd already jammed a whole one in his mouth and was eyeing up the rest of the plate.

"T'ey're 'orrible," Leo said, his hand over his mouth to block the crumbs. "You don' wan' 'em. Trus' me."

Leo Ross? Being greedy? What a delightful sight. I'd thought of him as the kind of annoying person who never wanted dessert at a restaurant.

Out of nowhere, a low-down part of me wondered: What other sweet things did he like to devour?

I blinked away that erotic train of thought, quickly plucked one of the cookies off the plate. "You lie so beautifully." I took a bite and got a direct hit of creamy, crunchy sweetness, a happy sigh coming out of my mouth.

Tommy eased himself down into a beige armchair that had a body-shaped indent in the cushions. "Now that I've been sufficiently hospitable, what do you want from me?" He nodded to Leo. "I know a bona fide Londoner such as yourself wouldn't come to the deepest, darkest countryside unless he felt he had to. Another celebration for the great literary tastemaker Alexander Ross?"

His tone was light, but I could hear a thread of contempt, too. Judith had tensed up when I'd pressed her about what had caused Tommy and Alexander's break. She squeezed out a terse "artistic differences," before she'd changed the subject.

I glanced at Leo and he dipped his chin to tell me to

take the lead. I took a deep breath to start my song and dance and gave Tommy a big smile. "No, not at all." I explained our plan, to draw in the community around the store, to think about what the future of Ross & Co. could be, instead of living in the past.

I inhaled for the big finale, but a harsh rattle in my chest stopped the words and a round of machine-gun coughs bent me over. It was like the flu had one last tentacle that was refusing to let me go.

"Do you need water, Mari?"

Leo's concerned voice was a lifeline, and everything in me reached for that safety. I nodded, too winded to speak.

"Kitchen's through there," Tommy said, worried. "Glasses to the right of the sink."

I concentrated on getting the oxygen back into my lungs, until Leo was in front of me again with a small glass and a paper napkin. The tap water was cold and soothing. I gulped it down, patted my mouth, cleared my poor throat.

Leo's hand rubbed gentle circles between my shoulder blades, and I closed my eyes for a second, let myself feel that reassurance.

"Better?" he asked, sounding closer, and I realized that I was leaning into him, a flower looking for a little bit of warmth. I looked up, my cheeks burning, about to back off and apologize for invading his personal space, when—

"I'll remind you that I'm an old man who probably shouldn't catch a lurgy like that," Tommy said querulously.

I shook my head as I sat up straight. "I was sick two weeks ago," I said a little hoarsely. "Sounds worse than it is, please don't worry."

"This trip was too soon," Leo said. "We should have waited."

I glared at him for that piece of high-handedness, and he snorted unrepentantly.

Tommy's eyes had zeroed in to where Leo's arm still stretched out to reach my back. "You're looking after her?" he asked, studying Leo's face.

Leo grimaced. "As much as she'll let me. But she's her own person."

And finally, Tommy's face softened. "It's the clever and bloody-minded ones that get you in the end. When they let you in, it's better than getting a Nobel Prize."

I enjoyed being called both smart and stubborn, but the rest of Tommy's words left me feeling like I'd been blinded by a spotlight. "We're not . . ."

"We're not like that." Leo talked over me in a rush. "We're just colleagues."

I nodded, ignoring the feeling that a link was forming between us, something stronger than just saving the store.

"Are you?" Tommy said, the words bone-dry. He looked at me and smiled kindly. "You made a good speech, Mari, but I'm still not certain you haven't wasted your time. Why should I travel all the way up to London to speak at this festival of yours, when I have no investment in the shop continuing to exist? My books sell perfectly well in other places. I certainly won't miss Ross and Co. if it closes." He picked up his mug, like he'd just played his ace and the hand was over.

Time for my trump card. "Judith would," I said quietly.

His teacup froze in front of his mouth, then he took a long sip.

A log popped and sparked in the stove. A crow cawed outside. Leo's eyes burned into the side of my face. I hadn't told him this part of the plan.

"You're old friends, right?" I asked carefully, not wanting to break the spell. "She said you were."

A blush swept over Tommy's cheeks. "Yes, we were friendly once upon a time."

I sat forward, waiting for him to make eye contact with me again. "Before you started writing as Cliff Thomas, you wrote a literary novel under your own name. *Unwisdom*?" I kept my voice low and warm, like I would tell him a secret if he told me one.

He waved a hand at me in dismissal as he put his mug down. "Oh, that pile of rubbish. I'd been reading far too much Updike and Cheever. Juvenilia. It's a blessing that it's been out of print for three decades."

But his red cheeks were telling me something else. "I found a copy and read it. I thought it was beautiful," I coaxed.

He mumbled, "I'm not certain what that says about your taste, but thanks very much all the same."

Leo's eyes on me were wide as I sneaked up to the line between literary discussion and prying. "You wrote about a young sculptor in love with the woman married to his much older patron."

Tommy turned his cup a precise inch to the right. "It's called fiction for a reason," he told it. "Couldn't sculpt my way out of a paper bag."

I opened the side pocket of my purse, took out and placed the picture of Judith and Elizabeth Jane Howard in front of him. I tapped young Tommy's narrow face in the background, his eyes totally focused on Judith. Like he was soaking her in. "That's you," I said quietly. "Looking at her."

His Adam's apple bobbed with a hard swallow, then he

sighed. "Such a terrible cliché, to fall madly in love with your benefactor's wife."

I could sense the held breath next to me, the words Leo was keeping back. His knee started to jiggle, and I put my hand lightly on top of it. He stilled instantly. "They call them tropes, these days," I said to Tommy.

"I mean, all of Alexander's young men fancied her, you see how ravishing she was." Tommy scratched his unshaven cheek. "But we could talk endlessly, she and I, about anything. She teased me into reading Georgette Heyer, you know. When we met, I was a snobbish bore, only wanted to read Great Literature."

"So what made you pull back from her? From them?" Leo asked.

"I couldn't tell her how I felt, though I suspected she knew and was trying to be gentle with me. But I watched her and your grandfather together and finally understood it was hopeless." Tommy shook his head. "They loved each other, even though he treated her like a dolly bird."

My brain caught on the new phrase. "Is that like arm candy?"

He nodded. "I finally had to leave London, I was going to go round the bend otherwise. I picked a fight with Alexander, said writing literary fiction was bollocks. I would write books that millions of people would read and make piles of money and that would be life for me." He smiled a little. "And I have enjoyed myself, don't get me wrong."

"But life has gone on," Leo said. "You're not the same person, and neither is she. She'd really appreciate your friendship."

"Then why isn't *she* here asking?" Tommy asked, hurt in his voice.

Leo knit his fingers together, let his worry show on his face. "She's in a lot of pain, these days, from her arthritis. Going into town is a major achievement for her, even with the best medicine. Some days she can't even make it down the road from her flat."

"I'm sorry to hear that," Tommy said, looking a little mournful. "I remember her as a whirlwind, always in bright dresses, half running from place to place." He glanced over at me. "How do you fit into all of this, then?"

I surfaced out of the sad fifty-year-old story and shrugged. "I'm just here until mid-April to help out. Then I go back to real life."

Tommy gazed at me, and I suddenly felt like he could see my bones and the lonely spaces in between. "Real life? That's a pity. I think you might be good for them. The Rosses." He turned to Leo. "I have one more question for you, boy. What do you think of Alexander, truly?"

Leo shifted in his seat, his mouth turning down, and uncertainty had me gripping the couch. Would Leo talk about the grandfather he loved and missed, or would he step back and look at the bigger picture of Alexander Ross?

"Alexander was important to me," he finally said, his voice a little wistful. "But he wasn't an easy man, or a perfect one." Leo sighed. "For a very long time I thought he was always right about everything. But . . . I think he was much more complicated than he let on."

I could see what it took out of him to be honest about the person he loved, and something in me wanted to honor that bravery. I put my hand on his shoulder and he smiled at me gratefully.

Tommy nodded once. "All right. Send me more information about this festival of yours and I'll see if I can clear space in my diary. It's usually very full, you know."

I raised my eyebrows at him. I'd bet money his calendar only had doctor's appointments in it, but if this was how he was going to play, I'd go along. "We appreciate you taking the time."

"A pleasure to meet you both," he said. Gravel crunched outside the house. "That must be your cab."

Tommy waved us off, and when we were in the back seat of a station wagon returning to Frome, Leo turned to me. "It worked," he said, sounding both elated and exhausted. "I can't believe that worked."

I shrugged. "I can." Leo raised his eyebrows in question, and I continued, "If he definitely wasn't going to say yes, he would have called and told us where to shove the whole idea. He just needed to know we weren't going to waste his time."

Leo's brow furrowed. "I'm not certain whether you're the most terrifying woman I've ever met, or the most perceptive. How do you get away with talking to people like that?" But he didn't sound scared at all. He sounded . . . respectful. Almost a little pleased.

And I liked pleasing him. The realization was a hot little shock, static in wool.

I grinned at him. "I like both those options. And I guess it's because I'm not from here. You guys have all these unspoken rules, but maybe being American gives me a pass."

"I suppose it does." He looked out the car window at a

horse running through a meadow. "I rather like having a secret weapon. Now I know how James Bond feels."

"You can call me Q," I said with a smile.

"Not Moneypenny?" He shook his head at himself, chuckling. "Absolutely not Moneypenny, don't be ridiculous. Of course you're Q. Never thought I'd be the brawn of an operation."

The laugh bubbled up inside me. "Glad we're on the same page."

"Me too." After a few seconds, our laughter faded, and he said again, his voice softer, "Me too."

CHAPTER THIRTEEN

Mari

Day after day, my lungs got better, until a week after the trip to see Tommy I could walk for half an hour around Bloomsbury and not need to sit on a park bench halfway through. Leo's and my working relationship was even healthier, too. WhatsApp messages and spreadsheet edits zipped back and forth between our screens, and we threw ideas around as we organized shelves and sold books.

We'd started to plot the rest of the lineup on the train back to London, and a week later, we had the framework of a festival. Seven events, each lasting forty-five minutes. The first event at eleven, featuring two YA romance writers, one contemporary and one historical, who had wholeheartedly agreed to join in when I'd slid into their DMs on Instagram. Tommy would be our headliner at five, swapping stories with an up-and-coming British-Nigerian thriller writer named Folarin Adegoke.

Then there were all the logistical puzzle pieces that went into organizing a book festival. Basic things like enough chairs for people to sit on, a sound system so our authors wouldn't have to yell. Any book festival worth its salt needed coffee and tea, but there was no way we were going to set up an entire café from scratch in the time we had. With Catriona's help, I'd worked out buying a few used drip coffee machines on Facebook Marketplace and making a setup with compostable cups and thermoses.

But finding all the stuff that made a festival was easy. Getting people in the door? That was going to be a whole new ballgame. There was no way we could rely just on word of mouth—customers were still trickling in instead of flowing like we needed. We had to have an up-to-date website, an online store for selling tickets, and definitely a social media presence to reach the broadest possible audience.

But when I wasn't contemplating the problem, I caught myself contemplating Leo.

How elegant his long hands were when they picked up books and turned the pages. How his eyes were the color of a glass of bourbon in candlelight, and how they widened a little when he asked Sayeeda and Neil what they thought of the current cookbook selection.

I also thought about how they closed in pleasure when he sipped his morning coffee, but that thought got smacked down faster than a mosquito.

Most of all, I thought about how he wore the same outfit every day, black dress pants and black cotton shirt buttoned to the very top button, and a black wool sweater over them when the bookstore thermostat was being really temperamental.

"Don't you know there are other colors, since you're an artist?" I asked him one day, as we were bickering over what we wanted the website to look like, because despite his muttering, Ross & Co. needed more of a brand identity than the name of the store in Times New Roman.

He blinked owlishly at me, which I guessed was fair for how suddenly I'd changed the subject. "I suppose you're not looking for a lecture about the visible spectrum?"

I ignored his sarcasm, gesturing to his outfit. "I mean, who would it hurt if you wore charcoal gray once in a while? Or really went wild and tried navy?"

He looked down at himself for a long second, then shrugged. "It just means there's one less thing to think about in the morning. Also, I have a black cat and she sheds."

"Kitty!" I blurted, then slapped my hand over my mouth. Even for me, that was a little too much enthusiasm. "I'm sorry, I just love cats. We have a bookstore cat at Orchard House named Emperor Norton, and he's one of my favorite things about it." I sighed, missing the lazy orange lump. "Cats are the best."

Leo shook his head and smiled. "Don't they know it. Half the time I don't know whether I'm my cat's favorite person or her hapless butler."

"Can I see a picture?" I asked eagerly.

He took a battered rectangle out of his pocket, tapped and swiped, then held out a picture of silky black fur curled up asleep on top of gray sheets. "This is Mog."

"What a perfect little panther," I crooned. "What does

Mog mean?" I asked in a more normal voice. "It sounds like a witchy name."

Leo shrugged as he put his phone away. "It's slang. Just means cat."

I raised my eyebrows. "You called your cat Cat? Bonus points for creativity."

He snorted, and when I felt the vibration, I realized how close I was sitting to him. When I inhaled, I could smell something simultaneously warm and clean, like bay leaves and spices crushed together.

"Something wrong with your nose?" Leo asked.

I blinked and finally took in his confused face. Oh my God, I'd practically been drooling on him. What was *wrong* with me? "Absolutely not. I was just . . . breathing."

"Breathing?" he said, because I was about as believable as a politician promising world peace.

"Deeply," I persevered. "I was sick recently, remember? My lungs need all the help they can get."

He considered this for what felt like a century, his lips twitching, then said, "All right."

"Moving on." I resisted the urge to press my hands against my red cheeks. We managed to get through the conversation without any more unprofessional outbursts, but thoughts of herbs and spices and that *ridiculous* top button danced through my brain afterward.

An hour later, Graham ambled up to the counter. "Want to go pick up some lunch with me?" he asked.

I blinked. "I thought you brought in food?" I suspected that in his spare time Graham was an amazing cook, since he came in on his work days with a neat pile of Tupperware, and droolworthy smells came from the break room when he was getting his lunch ready.

He shrugged. "Yeah, but it'll keep. Today I really fancy a toastie. Come out with me."

I thought for a second about the bajillion begging emails that I still needed to write. We wanted a historical fiction writer who didn't write about World War II to go with the two writers on the panel who did, and a literary fiction author who wasn't asking a speaking fee that would cost a month's salary. I needed to find a student coder who could take Leo's and my sketches and designs and turn them into an actual website. It was already the end of January, and we had nine weeks to create a festival from scratch, which was basically no time at all.

But maybe I needed to take a break to keep my morale high. I couldn't just eat tuna fish or hummus sandwiches in front of my computer every day. "Sure, why not?"

For a moment I felt eyes on my back, but when I turned around, Leo seemed to be studying his screen intently.

Fifteen minutes later, Graham and I sat in a tiny hippie-ish café tucked behind one of the UCL hospital buildings. He munched a massive grilled cheese sandwich packed with cheddar, red onions, and cilantro chutney, while I inhaled the steam off my lentil soup that smelled like coconut and spices, like a mini-vacation to somewhere a lot balmier than London.

We ate for a little while in appreciative silence, then Graham put his sandwich down, clearly listening to something. He hummed a little bit, then said with a smile, "I suppose today is nineties' throwback day on 6 Music."

"What's this song?" I asked, tearing a chunk off a roll to dip in my soup.

His eyebrows shot up. "It's Blur. One of their hits." His head cocked. "You know Blur? 'Song 2'?"

I squinted, trying to cast my brain back to listening to the radio in the car as a little kid. "Is that the woo-hoo song?"

He snorted. "Yeah, I suppose you could call it that. But this one is called 'To the End.' My dad was obsessed with this album, *Parklife*. I heard it all the time when I was a kid."

"Sounds like you're close to him. Your dad, I mean." Not that I knew anything about what that would be like.

He nodded. "He was a really good dad, growing up." He smiled shyly. "It's a little naff to say, but honestly, he's my best friend, especially now that I'm a grown-up."

I let curiosity override envy. "What do you mean?"

He tented his fingers. "We did all the usual father-son things growing up. Playing football, building Lego, going to see Spurs..."

"Spurs?"

"Tottenham Hotspur. Football team. Or *soccer*," he said, twanging the last word like a banjo string.

"That's what my accent sounds like to you? Jeez." Then I remembered Leo's joy list. "Wait, a football team like Arsenal?"

Graham hissed. "Yeah. They're our big rivals." His eyebrows went up. "Bagsy you're a Spurs supporter."

I laughed. "Sure, whatever you say." I did get the warm and fuzzies that he wanted me on his team, though. "So, your dad?"

"My dad, yeah. We did all those things, but I could talk to him about anything, too." He smiled. "He's not a hard man at all. I know he loves me and Dan and Tim to pieces because he's told us so many times. And he'd always tell me it was all right to cry when I was sad, that I shouldn't bottle everything up." A little chuckle. "It could be all the poetry he reads. But enough about me. What about your dad?"

I took a deep breath. Talking about my mom with Leo made this a little bit easier. "I don't have one." I shook my head when his mouth opened. "I mean, I do, biologically I do. But he was a sperm donor, basically. A guy my mom slept with when she and my stepdad were on a break."

Graham tilted his head, his eyes getting sharper. "He didn't have a name?"

"Nope," I said, punching the *p*. "My mom said she was just with him for one drunken night, then he disappeared."

I took a long sip of my soup, seeking warmth as he chewed over my sob story. Then he leaned forward and said, voice low, "Have you ever done something like 23andMe? I mean, you're how old now? You could look for him, if you wanted."

"I'm turning thirty in May." I pressed my fingers into my forehead. "My mom made me promise not to look. To think of Greg, my stepdad, as my dad. But Greg cut me off right before I graduated from college."

Graham's expression tightened. "Cut you off?"

I winced a little, picking at the scar tissue of this particular memory. "He packed up all his stuff and moved away. He didn't leave a forwarding address, and his old phone number was disconnected." I shrugged. "We weren't close, to say the least. My mom died when I was nine, and he looked after me because there wasn't anyone else. Once I was an adult, he went to go live his own life."

He studied my face. "What an absolute c—" He

paused, then said, "Twat. And I'm so sorry about your mum."

I shrugged. "Thanks. I turned out OK. At least he taught me the life skills I needed. But no, I've never done 23andMe, or looked for my bio dad at all." I was going to climb out of my skin if Graham kept looking at me with puppy-dog pity eyes. "But guess what? I'm meeting Leo to go look at some art tomorrow morning. There's this gallery called the Ralston he wants me to see."

Graham breathed out a laugh. "You're going to a museum with Leo? Really? Isn't that a turn-up for the books? Though you two have been a lot cozier since you went to Somerset."

I shrugged lightly. "We just needed to communicate." I raised my eyebrows at him. "Maybe something for you to think about the next time you and Catriona start bickering over nothing?"

His cheeks turned bright red. "I have no idea what you're talking about, you absolute shit-stirrer."

I scoffed. "So much for being comfortable feeling your feelings."

He folded his arms and clamped his lips like a sulky toddler. I mirrored his posture, trying to make him see how ridiculous he was being.

Finally he exhaled. "I don't know how to fix it. She's so bloody stubborn."

"'Sorry' is usually a good way to start."

He growled, "I *have* bloody apologized, a thousand fucking times."

I rested my chin on my hand, keeping my voice innocent. "For what? Tell me exactly what you apologized for."

Graham's eyes darted around my face. "I apologized that it happened. That she felt bad."

I couldn't help myself, I cracked up. "Oh, for someone so smart, you are such a *schmuck*." I kept going in response to his glare. "What about what *you* did?"

"I DIDN'T—" Graham saw the staring faces around us and immediately stopped yelling. He leaned across the table. "I didn't do anything," he whispered adamantly.

I met him in the middle. "Say it again," I whispered back.

He stared at me like I'd grown an extra head, but repeated, "I didn't do anything."

I sat silently, waiting for him to notice the big fat epiphany waving its arms and jumping up and down. But his puzzled expression made it look like it wouldn't happen today. I leaned back and smiled. "Oh well. You'll figure it out. Back to work?"

He blinked out of whatever thought he was having and nodded. I was halfway out of my chair when he said, "Mari? How would you feel if you met your dad?"

My butt met the seat with a *thunk*. I swallowed hard once, twice. "I don't know how I'd feel," I said slowly. "I don't need a father anymore."

"But would you like one?"

It was like someone asking me if I wanted to take a jetpack and fly to Mars, a hypothetical that had no relationship with reality. "That's such a weird question."

"Come on." He was smiling, but there was something intent in the way he looked at me, like he was really invested in my answer.

For a moment, I let myself imagine my father, the way I had as a kid after Greg put me in time-out for the umpteenth time because I'd made a noise louder than a whisper.

My dad would have my round cheeks and wide mouth. He'd be easygoing, relaxed and quiet where Greg had always felt the need to impose himself on everything and everyone around him. Fantasy Dad would hug me hello whenever he saw me, ask how my work was going and care about the answer. He'd swap books with me, go running with me, but also introduce me to new things, like soccer or classical music or . . . who knows, woodworking. That was a very dad kind of hobby.

"Yeah," I finally said, my voice shaking a little. "Hypothetically, I guess I'd like to have a dad. But the chances of just running into him are, like, less than zero."

Graham shrugged. "You might be surprised."

As he collected our empty plates and took them to the counter, I turned over that phrase, looking for any hidden compartments. Was Graham just being optimistic? It was a conversation that made me feel like I'd walked into a dark forest with no idea where the trail would take me.

CHAPTER FOURTEEN

Leo

I blew on my fingers to warm them up, then shoved them in my pockets again as I waited for Mari outside the Ralston Gallery. Across the street, the trees in Lincoln's Inn Fields were bare, its lawns sodden, and the day was so murky it felt like the sun hadn't bothered to rise. My anticipation at showing Mari some of my favorite paintings was fading, and my mood was starting to echo the gray and mud.

I checked my watch again. Quarter past ten. I was used to giving fifteen minutes' grace to anyone trying to travel in London. Buses could be caught in traffic, Tube trains could be stopped for no reason, someone walking could be waylaid by a chugger wielding a clipboard for direct debit donations, or a tourist asking for directions.

But the Ralston was only twenty minutes' walk from

the shop. Twenty-five, if Mari was pausing to take in the scenery, which she had every right to.

A few minutes passed, and now she was definitely late. Was she just being kind, when she said she wanted me to show her around? Maybe she'd rather be doing this with Graham. The two of them had their little happy conspiracy now, and some small, Gollum-esque part of me wondered if I'd catch them kissing in a corner before too long.

A few tourists climbed up the steps past me on the way into the gallery. My eyes found the toes of my boots, stark black against the pale gray stone of the Ralston Gallery's front steps. I shivered as an icy wind blew across the pavements, sending a few crumpled brown leaves skittering.

The thought of Mari and Graham kissing made me kick another leaf across the step.

My phone buzzed in my pocket and I yanked it out, but the name on the screen wasn't the one I'd hoped for. "Since when do you ring me?" I asked Vinay.

"Can't we ring each other when we have exciting news?"

I rubbed my eyes under my glasses. "Of course we can, I'm such a wanker."

"No, you're not," he said easily. "Are you in the middle of something at the shop?"

I stomped my feet, trying to warm myself up a degree. "Er, no. Not at the shop. I'm at the Ralston Gallery, waiting for Mari."

"Ooh, you're spending time with her outside of work? Interesting." Vinay drew out the last word to be five seconds long.

"It's not like that," I said, trying to convince myself as

much as him. "We work together. Nothing could ever happen."

A pause. "Did Alexander ever make any rules about fraternizing?"

I stared blankly at the Fields as the realization hit me. "No, he didn't." I pressed my hand to my forehead. "And Catriona and Graham were together when they both started working at the shop." Something that was easy to forget with the way they picked fights with each other now. "But I'm technically her line manager, too."

"Didn't you say she was a consultant? It's not like she's really your direct report."

"She isn't, quite. She's the manager of another shop, she's just helping us for a little while."

"Well, then. Don't make it a problem if it's not a problem," Vinay said, sounding just a bit smug.

"But that's my favorite thing to do," I grumbled. "Enough about me. What's your news?"

"Sonali's pregnant with twins. You're going to be an uncle."

My mouth opened and I pumped my fist. "Congratulations, mate," I said, feeling nothing but joy. "I'm delighted for you. I know you both have wanted this forever."

"Yeah, the third round of IVF was the charm. It's just . . . mad. We've been holding on to the news for weeks, not certain if it would take, and it finally has."

"Wonderful," I exhaled.

"And given that circumstances are about to change in a big way—" He paused, and I straightened up, heard a discordant note in his voice. "I'd like to earn another commission, given that we have to buy two sets of baby things, not one. My boss is still wondering about you and your family, if there's something that would make you more interested in selling."

Now I was glad that Mari was late. If Vinay had tried this a few weeks ago, I might have been a bit more open to it. But Mari and I were on the same page, and she was going to fix things, she was going to help resurrect the shop the way Alexander would have wanted.

Her faith bolstered mine.

"I understand, mate," I said gently. "But my answer's still the same."

Vinay's sigh resonated. "I thought it might be. Just . . . if you change your mind, will you let me know?"

I told him I would, and we said our goodbyes.

I sighed as I looked around the empty square, hoping for a hint of chestnut hair. But Mari hadn't come. Maybe she wanted to keep our relationship strictly professional, especially now that she and Graham were getting close. Maybe the hints of something more that I'd felt when we'd talked about books, when I'd soothed her when she was ill, had just been my imagination.

I tapped out a text to her, then shouldered my bag and went inside the gallery, ignoring the way my feet dragged, ignoring the empty space in my chest.

Mari

It was a lot harder to sprint in jeans and Converse than in shorts and running shoes, but I was giving it my best shot, ducking and weaving through other pedestrians as I ran from Ross & Co. to the Ralston Gallery.

Stupid alarm not doing its job, I cursed mentally as I hauled ass down Southampton Row. Stupid early-in-the-morning Mari for switching it off, then turning over and falling back asleep.

I'd told Leo I'd meet him at the gallery when it opened at ten, but when I'd woken up, the digital numbers had flashed 10:20. Adrenaline was a hell of a drug, powering me as I showered, dressed, and inhaled a granola bar.

Go faster, I muttered to myself as I picked up speed. Dive up the front steps, skid to a stop in front of the ticket desk. Racewalk through the gallery; breathe, breathe, breathe because you spend too much time sitting and not enough time running.

Colors and shapes on the walls skipped across my vision as I looked for a skinny, five-foot-nine man wearing all black clothes. Finally, on the second floor, I saw him through an entryway, sitting on a bench. My mouth opened to call his name, to apologize, but my words stopped.

He was alone, silent, and I didn't want to pop whatever creative bubble he was in.

Peace radiated from him as he bent over the sketchbook in his lap. A flat box of colored pencils lay open next the line of the petal just so. I leaned in an inch to get a closer look and got that hint of green and spice on his skin.

And now I could feel his eyes on me. "That's pretty," I said quickly.

His pencil paused on the page. "It's nothing much."

I blinked at the drawing, which looked like it had been picked from a real garden a second ago. "Nothing much?"

"No, I mean . . . thank you. I try to practice. Do you draw?"

"Ha. Do stick figures count?" I looked up at the paintings. "Yeah, no, I suck at Pictionary. But I like looking at art. It's rejuvenating, soaking in beautiful things."

I glanced at him, and he wasn't looking at his drawing. He was taking me in, instead. Like he was going to draw me next. "Rejuvenating. I like that."

After another minute of him drawing and me looking, words bubbled up. "Can I ask you something?"

He put his pencil down and turned to me. "Of course you can."

I pointed at the page he was working on. "Why are you using green in the petal? It's yellow, right? Like an orangey-yellow?"

He shook his head. "At first glance, of course. But nothing's all one color, if you look closely for a long time. It's got all these different shades. I just . . . see them all, and put them down on paper.

"Like your hair." He pivoted a little, his knee nudging against mine, and reached out, using his pencil as a pointer from the top of my head down to my shoulder. "It's definitely chestnut-colored, but under these lights, and with the green walls, the waves have got lilac and mauve in them."

His attention was warm, a lamp burning in the winter dark. Every molecule of my body was alert to how our knees nudged against each other, how the fingertips of my left hand were only a few inches from his right thigh. How his eyes were focused on my blushing cheeks, mouth. How my lips parted.

No, wait. I shouldn't do this. Not with him. He was too familiar now, too close.

"I wish someone had told me that when I tried to dye my hair purple in high school," I said to pop the bubble. "The bathroom looked like Barney the Dinosaur spontaneously combusted."

Leo snorted, shaking his head.

"But seriously, this makes you really happy. And you're, like, genuinely gifted at it."

"I'd be better if I'd studied properly." He looked down at his pad. "But maybe I wouldn't love it in the same way. This way, it's just fun."

I would have believed him if he'd said it with more enthusiasm, but instead all I got was wistfulness. I guessed art school was his road not taken. "But you could still study, right? Adult education is a thing here?"

"It is. But the shop is the priority, which is how it should be."

I couldn't argue with that. It was the reason I was here in the first place. And Leo's hunched shoulders told me I should change the subject. "Does this place have a café? I was so late I didn't get any caffeine, and I'm starting to get a headache."

Leo shut his sketchbook, the sound punctuating the end of his fun. "Of course, come on."

Fifteen minutes later, I hummed happily as I tackled a

wedge of coffee-and-walnut cake, which I hadn't been able to resist ordering with my cappuccino. "How do we not have this cake in the States? It's delicious. It's, like, mapley and nutty and rich. So good."

Leo smirked a little as he sipped his tea. "I suppose the most powerful country in the world can't have everything. Yes to an enormous nuclear arsenal, no to walnut sponge."

I snorted. "I'd want the sponge, not the nukes, but that's just me." I waved my fork at him. "Also, can we talk about Ribena? And blackcurrant things in general? Graham gave me some British Skittles the other day, and there should be blackcurrant-flavored everything as far as I'm concerned."

"Even lube?"

My mouth gaped. Leo clapped his hand over his mouth, eyes wide.

The laugh burst out of me like water from a fire hose. "Lube? *Lube?!*"

He closed his eyes like he was a small child, pretending the world disappeared when he couldn't see it. "I'm sorry," he mumbled through his fingers. "I don't know what came over me."

"No, no, don't apologize," I said through my giggles. "You, Leo Ross, have hidden depths."

Now his hand covered his whole face. "That was a depth that should probably have stayed hidden."

I put my fork down, reached out and tugged on his hand, pulled it away so I could see him. "Why? You're funny."

He looked down at where I was holding his hand in mine, surprise written across his face. "You're the only person who's ever said that."

"Bashful" wasn't an adjective I usually applied to myself, but I could feel my cheeks getting pink and an awkward chuckle sneaking out of my mouth. "Well, you are." I let him go, tried to find the composure that had gone AWOL.

I'd forked up another bite of cake to shut myself up when he blurted, "You should come for Friday-night dinner sometime soon."

I blinked. "You want me to come for Shabbos?" That felt . . . intimate. Too intimate? Shabbos was usually for family, and I definitely wasn't family.

He nodded eagerly. "It'd delight Judith, and you could join my sisters' little coven. Wait, are you Jewish?"

"I'm not, but you know Suzanne is. She sometimes made a Friday-night dinner when she missed her mom. It made her feel like she was still here." I smiled a little. "I don't really get noodle kugel. Cheesy noodles with raisins and cinnamon is such a weird side dish."

"Mum doesn't make lokshen pudding, but she loves to cook all sorts of things." His eyes went wide. "But will you come? Please?"

I looked at his earnest face and the automatic *No* dissolved in my mouth. I knew from going to Suzanne's that Friday-night dinner was more than just food. It was ritual, warmth, and light. It sounded tempting in the middle of the London winter.

"Are you sure you want me there?" I still asked.

Leo hesitated, smiled shyly. "I'm not your boss, Mari. You don't have to come if you don't want."

That shy smile was a taste of honey, and I wanted more of it. And he was right, he wasn't in charge of me. I could decide how close we would get. "Yes, I'll come. Thank you for inviting me."

He exhaled. "Good. I'm glad. And you're welcome." He sat back in his chair. "And I'll make sure Mum makes something you can eat. She's cooked salmon before."

I waved him off. "Oh, I've eaten just side dishes plenty of times. I don't want to be a pain."

He shook his head hard. "My mum's big on being hospitable. She'll be upset if you can't eat everything."

I was about to protest at the fuss involved, but then I thought of his hand on my back at Tommy's, the glass of water, the look of concern. His acts of care hadn't irritated me. They hadn't made me want to throw up spikes and sharp edges.

I liked it when he fussed over me. So why not let him do it? It wouldn't necessarily lead to anything deeper.

CHAPTER FIFTEEN

Leo

It was one thing to invite a colleague over for Friday-night dinner, particularly one who was visiting from abroad. That was being warm and welcoming, that was being hospitable.

It was another to invite over the colleague whose raucous laugh I'd found myself listening for over the last week, whose gentle hand on mine in the Ralston Gallery café had made me want to take it and kiss it.

I paced the floor of my bedroom, counting the seconds until Mari arrived, not knowing whether I wanted to stop time or speed it up. Bex had always said she was never quite sure what I was thinking because of how quick I was to agree with her about everything. Toward the end, we'd grown so far apart that trying to say something meaningful would have been like trying to shout from miles away. But now, whenever I saw Mari, I felt like some mischievous higher power had taken a Sharpie and scribbled my dreams and longings all over my face.

If I didn't want her to notice I fancied her, I was doing an absolutely brilliant job.

As I turned for another pass across the room, Mog meowed grumpily at me from her perch at the end of my bed.

I pulled my fingers out of my hair and sighed. "Yes, Your Majesty, I know you don't like it when I stomp around. Especially when I could be petting you."

I sat down next to the little loaf and dug my fingers into her favorite spot behind her ears, telling her how good and sweet she was. She shut her eyes in feline bliss, purring like a moped engine.

My door opened, and Mari slipped through the gap. "Hello, Leo, and hello, precious little void."

At the sound of her cheerful voice, my hands involuntarily went to my hair to smooth it down, my cheeks flushing.

Mog narrowed her eyes at the intruder, but Mari turned to me, politely ignoring the cat in the way all cat people know to do. "Your mom sent me up here," she said, miraculously not noticing my stricken face. "Dinner in ten minutes, she says."

I inhaled the scent of frying onions and herbs, my stomach torn between hunger and trepidation. "Did you make it here all right?" I asked, trying to keep the stress out of my voice. "Hard to find your way to a new place in the dark." *Well done, Leo, that wasn't asinine at all.*

But Mari nodded. "Oh yeah, fine. I'm glad I left on time, it started to rain when I turned onto your street.

But it's pretty here. Villagey." She paused, and her mouth turned down slightly.

I sat upright. I didn't mean for my unhappiness to ruin her evening. "What's wrong?"

"Nothing," she said too quickly. I waited for the lie to dissipate, and she shoved her hands in her jeans pockets. For a moment she looked almost... shy. "I don't think your mom liked my hostess gift."

I blinked at the old-fashioned phrase. "You brought a hostess gift?"

She rolled her eyes. "Of course I did. Suzanne would fly here and kick my butt if I didn't."

I shook my head. Just because Mari dressed casually and didn't stand on ceremony 95 percent of the time didn't mean she didn't know something about manners. "So what did you bring?"

"Some pink gerbera daisies? The big, cartoony-looking ones?" She half smiled. "I can see from downstairs where you inherited your dislike of color from. I've never seen so many different shades of beige. Or would you say it's greige?"

I winced. My mother redecorated every few years, but always with the same neutral palette. "Yes, it's greige. But *I* like color."

"To draw with, sure. But nowhere else," she argued back.

"I like it when you wear it," I blurted, barely resisting the urge to slap my hand over my mouth after saying it, like I had when I'd made that idiotic comment about blackcurrant lube.

Astonishment widened Mari's eyes.

I'd gone so long without being embarrassed, but this

pretty American woman had blasted a gaping hole in my filter. Now I flailed my hand at her jumper, fuzzy wool the color of a tropical sea. "It suits you. You're a colorful person."

Her eyes narrowed. "I'm not sure that's a compliment."

I just barely stopped myself from mussing my hair again. For fuck's sake, I could use my words better than that. But I couldn't use just any words, because revealing to my coworker that I'd developed a schoolboy crush on her would be disastrous on multiple levels. "You know what it's like when you see a rainbow?" I said carefully, like I was walking along a narrow, high wall, resisting the urge to put my arms out for balance.

"Yeah?" she answered just as slowly.

"Like everyone stops to look at it, to appreciate it, because you can't help but take in all those colors? That's what it's been like, having you at the shop. You walk into a room and everything gets more vivid, and people can't help but feel . . . joyful."

My unspoken words floated in the air between us.

You make me smile. You make me laugh. When you open your mouth and say something saucy, all I can think about is the curve of your lips.

"Joyful?" Mari's face was uncertain, her fingers knotted together. "I . . ." she started, her sweet face blushing daisy pink.

As subtly as I could, I gripped my duvet. I couldn't reach for her, couldn't untangle those fingers and kiss each one.

But now she shook her head, putting her easy smile back on. "Never mind. Thank you. What's Mog's story? When did you get her?"

I exhaled, reached over to scratch Mog's head until she closed her eyes in pleasure. "I didn't so much get her as she got me. I'd just turned nineteen, and I was taking out the rubbish at the shop on Fireworks Night and heard this tiny little squeak from under one of the bins. When I looked underneath, I found this ball of black fluff with yellow eyes, who hissed at me like a little angry panther. I managed to lure her out with some cheese and took her to the vet near here." I held up my right hand so she could see the fine scars from baby Mog's claws across my knuckles. "Got these for my pains. But the vet said the local RSPCA was full up of stray cats, and deep down I knew I wanted to be the one who looked after her. So I took her home."

"Why did you want that, when she'd scratched the shit out of you? Because you felt responsible?"

I didn't fully understand why Mari's brow was furrowed, but all at once I wanted her to know this, know *me*. "No. I wanted to care for her because I liked her from the first moment I saw her. She was adorable and ferocious at the same time, and I wanted . . ." I swallowed as the truth of Mog and the truth of Mari hit me at the same time. "I wanted to win her trust."

It was like some higher power had pressed pause on the moment, leaving my heartfelt words floating between us. Mari's mouth gaped slightly.

"And she does trust me, most of the time," I said, forcing lightness into my voice. "As long as I do what she wants. Which I do, often."

Mari paused for a long second, indecision on her face, until she smiled at Mog. "Well, I can't totally blame you, because she's gorgeous, aren't you, sweet girl?"

Mog looked over at Mari, then reached out her long legs in a luxurious stretch, maintaining eye contact. In a classic move, she lazily flopped over to show her stomach for admiration and pets.

But Mari's eyes narrowed. "Oh, no. That's the Belly of Deception. If I pet you there, you'll shred the meat from my bones."

I snorted. "Belly of Deception. Very good." I reached out and ran my hand down the especially soft fur, and Mog arched to give me more to touch. "But she's weirdly all right with it, honestly."

Mari hesitated for a moment, then sat down on the mattress on Mog's other side and trailed her hand down the cat's belly. "Aren't you a fuzzy little weirdo," she said as Mog thrummed. "Where's your sense of danger, huh?"

Mog closed her eyes and purred louder in response.

"She likes you," I said softly.

"I don't know why." Mari's mouth turned up in a gentle smile. "But I'm honored."

"Dinner!" my mother called up the stairs, and all at once Mog rolled over, hopped off the bed, and trotted out the door.

Mari and I got up to follow. She chuckled a little and said, "I should have asked you. About the hostess gift. I could have gotten a box of chocolates or something."

I smiled involuntarily and shook my head.

Mari barked out a laugh. "Your mother doesn't eat chocolate either, huh? I guess some people just don't like pleasure."

She turned for the door, and a flush crept up my neck. *Pleasure.* That word was in my vocabulary for tiny, furtive things. Pink marshmallows melting on my tongue, the scratch of a sharp colored pencil across a fresh sheet of paper.

It wasn't a word I associated with Mari Cole. I couldn't, for the sake of the shop, for the sake of my sanity. It was no use, hoping for impossible things.

CHAPTER SIXTEEN

Mari

I winced at the sight of my daisies in a gray vase in the middle of the black dining room table. They had looked so cheerful in the grocery store, but now they looked as garish as a flamingo on the tundra.

Had my blush been as pink when Leo had said how joyful I made everything? I was pretty sure it had. It definitely was when he'd talked about Mog, how he wanted this prickly little animal to feel safe with him, and for a split second I'd wished he were talking about me.

Steadiness was an illusion, I knew that. People changed their minds from second to second, strung you along, left with no warning.

But Leo was real, and solid, and he didn't say things he didn't mean. At least, I didn't think he did.

"I like the flowers," Judith said kindly from her seat next to me. "So bright."

"So do I," Leo's sister Sophie said immediately. "I wanted to paint my side of our bedroom hot pink, but Mum said no."

Her sister, Gabi, chimed in with a shy grin. "And I wanted to do my side aqua green, so it would be like Miami colors."

"You can paint your rooms whatever color you like when you live in your own house, my loves," Leo's mother, Elaine, said, her smile harried.

Leo leaned over to Sophie. "When you do, I'll come help."

I smiled back at the Rosses weakly. I would have felt better about the color explosion if all the Ross family members weren't also wearing black, though Judith had at least wrapped a black-and-white polka-dot scarf around her neck.

"Do you like the Riesling, Mari?" Elaine asked. She was slender, with Leo's almond-shaped eyes and pointed face, her ash-blond hair contrasting with her almost-black brows. "You must be used to good wine where you come from."

"This is nice, thank you," I lied politely. I could tell it was good wine, but it was the kind of minerally white that tasted like sucking on a chunk of granite. What did people have against wine that tasted like fruit?

Mr. Ross's chair sat at the table, empty. I didn't know how he could resist the smells coming from the dishes on the table. There was a side of salmon topped with frizzled onions and lots of capers and dill, a bowlful of rice pilaf glistening with butter, a huge plate of cut-up raw vegetables with what looked like a yogurt and herb dip, a golden loaf of challah dotted with black and white sesame seeds.

"Shall we eat while it's hot?" Judith asked Elaine.

"David knows dinner is ready," Elaine said tightly. "He'll come before too long. You know how he is when local elections are so soon."

A few minutes later, I heard footsteps. "Dinner! Why didn't you call me?" David said briskly as he came into the room.

Judith rolled her eyes at me.

"Ooh, salmon. Looks like we're ringing the changes here." David sat down at the head of the table. "What happened to the Shabbos chicken, my love?"

"Our guest doesn't eat meat, Leo told me. I took it as an opportunity to try out some new dishes." She nodded to me. "I also made special custard with oat milk to have with pudding."

I blinked at Leo. I hadn't said explicitly that I was lactose intolerant, but he'd brought me coffee at the store enough times that he could make an educated guess. "Thank you for thinking of me. I could have just skipped the custard."

Leo looked at me in horror. "No one should ever have to miss custard."

I cracked up a little at how adamant he was. It was a welcome break from Elaine's polite smiles.

"So, are you two pulling the shop back from the brink of death?" David said, the cheerfulness in his voice undercut with something sour.

Leo's hand was going to have marks on it from how tightly he was gripping his knife. "Yes. Mari's doing a wonderful job. Her help was just what we needed."

It was hard to bask in the compliment when it was actually a barb aimed at someone else. Elaine's eyes darted between her husband and son, and some instinct I didn't know I had made me want to smooth those sharp edges. "We don't have to talk about work here. I'm just happy to eat a nice meal. I've been eating a lot of canned soup and microwave meals in the attic, and this all smells heavenly. Where did you get the recipe for the salmon, Mrs. Ross?"

Leo's eyebrows went sky-high at my rapid-fire speech, but he was smart enough to keep his mouth shut.

"Oh, goodness, please call me Elaine," she said. "And it's an American recipe, actually."

"Elaine's a brilliant cook," David said, and it was the first time I'd seen him smile. "You should see her collection of cookbooks. I had someone build floor-to-ceiling bookcases when we redid the kitchen, and she filled them in just a few months."

Elaine chuckled. "I can't help myself. They keep publishing new ones all the time, and I get so excited at the prospect of trying something new."

I asked her about her favorite writers, and we settled into bookish conversation, swapping recommendations. I promised to order *Crying In H Mart* for her, and to hunt down a copy of *Good Things* by Jane Grigson for myself.

As I made a note on my phone, she looked over at where Leo was focused on his meal. "I should make this salmon again, Leo. You've almost finished your plate."

He froze with his fork halfway to his mouth.

"Leave him alone, Elaine," David said wearily.

"I was just noticing he was enjoying the food, nothing more."

David raised his eyebrows. "Were you?"

Understandably, Leo put his full fork down. Who'd want to eat when everyone was looking at him like he was behind bars in a zoo?

"Leo showed me around the Ralston Gallery," I piped up. "You guys are so lucky to have such amazing art on your doorstep."

I almost sighed with relief when Judith's mouth twitched. "Did he now? It used to be his and Alexander's favorite place to go. Alexander would say he practically had to carry Leo out of there. If he could, he would have stayed all day to draw."

I nodded eagerly. "I know, I saw him sketching."

Now Elaine put her fork down. "You *saw*?"

I blinked at her surprise, but now Sophie and Gabi sat up in their seats. "If you're doing art properly again, can we have more stuff for our walls?" Gabi asked Leo.

Leo reached for his napkin and wiped his mouth, even though as far as I could tell there hadn't been any mess. "Of course you can," he finally said, smiling shyly. "What would you like?"

As Gabi and Sophie talked over each other, making requests for flowers and animals and landscapes, Elaine bustled around the table clearing dishes while David disappeared to make another work call. Judith reached over and squeezed my hand.

"I'm so glad you joined us," she said. "Leo's not asked anyone to dinner in a long time. I hope you can come again before you return to America."

Her last words felt like someone had turned on a harsh light in the cozy room. I was leaving in less than two months. This wasn't my family. It couldn't be mine. I needed to stop drinking from this well. "We'll see. I think we'll be pretty busy as we get closer to the festival."

Judith's forehead wrinkled. "I understand. I know you two are working so hard."

I nodded at her words, ignoring the sadness in her tone. "We are. Ooh, that looks great, Elaine." I speed-ate a bowl of the deliciously tart rhubarb crumble she served me, then stood up from the table and made noises about a long week, an early night.

But once I'd put my parka and shoes on, Elaine opened the door to what looked like an ice monsoon, rain and snow mushed together. "Oh no. We can't possibly let you walk to the station in that. The sleet's practically horizontal."

Leo squinted at his phone. "There's a yellow warning until three A.M."

"You should stay with me downstairs overnight," Judith said warmly, putting her hand on my arm. "It's filthy out there. You can sleep on my sofa bed."

I couldn't bear to stay in this place a second longer than I had to. It made me want too much. "No, thank you. I couldn't impose on you like that."

"You wouldn't be imposing," Leo said.

I ignored the warm feeling in my chest from his kind expression and shook my head. "It's really hard for me to sleep in a new place. I'll be a lot happier in my own bed."

"Then we'll call you a taxi," he said firmly.

Judith nodded. "That's a good idea."

"But that's hella expensive," I interrupted.

"We're your hosts, we'll pay," she replied, then said more quietly, "I know we're struggling, Mari, but we're not so desperate as that."

How did I explain that it wasn't about the money, that I couldn't handle that kind of generosity? But it was like speaking a foreign language to them.

Leo's mouth turned down. "The taxi's website says it'll be at least an hour's wait."

Uber would probably be on surge pricing, if a car would show up in the first place. "I'm just going to go to the station," I said finally. "It's not that bad."

The last word was punctuated by the sleet suddenly picking up, sounding like hundreds of water balloons exploding.

Judith looked back and forth between Leo and me, and I could have sworn I saw the tiniest smile on her lips. "We can't let you go alone. It's not safe when it's like this." She waved to Leo. "Go with Mari, make sure she's all right."

Rejection opened my mouth. I wasn't fragile. I just didn't know what to do with Leo's hopeful looks and Judith's thoughtful ones. "I don't need . . ." I tried one more time.

Judith stared me down. "For my sanity, please let him go with you."

I knew something about Jewish guilt from Suzanne. Only an idiot would try to hold out. I sighed. "Fine. At least it's not a blizzard, I guess."

I waited while Leo shoved his feet into his boots and zipped himself into a black rain jacket with a hood. I turned up my parka's hood, though I was sure the wet down was going to feel like wearing cement by the time I got home.

Once we were standing outside on the front step, the saffron-warm light of the Ross house shining on us from the windows, I asked Leo, "How fast can you walk?"

He raised his eyebrows at me. "I grew up in London. It's illegal to walk slowly. They'll arrest you and everything."

"You're still funny," I said, raising my eyebrows back. "Race you to Hampstead?"

Instead of telling me I was ridiculously immature, he smiled slowly, and an answering little flame lit up in my chest.

"Ready to lose?" he asked.

"Never." I bumped him lightly with my shoulder to knock him off balance, then jumped down the steps and raced off into the sleet, going as fast as I could toward the station. Leo's feet slapped the wet sidewalk behind me, and I could feel cold water splashing up my legs, but I was single-mindedly focused on my destination, getting to warmth and shelter as quickly as possible.

In spite of the race, we were still soaked when we got to the station, and I could feel my parka steaming and the damp denim of my jeans becoming itchy as we descended in the elevator and walked to the southbound platform. It was busy with bodies, and the sign showed we still had another five minutes to wait until the next train. Five minutes was a long time when the surrounding air was an old wool blanket, prickly and stale and too warm. More and more people filtered onto the platform, and I started shifting on my feet, looking to make sure the exit was still there. I tried to concentrate on my breathing, count four seconds out and four seconds in, but before long those four seconds were more like one.

"Is there a bus?" I finally asked Leo.

His eyes were barely visible behind the steam on his glasses. "Yes. But it's not frequent, and you'd have to change to get to Bloomsbury. The only real option would be to go back to the house and wait for a cab, like I suggested the first time."

I didn't bother to answer that last high-handed comment, just stood there staring at the screen until the Northern line train finally arrived. All the seats were taken, but there was room to stand. I thought I would be OK, but the train filled up more and more as we traveled south, and my tolerance shrank and shrank, until at Euston I was repressing the urge to scream at the invasiveness of it all, the noises and closeness and tension.

"Leo?" I said instead. I hated how small my voice sounded.

He took one look at my face, grabbed my hand, and tugged me close to him as more people piled into the car. I tried to close my eyes, tried to breathe deeply. An exhale came out of me that sounded a lot like a whimper.

Leo's mouth was tight, his brow furrowed. "What's wrong?"

"I'm..." I tried to say but choked on my own panic. It was so stupid, but how was I supposed to have known this before? I'd grown up practically in the middle of nowhere, I'd always driven places, and the biggest city I'd been to, San Francisco, was a toy village compared to London. "I think I'm a little claustrophobic," I said, trying to keep my voice easygoing and failing miserably.

"How much is a little?" He squeezed my hand gently, grounding me.

"I'm like a six out of ten." I tried to smile. "Zero meaning I fantasize about sleeping in a coffin, ten meaning I've already moved to a cabin in Alaska."

"Mari, stop joking and tell me what you need."

His voice was urgent and a little stern, and I gave up

the pretense that I was anywhere in the vicinity of OK. "I don't know," I said, my voice thin.

He bit his lip and looked over my head, down the Tube car. "I'll get you off the train at the next stop," he said into my ear. "Until then, hold on to me. It means you'll be close to me, instead of a stranger." He suddenly gulped. "Unless that's too much."

"I don't like that you keep having to take care of me," I complained half-jokingly.

The corner of his mouth curled up. "I won't get used to it, I promise."

I eased into him. Keeping one hand on the pole, he carefully slid his other hand under my jacket and around my waist, a gentle support. I pressed my cheek against his chest, soft black wool and the faint thump of his heart, and exhaled again.

"That's it, keep breathing," he said, his chest vibrating under my ear as he spoke.

We swayed together with the movement of the train, and I closed my eyes so I couldn't see the crowds around us. Shutting down one sense sharpened the others: Leo smelled damp from running through the sleet, but underneath was the scent that was all him, bay leaves and warm spices, clean and comforting.

"You're doing so well, darling," he whispered. "Not much longer now."

All of a sudden, the train slowed down, then jerked to a stop, nudging us into each other. I opened my eyes and glanced out the window, but I could only see darkness, think about that small, coaxing word.

Darling?

"We're being held at a red signal," a distorted, buzzing voice said. "We should be on the move shortly."

A deep groan went through the car. Leo's arm tightened and I burrowed into him.

Another crackle, then, "Sorry for the delay," the announcer buzzed. "There appears to be an issue with a passenger at Warren Street. We've been asked to hold here until the situation is resolved."

Groans of *Fuck's sake* and *Shit* echoed around me, but Leo kept quiet, running his hand up and down my back in long, soft passes. "I have you, Mari," he whispered. "You're safe with me."

No one had said anything like that and meant it. But something deep down inside me, for once, believed him.

I said Leo's name again, but this time it was a sigh. His hand pressed gently, and I shifted that little bit closer. When I looked up at him, our faces were so close that he was just shapes in the dim light—slash of black eyebrow, pale blade of nose, his full mouth an outline. I couldn't help but focus on it. It would be so easy, a perfect little peck on his full bottom lip. That devilish mouth made for smiling and laughing and other more lascivious things.

His eyelids drooped a little as he caught me staring, and his gaze dropped to my mouth. He exhaled softly, his breath warm on my face, and a shiver shot through me, shoulders to stomach to knees. I tilted my head, let my eyelids flutter shut.

The train jerked to life, and Leo tripped backward. Suddenly, we had a few inches of space. Space that suddenly felt like a chasm when he looked at me, dark-eyed and flushed.

"I'm sorry, I didn't mean—" he blurted.

"Warren Street," the announcer finally called.

Mean what? I thought, stricken by the cliffhanger, but in the massive shove to get off the train, I didn't get the question out. A wave of strangers turned and walked toward the "Way Out" sign, but I hung back. I took huge lungfuls of the stale warm air, waved my arms around and bounced up and down, then did a few jumping jacks for extra energy.

"Why on earth are you doing star jumps?" Leo asked incredulously, his hands on his hips.

"Reclaiming. My. Personal. Space," I said, punctuating each word with a jumping jack. "Do you call these star jumps? I think *this* is a star jump." I crouched down to the floor in a ball and then leaped straight up, exploding out my arms and legs.

He looked up and down the platform, uncertain. A few people were clustered near the exit, but the crowds had disappeared.

"Come on, Leo," I challenged. "You're never going to see those people again. We can just be two weirdos together."

For a second I thought he'd just roll his eyes at me and walk off. But then his arms windmilled, his legs kicked out, and I got to see Leo Ross *let go*, pogoing like we were a two-person mosh pit, his salt-and-pepper hair flying, his cheeks flushing.

"Yeah, dude," I said too loudly, "that's it."

"I can't believe I'm throwing shapes on a Tube platform in the middle of the night," he said, laughing.

"I can't believe you're doing it, either!" I jumped into the air and whooped, and for thirty seconds we danced to music only we could hear until all the stress had left our bodies and we were gasping for breath. Gasps that suddenly sounded like we were out of breath from doing something else entirely.

Leo straightened up and shook his head. "Let's get you home," he said, somehow both firm and breathless. "We have work in the morning."

I studied his pink cheeks, the brightness in his brown eyes, and the urge to do another wild, weird, crazy thing almost overwhelmed me: to ask him to come home with me. Not to ask. *Beg.* Beg for his full mouth on mine, his artist's hands on my skin.

But he was right. We had work in the morning. More importantly, he was too good, too soft to understand that all I wanted was one wild night. That I didn't do deeper feelings. That I couldn't.

So I kept my mouth shut and followed him to the "Way Out" sign.

CHAPTER SEVENTEEN

Leo

Mari's eyes, soft and trusting in the dark of the Tube carriage.

I opened my own eyes and shook my head hard. I was crouched on the ground in front of Ross & Co.'s doors. After last night's sleet, Saturday had dawned below freezing, the sky a high, pale blue, the kind of day that was perfect for a long tromp across the Heath, feeling ice crunch under my boots. Not that I had a chance of that kind of luxury today. I had a festival to organize, but all my brain wanted to do was replay those three minutes of the trip home last night.

Mari's body, warm and curved and so close to mine.

The closeness of her, her tropical scent, had left me vibrating, needy and craving, and even though I'd used my hand and some soap to take the edge off when I'd finally gotten home and defrosted in a hot shower, I'd still been wide awake before my alarm. Graham was meant to open the shop, but I was sure he wouldn't complain if I got the boiler going before he arrived. The gate rose with a complaining screech, the metal dull cold even through my glove as I shoved it open.

I walked into the shop, not bothering to take off my coat and hat. Bluish winter light streamed dustily through the windows. Mari must not have been out of the garret yet. No, I couldn't think of her still snug in her bed—it would be far too tempting to go up the stairs and knock on her door, ask if I could climb into all that warmth and softness, hold her close like I had the night before.

I set the heating to turn the shop from freezing to just-barely-warm-enough. In the break room I put the kettle on to boil, put a tablespoon of instant coffee and a packet of hot cocoa mix into a chipped blue mug. A little powder spilled next to it, and I absent-mindedly dabbed it with my fingertip. But when I popped my finger in my mouth...

Mari's mouth, full and pink and just the tiniest bit open.

I groaned. Oh God, I had wanted to kiss her more than I'd ever wanted chocolate. I'd have given up sugar in an instant if it meant I could touch her lips with mine.

Touch? More like devour. And not just her mouth, either.

"Gorgeous out there," Graham said behind me. "Cold as brass monkeys, but gorgeous."

My fantasy evaporated, and I coughed, mortified. "Yeah. Lovely."

"Kettle's on too, fantastic." He shuffled up next to me. "Any reason you're in so early? I know this place is your life, but surely you don't want to be here every hour of the day?"

His smile said he was waiting for a joke. "No," I said stiffly, consumed with thoughts of Mari.

He blinked. "All right, mate. I'll check on the computers, shall I?" I didn't know how he was relaxed even in the face of my coldness. God, what would Mari want with me? He was so cheerful and at ease with himself. I was awkward and withdrawn, a bunch of nettles in human form.

"Hi, boys," my brain's singular obsession said warmly from the doorway. "Any hot chocolate for me? It's frosty today."

"Sure," Graham said. "Leo could make you one of his mochas, if you wanted. They're somehow rubbish and delicious at the same time."

I turned around as Graham left and Mari nodded to him with a smile. There was no sign that she'd been affected by me, by us being wrapped in each other, practically inhaling each other's breath. I looked for a flush on her cheek, a tremble in her hands.

"A rubbish mocha sounds good right now," she said.

Without saying anything, I boiled more water, focused intently on measuring out coffee and cocoa, added a big splash of oat milk. When I handed her the hot mug, I could have sworn our fingertips touched, but that must have been wishful thinking on my part. "We have a meeting later," I said abruptly. "About the ticket sales for the festival."

"Yeah," she said softly. "Of course."

Wait. She hadn't yet made any eye contact with me. "Mari?" I asked tentatively.

"Yeah?" I waited, and finally she looked into my eyes.

Her cheeks blushed a shade of cherry-blossom pink I wanted to capture with watercolors, a wash of spring on snowy paper. I wanted to see that blush on the rest of her skin too, wanted to follow its path with my hands and my mouth.

"Leo? Did you want to say something?"

Oh, I was an unprofessional horny bugger, standing here staring at her. "I forgot. Carry on."

"OK, then," she sounded out slowly. "I guess I'll see you at two." She turned and ambled out. "Blondie," I heard her call, "I watched some of that 1980s crime show you told me to. That was nuts. I can't believe they stole all that gold by accident."

The masochist inside me stuck my head out the door to see Mari and Graham grinning at each other, and my stomach fell into my shoes. I was pining for her like a desperate Romantic poet without the good lines, but she simply didn't feel the same way about me. The sooner I got that through my head, the better.

Mari

I was pretty sure last night on the train hadn't been an extremely sexy hallucination, but Leo's body language in the kitchen said I must have been imagining things. Or that he wanted me to think I'd been imagining things. A rock of disappointment had sunk in my belly when he'd held himself away, eyes down.

The whole dance that Leo and I seemed to be moving through was new to me. Two steps forward, one and a half steps back, moving forward but never getting there. A Zeno's paradox of yearning.

A life of flings didn't leave room for yearning, and I'd been fine with that. I didn't love feeling on edge like this.

It really didn't help that my sex brain was writing a long to-do list in multiple senses of *doing*. I was in general pretty vanilla, but something about the combination of Leo's quiet reserve and his proper accent and *that one stupid top button* made me want to break his composure in the filthiest possible way, so that all he'd want to do was take me to bed and do filthy things to me back. The kind of things that had me waking up wet and gasping.

I paused in the middle of writing my action list for the day and smacked myself gently on the forehead with my pen. I couldn't fantasize in the middle of the store. Even I had limits.

The morning went by in a blur of logistics emails to all

the different vendors we needed for the festival. The chair guy, the sound guy, the printer for programs and schedules. I sipped canned tomato soup from a mug as I wrote, and at lunchtime I slipped out for a quick walk to soak in the frosty blue sky and white light. But I couldn't stop checking my watch, urging the winter shadows to move faster across the bookstore floor.

When two o'clock rolled around, I tapped on Leo's office door, then opened it. He shot out of his chair like I'd electrocuted him.

"Sorry, didn't mean to surprise you," I said, surprised myself.

"You didn't," he said as he sat back down. "It's fine. Just away with the fairies, that's all." He shuffled some papers, cleared space. "Ticket sales."

I shook my head and sat on the wooden chair beside his desk. "Yeah, ticket sales. There's a little bit of movement after hanging flyers in the student union and in the cafés around here, but it's not enough. I was thinking we might want to involve some Bookstagrammers and BookTokkers based here. Offer a free ticket in return for some promotion on their accounts."

"What would that look like?" he asked, sounding curious and not dismissive like he would have done when I first arrived. "And wouldn't we need an account of our own? We've never done social media, and I wouldn't know where to begin."

I resisted the urge to ask him what century he'd been born in. "Ross and Co. has an Instagram account," I confessed instead.

He blinked at me. "We do? But I haven't . . ."

"No, I set one up on my own." His mouth opened, and

I put my hand up. "I swear on Louisa May Alcott's grave that I haven't done anything with it. It's set to private, I'm not following anyone, and there are no posts. But I wanted to claim the right handle before anyone else could."

Six weeks ago he would have been outraged, and part of me was holding my breath that I hadn't moved us back in time, that I hadn't lost his trust, so hard-won. But now he sighed. "All right, fine, show me."

I told him the login details and introduced him to the wild world of Bookstagram. "People really are keen on this, aren't they?" he said thoughtfully as he flicked through reels of people raving about books. "They love the stories and they love books as objects, too. It's all very emotional."

I nodded eagerly. "People have a lot of feelings tied up in reading. I definitely have some books I read for comfort."

"Like *Paddington*?"

I smiled. "Like *Paddington*."

He flipped over another Instagram reel and I leaned over to watch it with him. Bay leaves, spices, his watchful quiet, they drew my attention even more than the cheerful woman holding up the latest Sarah J. Maas on the screen.

My bun collapsed and the long braid fell down onto my shoulder, close to his face. "Shit, sorry, one second," I stuttered. "I need to buy more pins. I keep losing them, it's stupid." I looked down at him. "I call them bobby pins, but maybe they have some other name here?"

"No," he growled.

My fingers froze at the sound, his voice deeper than I'd ever heard it. "No? They're called bobby pins here?"

Which was a ridiculous question to ask, because Leo's facial expression said he wasn't interested in the correct words for anything. His whiskey eyes were dark, focused, predatory. But then his face fell and he looked down at the desk. "Kirby grips," he said in his normal voice. "That's what they're called."

For a second, disappointment surged in my chest, then I straightened my spine. I couldn't let him avoid this, not when he kept giving me hot looks and then getting upset about it. "We should talk about last night."

"I don't see why that's necessary." But his face was turned away from me, his usual composure showing cracks. Like it wouldn't take much to reveal the man underneath.

"I thought about kissing you," I said softly. "And I'm pretty sure you thought about kissing me."

I took the risk, touched his shoulder, and he buried his face in his hands. "You're not wrong," he said, muffled. "But I don't have any right to that."

The feminist inside me snapped awake. "What do you mean, *right*? I kiss who I want."

He sat up and pinched the bridge of his nose. "No, I am not a caveman. But you . . ."

I sensed where this was going, but not talking to each other had landed us in the shit already. "I don't do this whole British leaving-words-unspoken thing."

"You don't fancy me the way I fancy you!" he almost yelled. "That's why I don't have the right," he said more quietly. "You're going to end up with Graham, anyway. You two are more right for each other."

I snorted involuntarily, and Leo glared at me. "No fucking way," I said, half laughing.

"But he makes you laugh all the time," he said stubbornly. "You call him Blondie."

"I do. *Friends* make fun of each other and give each other stupid nicknames. But you know he and Catriona are meant to be, which they'd figure out if they stopped sniping for long enough." I could see that Leo still didn't really believe me. I needed to be honest here. I sat down on the edge of his desk, facing him. "Look. I do have something special with Graham. We've talked about it. But it's not sexy. It's more like . . . I look at him and he looks at me and we just *understand* each other. No pretense or trying to be cool."

"That sounds like it *could* be something sexy."

"I know, but it isn't. I just . . . feel like I've known him forever." I reached up and tugged on my braid, a little nervous. "I don't know what else to say to make you believe that our relationship is platonic."

Leo let out a long exhale. "So you don't want to . . ." He hesitated, and I stared at him. "Shag him," he finally said, two pink flags appearing on his cheeks.

I couldn't help my smile. "I thought 'shagging' was a word Austin Powers made up, but I guess not." I leaned forward and said softly, "I would not shag Graham Beckett ever." Because apparently, deep down, my type was this man, whose black hair was threaded with gray from carrying the worries of the world. But underneath all the anxiety and the shyness was dry wit and warmth and . . . tenderness, and for the first time in years, I thought I could trust that sweet feeling. That he wouldn't snatch it away.

A wild kind of bravery rose up inside me. "Now, what do you want to do with me?"

I saw Leo's face change when he understood I was serious. Uncertainty gave way to something new. He reached out and tugged gently on my braid. "This drives me mad," he said, his voice an octave deeper. He pulled again, and I shivered at the fire in his eyes and the tease on my scalp. "I want to see it down," he said. "You never wear it down."

"You want to muss me," I said, wonder in my voice. His bossiness shone in a new light. Did it grow out of desire, not just responsibility?

Leo's eyes fluttered. "Fuck, yes," he sighed.

I cracked up a little with the tension. "Well, look at you, Mr. Secret Alpha."

"I don't know what that means," he said, his voice teasing.

I groaned. "Because you still haven't read any romance novels."

"I think it's fairly obvious I don't want to read right now." He stared at me, his whiskey eyes luminous behind his glasses, and I found myself holding out my braid to him. Wishing for more from him.

"Undo it, please," I asked, a tiny earthquake somewhere making my voice shake.

He bit his lip, tugged off the rubber band that tied the end, pulled the three strands of the braid apart. It flowed down past my shoulders, covered my breasts. His fingers combed through it, and I hummed with the tug on my scalp.

"You have princess hair," he said, pressing his lips against the strands.

The word "reverent" popped into my head, but I pushed it away. "I'm no princess." If I was anything, I was the scrappy orphan, making my way in the world with only my wits.

He gave me a slow, wicked smile. "Then why do I want to kneel for you?"

I felt us racing toward an edge, about to jump in the air, and I wanted more than anything to fly with him. I felt a rush of joy as I pushed him until he was leaning back in his desk chair. "Leo Ross, I want to sit in your lap and kiss you senseless. Any objections?"

He squeaked out a laugh. "By all means."

I straddled him and planted my mouth on his, and his gasp of surprise vibrated against my lips. But then he dove in, his chocolate mouth hot and hungry on mine, vibrating as our tongues touched, and I handed the kiss over to him, let him decide whether we were soft or hard, whether we were fast or slow.

For a few seconds he was with me, his hands strong on my waist and the back of my neck. But then I felt his shoulders tense under my fingers, the hand that had so confidently slid up into my wild mane of hair lose its way. I had to keep us flying, didn't want to plunge to the ground. I bit his lip lightly and pulled back. "Stop thinking."

I saw his face start to close. "What?"

"Stop thinking and just kiss me."

He gaped at me for a second. "I wasn't . . ."

I tugged his black sweater with each word. "I want you. You want me. It's that simple."

His devilish smile came back. "Truly?"

I gave in to the urge to run my fingertips along his lips, the unlikely wicked curve on such a shy man. "So fucking British. Yes, *truly*. You keep showing up in my fantasies and I need to know if Real You lives up to my sex brain's hype. Why do you look relieved?" I asked, laughing.

He chuckled, took my fingers and kissed them softly.

"I feel better now. I've been touching myself and thinking of you for weeks."

I couldn't hold back the shiver that that image set off, thinking of his lean body stretched on gray sheets, his face concentrated in pleasure. "I'd like to see that," I confessed.

Leo didn't answer, just tugged me close and found my mouth again, his kisses just as hungry but more determined now. I couldn't help but notice that he had next to no finesse—he didn't seem to know whether he wanted his hands in my hair, on my waist, or under my sweater and making inroads toward my breasts. His mouth dove between my mouth, my jaw, my temple, even my ear. I felt his hardness through my jeans and his pants, and when I tilted my hips just enough, the delicious friction made me gasp.

"Do that again, darling," he said into my ear. "That was the sexiest little sound."

Darling. No one had ever used that endearment for me before. But it turned out that that word, in Leo's crisp accent, was pure fire, affection and protectiveness all mixed up together. I moaned and rolled my hips again, his strong grip encouraging me. "Yes, that's it, let me give you what you need," he coaxed.

Several more rocks, and my body was tensing up, my moans getting higher. Leo started paying special attention to my neck, kissing it open-mouthed with a little scrape of teeth. I'd unleashed this beast, and all he wanted was to devour me, and I was loving it so much that if he kept pushing me down onto his lap, I was going to explode right here.

"Leo? Are you in there?" Catriona called right outside the office door, and our mouths froze mid-kiss.

"He's in a meeting with Mari, Cat," Graham said from farther away. "It's in the diary."

Leo's hands clamped on my hips, and I jammed a hand over my mouth to stifle my whimper.

"Don't call me Cat. And the meeting should have been done ten minutes ago. It's not like Leo to run late."

Thankfully, we heard footsteps as their bickering went down the stairs, away from us.

I moaned softly in pain and unsatisfied lust.

"Are you all right?" Leo whispered.

I half laughed. "No."

All of a sudden, he looked stricken. "Did I hurt you?"

Now I laughed all the way. "Of course not. Unless you count the worst case of blue balls in world history as hurting. And I know I don't have balls, but *Jesus*."

His mouth twisted. "You're not suffering alone."

"Fuck, that was close." I pressed my hands to my hot cheeks. "Wow."

Leo slumped back into his chair, and I eased myself off his lap and onto his desk.

"How am I supposed to get any work done after *that*?" he said, bewildered. He held up his hand and I could see it trembling. "I'm so worked up my hands are actually fucking shaking. That only happens in novels." He pushed his glasses back up his nose, then stared at me. "You are a siren."

I took in my handiwork—his ruffled hair, his flushed cheeks, his swollen lips and swollen . . . other things, and blushed hard. "Thank you. There's always seeing to yourself. I know what my plans are for tonight, anyway."

His laugh sounded like he'd took a huge gulp of helium. "Oh, fantastic, now I'll imagine you with your hand between your legs, thanks very much."

I leaned back on the desk and made eye contact with him. "Leo . . . why didn't you kiss me last night?"

He sighed. "Several reasons. One, you'd been so frightened, and I would have never taken advantage of you. Two, I was afraid, too." He reached out and squeezed my knee gently. "I didn't know what you wanted, and I wasn't about to do what I liked without asking you. What we have, this spark, is special to me."

I hadn't had anything special in so long, and out of nowhere I craved it, that feeling of the outside world falling away. "I'm here for it, don't worry. So, what *do* you want to do to me?"

He raised his eyebrows. "No messing about, then? All right. I'd like to spread your naked body on a mattress and taste every inch of you, for starters."

I shoved down the butterflies that his kisses and his filthy words had sent flying in my stomach. "Yes, Leo, we're absolutely going to fuck like bunnies," I said matter-of-factly. "And you're hella cute when you blush."

He laughed. "Shut up. You're so fucking erotic when you're blunt and I need to *think*." He let off another high giggle. "Clearly we can't do it in the office."

"It would be highly unprofessional to bend me over your desk, yes," I said dryly.

He scooted closer and pinched my belly lightly. "Cheeky thing. So where can we go?"

His teasing little touch was a spark, and I wanted more of that fire. I rested my forearms on his shoulders, my mouth curling up as he settled into me.

I jerked my head in the direction of the attic. "My place?"

"Far too close to work."

"Your place?"

He cringed. "Please never speak about having sex in proximity to my family ever again. Hotel?"

I snorted, already hearing my wallet's scream of protest. "In this town? Pity me, I'm only a bookstore employee."

"Any possibility that you'll let me pay for it?" he asked tentatively.

I shook my head, the soothing slide of my hands down his chest an apology. I couldn't owe him anything.

His sigh rolled under my touch. "Leave it to me. I'll find something."

I pulled back, needing not to be touching him to get this next part out. "I want to be clear about something." I waited until his face was all attention. "I have an IUD, but it's important to me that we use condoms, too." I wouldn't risk doing to a child what had been done to me. "I got the all clear for STDs right before I came here. Have you been tested?"

"I haven't, but of course I will," Leo said immediately. "There's a place near UCH, I'll go later." He reached out and put his hand on my knee, a gentle but solid hold. "I appreciate you asking me. I meant what I said, on the Tube. That you're safe with me." He squeezed. "But Mari, I also need to be clear about something. If we do this, you won't be my friend with benefits."

I held very still. We clearly weren't going to be enemies with benefits, and I didn't like the other options. "What will I be?"

He held my gaze. "Mine."

I stiffened and opened my mouth to object.

"Not forever. I know that. But until you go, as long as

we're sleeping together, we belong to each other, no one else. If you can't handle that, I can't go to bed with you."

My first thought was a hard no. I was an independent woman and this was the 2020s, for God's sake.

"You're hardcore," I said, delaying.

He shook his head. "All or nothing, Mari, that's what I can offer. Otherwise I'll go mad."

I took in his face, vulnerable and stern at the same time. He needed to know that he was safe with me, too. I breathed deep, then said, "OK. No one else, until I go back to California." I leaned in and kissed him softly to seal the deal, a tender little promise, then pulled back before the temptation to climb into his lap again got to be too much. "Well, I'm going to go back to work." I paused. "One last thing."

His eyebrows shot up. "What last thing?"

I reached slowly for his throat, and Leo went still, watchful. His shirt's top button fought me for a second, then gave in. There it was, a perfect little patch of white throat.

His Adam's apple shifted under my thumb when he swallowed hard. "What was wrong with it?" he asked, his voice rough.

I smiled. "I want to think about kissing you there when the time comes."

CHAPTER EIGHTEEN

Mari

In the end, it took four days to find somewhere for us to be alone and naked. Ninety-six whole hours before Leo texted me:

Sorted. Meet me tonight. Followed by an address, strings of unfamiliar letters and numbers.

Of course we saw each other in the store, but we kept our professional faces on. Day by day the shop was getting a little busier, and we had a big festival to prepare for, and of course there was no way we could make out in front of customers. But I couldn't help but notice that he was avoiding being alone with me, period. It only made sense once we ran into each other in a deserted corner of Natural Sciences and he stole a kiss.

Though "kiss" was the understatement of the year. He

pinned me to one of the shelves and feasted on me, shoved his fingers into my hair, pressed into me like he was trying to leave an imprint, and I melted everywhere from his heat, clinging to his shoulders so I wouldn't slide down to the floor. But when I moaned into his mouth, he pulled away and groaned, "I *knew* snogging you would just make it worse, fuck's sake." He stormed off, leaving me with my mouth swollen, my bun askew, and little chirping birds floating around my head like a dazed cartoon character.

Now I punched the address into my maps app to navigate London's transportation system. One Tube ride, one train ride, and a short walk across a park later, a new four-story apartment building in beige brick stood in front of me, its tall windows warm yellow in the dark. When I looked around me, I felt my shoulders drop from around my ears. I mostly liked the bustle of Central London, the way a million stories flowed around me like the Thames flowed through the city. But it was nice, to have a little vacation from feeling like my personal space was public property. I looked around the park I'd just crossed. People chatted with each other under the glowing streetlights, carrying bags of groceries, and others walked dogs along the paths scattered with brown leaves. This was a place where people lived, not just where they worked. It almost felt like a small town in the city.

I turned back to the apartment building and saw a skinny, dark silhouette hovering in one of the windows. I waved eagerly, and Leo raised a hand back. It was almost like we'd done this hundreds of times before.

I blinked that image of long-term domesticity away, pressed the buzzer for him to let me in. When I came out of the elevator on the third floor, he already had the apartment door open. A little part of me rubbed its hands gleefully when I saw the top button of his shirt was unbuttoned. He closed the door behind me and raked his fingers through his salt-and-pepper hair. "Is this all right? It's basic, but it's nice enough and I've always liked the neighborhood. It's not too bad to get to from the shop, either," he babbled.

The apartment looked like it had been furnished with IKEA's cheapest line, all white plastic and plywood. I doubted the cream sofa was comfortable to sit on for longer than ten minutes, and the art on the walls looked printed straight from a stock image website.

But this sweet, awkward man standing beside me was beautiful, lanky and dark-eyed, and I wanted to burn up his shyness with multiple orgasms. "Is there a bed?" I asked bluntly.

He rolled his eyes. "No, I thought we'd use our clothing to make a nest on the floor. Yes, smartarse, there's a bed. Frame, mattress, even a duvet."

I stepped into him. "Then what are you waiting for?"

I wanted to take his slow smile and save it for my wildest fantasies, of him holding my wrists and whispering sexy nothings in my ear. "For you to take your hair down, darling."

"What is it about you and my hair?" I asked, half laughing as I pulled out the first pins and put them in my pockets. "It's just wavy and brown."

"You see brown." He pulled the rubber band off the end of the braid when it fell and started to unravel it. "I see chocolate and nutmeg and cinnamon..."

I raised my eyebrows. "I think you might need some nonedible adjectives. It's like you want to eat me."

He raised his eyebrows back. "Don't I?"

A giggle bubbled up. "Touché."

"No food words. Bronze, then. Mahogany. Amber, when you're in the right light." He trailed his fingers through it, and I closed my eyes with how good it felt. "It makes me think of luxurious things. Precious things."

I blushed hard. I wasn't anyone's idea of a luxury, no jewel or fur coat. Being wanted this way, it was like surfing a tidal wave, when I'd spent the last seven years floating in the shallow end. I tried to joke, "I don't know why I haven't slept with an artist before. You're amazing at compliments."

But Leo wasn't going to let me dodge. "I mean it, Mari. All of it." He brushed a gentle fingertip along my cheekbone, down my nose, along the swoop of my Cupid's bow. "I don't know anyone else like you. You're special."

I couldn't handle those kinds of feelings. The seriousness, the sincerity. As far as I knew, they all ended in heartbreak, in grief. I knew we'd have to negotiate this before we could sleep together again, but for now I wanted him too badly to care. "Thank you," I said lightly. "But you wrote a check when you kissed me in the store the other day, and as long as we're standing here, I can't cash it."

Something hesitant flickered in his eyes, but bravado quickly overcame it. "Cheeky," he said with a smile, then pressed his mouth to mine.

Leo

It was icy cold and dark outside, but in this room, in Mari's arms, lost in her hungry kisses, it was like the hours and days sped up. The petal softness of her lips, the lush curves of her under my hands, made me feel like a plant growing in fast-forward, unfurling and reaching toward light.

I gloried in her, in us together, as we made our way across the spartan Airbnb, as I found the bedroom door handle with the hand that wasn't occupied with clinging to her, as I dropped my glasses onto the nightstand and tipped us both onto the hard mattress, Mari laughing a little with surprise as we bounced. I wanted to savor that giggle, wanted to make her do it again a thousand times.

I pressed up onto my arms and looked down at her, excitement and anticipation surging inside me like a burst of sunshine-yellow paint. She was effervescence, green spring and new life, flowers blooming on her skin.

I wanted to bask in her.

She blushed deliciously pink, pulled me back down to her and kissed me hard with her wide mouth that tasted like tea and spices, and I pushed back, consumed her like she consumed me, filled my hands with her glorious arse and squeezed, slid my hand under her soft blue jumper to find skin like silk under my fingertips.

She stiffened, yelped into my mouth.

I took my hands away like she was on fire. "I hurt you—

fuck. Are you all right?" I asked, panic coursing through me.

"No," she gasped, but all at once Becca's pained, grimacing face appeared in front of me, and I pulled back, rolled away with my hands on my face. What a cruel joke, for fate to give me a woman who actually desired me and for me to fuck it up so quickly.

"Where are you going?" she laughed, brushing her hand across my back. "You didn't hurt me, I'm just really ticklish. When you touch me like that on my ribs, too soft, I can't handle it."

Her explanation did about as much good as throwing a pebble at a stone wall. I was still clumsy, still not good enough. "I can't do this," I blurted as I sat upright, fumbling for my glasses.

"Wait, what? Why?"

I looked around on the floor for my shirt. "I just . . . can't."

A second passed.

"Leo," she said, soft and plaintive. It would be like stabbing myself in the chest to ignore that. I turned around and saw her eyes were round and wide, that she was holding her knees like she needed comfort. "Did I do something wrong?"

Self-pity disappeared just as quickly as it had come. My fingers dragged painfully through my hair at the thought that I'd hurt her feelings. "It's not you. It's not remotely you. It's me. I . . ." The words knotted in my mouth.

"You *what*?"

"I'm shit at sex!" I answered far too loudly.

Unbelievably, she didn't burst out laughing. She just sat for a moment, blinking. "What do you mean?" she finally asked.

I was tempted to crawl under the bed and die of sheer humiliation. "I don't know what I'm doing. I just wanted you so much that I thought it would be all right, but now you're here, and gorgeous, and I'm *rubbish*. I've only slept with one other person in my life and even then not that many times, because she didn't like what I did to her."

Mari eased into a cross-legged position facing me, rested her elbows on her knees, then put her chin on her fists. "I'd like to think I know you well enough that you weren't forcing her to do anything," she said gently. "Were you both inexperienced?"

I nodded, embarrassment reddening my cheeks.

"So you didn't know how to make her feel good, and maybe she didn't know how to tell you what she liked. That's not just your fault, Leo."

I stared at my twisting fingers. "I wasn't the one who was hurt."

"But you were the one who felt like a monster. That's its own kind of hurt." She rose up on her knees and put her hand on my chest, over my heart still wild for her touch. "I know you're not a bad guy."

I wished with everything I had that it were true. But I knew I was awkward, prickly, clumsy. No one's idea of a hero. If I'd been left to my own devices, I would have crashed Alexander's legacy onto the rocks and wrung my hands while it sank.

But could I still run the shop after Mari left in April? More than that, would I *want* to?

Doubt felt like a widening crack in the path ahead, one I'd fall into, and I mentally backed away as quickly as I could.

"And not being perfectly in tune with your partner's

desires doesn't make you a monster," Mari continued now. "We're brand new, Leo. We have so much to learn about each other. But that's why we have to talk."

She was asking me to be present, to be with her, and I pushed down thoughts of the future. "I always like talking to you," I offered tentatively.

A saucy little grin teased me from the corner of her mouth. "Even if I'm telling you to change something?"

I smiled. "Even then."

She rewarded my honesty with a tender little kiss. "Let's play a game."

Curiosity flickered to life. "What kind of game?"

"Show and Tell." She tilted her head toward the plain wooden chair in the corner. "Go sit over there."

I obeyed her, and she scooted to the end of the bed, facing me, two meters away that felt like two miles.

"You're a great kisser," she began quietly, looking me in the eye. "Your mouth felt incredible on mine, and you were soft when I wanted you to be soft, and hungry when I wanted you to be hungry." She trailed her small, delicate fingers down her throat. "I'm really sensitive on my neck and shoulders, and I'd love it if you sat behind me on the bed and just kissed and sucked and bit me there. I can get halfway to coming just from that."

Without thinking, I was out of my chair before she put her hand up. "No touching."

"But I want to do that." God, the thought of having her that way, soft and trusting, made me feel almost feral.

"Wait," she said with a smile.

I growled and sat back down.

She pulled her jumper, T-shirt, and something wine-colored and lacy that I wanted to study later over her head, and I laughed and gasped at the same time at the sight of her bare breasts. "Oh, fuck *me*."

"That's the plan," she snarked, and I snorted. "You like what you see?"

"I want to taste them," I said from the pit of lust that had opened inside me. "They look so sweet."

Then things got very serious as she cupped them in her hands, and my trousers were starting to feel unbearable. "All right," she said, her voice husky, "but I like fingers here, too. I'd like it if you stroked me with your whole hand, or if you tugged and flicked here." She sighed as she matched action to words, then looked at me with hooded eyes. "Do you like to be touched there?"

I hadn't realized my jaw was wide open until I snapped it shut. Of course I *had* nipples, but they were just *there*. "I . . . fuck. I don't know."

She tilted her chin in challenge. "Take off your shirt and try."

My fingers were slow and fumbling on my shirt buttons as self-consciousness fought for space with need. I'd never been much to look at with no clothes on, never spent time at the gym or in the sun. But as I put my shirt to the side, Mari's eyes stared fascinated at the sparse black patch of hair on my chest, then dropped to the clearer line that led down to my waistband. Her hot gaze made me brave, and I ran my hands up my chest, stroked, flicked, sparks skittering across my skin.

"Nice?" she murmured.

Her eyes on me magnified every sensation. "Very nice," I breathed. "Would be even nicer if you did it." I thought of her pressing sweet kisses down my chest toward where

I was desperately hard for her and almost gave up right there.

"Duly noted." The heat in her eyes was a heady contrast with the formal words. "Are you going to have a heart attack if I take my pants off?"

I couldn't hold back a mirthless laugh. "Probably. But do it anyway."

She slid her jeans down her legs, leaving silky light blue knickers on. I wondered how that fabric would feel against my fingertips, if she smelled delicious there, if she'd squirm if I nuzzled and licked her through it. I jammed my hand hard between my legs. No good thinking about her knickers if I died of sheer arousal before I got between her thighs.

"Now yours," she said from miles away.

Oh, thank fuck, my erection was about to fall off in protest. As fast as I could, I unbuckled and got rid of my trousers.

She started to rub slow circles between her legs. "How do you get yourself off?"

I shook my head. "If you want me inside you tonight, I can't touch myself. I'm about to come in my pants as it is."

A lazy smile touched her lips. "Then just tell me."

"I like it hard," I forced out. "Wet, tight, fast."

She moaned softly and her hand moved more quickly. "Do you use lube?"

My hands clamped onto my hair, and I gulped. "I do."

"I'd love to go down on you," she sighed. "Get you all wet and messy that way."

Fuck, I was going to combust right here. They'd find a little pile of ashes with my bent and shattered glasses on top, all because I was imagining Mari Cole kneeling in front of me, her pink, full mouth between my legs. "Promises, promises."

She opened her eyes, and the look in them was hazy. "No, I would. It makes me incredibly hot. I want to know the sounds you'd make, how big you'd get in my mouth, what you'd taste like."

I was out of the chair and almost on the bed when she said, her voice shaking, "No. No touching yet."

I sat back down, about to howl with frustration. "I can't stand this. Let me do *something*."

She stared at me, the challenge clear. "Touch yourself as much as you can handle and tell me what *you* want."

My hand slid down of its own volition and pressed hard, then gripped tight. "I want to taste you so badly," I confessed. "I want to bury my face between your thighs and never come up for air."

A smile curved her mouth, even as she shivered. "And I'd let you. But I wouldn't want you to go too fast. Some people go right for the prize and it's too much. I love being teased." She slid her hand inside her knickers. "Licked up and down, tasted everywhere until I'm shaking and pulling your hair and begging for your fingers inside me." She sighed. "I love being full when I'm being licked."

Now my hips were shifting on the seat, my body as desperate as my mind, my control totally unraveled. I was beyond self-consciousness, beyond uncertainty, beyond the most basic fear. "Let me taste you, Mari. Please, I have to, *please*."

She studied me for a moment, and I was about to die, until she slid back on the bed and spread her legs for me. "All yours."

I dove onto the bed, ripped her knickers down and threw them across the room to the sound of her laughter. Scattered wet open-mouthed kisses over her delicious breasts, her rounded stomach, until I dropped onto my front on the mattress and finally put my mouth on her with a groan that could have been heard across the river. I was *gone*, lost in her wetness, her taste, the softness and the warmth of her.

"Aaah, easy," she gasped.

I instantly stopped. "Sorry, that was too much. I didn't mean to . . ."

A hard tug on my hair interrupted my flood of apologies. "I swear to God, if you leave me hanging again, I will actually kill you," she said, sounding half-hysterical.

I pushed up so I could look her in the eye. "Are you certain?"

She sat up and we were face-to-face, her shaking hands cupping my jaw. "Listen to me. I need your mouth so bad, Leo, it just has to be gentle. *Please* don't stop."

The world went still. A lush, clever, sweet woman, spread out underneath me, begging for *my* touch, *my* kiss. It was a feeling like a door I hadn't known was there had unlocked inside me, letting a part of myself out into the light. "Did you just say please?" I asked, my voice low and quiet.

Mari

Just like in his office, this shy, tentative man transformed into something hot-eyed and hungry when I begged, when I offered myself to him. I wanted that heat to touch me, to wrap itself around me and overwhelm every barrier I'd ever put up. I reached up and carefully tugged his glasses off, put them back on the nightstand where they belonged. "I'm yours. Right here and now, I'm yours. *Please* take me."

A quick hard press of his smile to mine, then he slid down the bed again. Instead of diving in like he had before, he explored me, slow and soft, rubbing his tongue across every inch of me, seeing what made me sigh. "You make the most gorgeous little sounds when you feel good," he said thoughtfully, after I let off a particularly horny moan. "I wonder how many different ones you have."

"Keep going and you'll see," I got out.

He flicked his tongue lightly in exactly the right place, and I gasped. "Oh, I wouldn't stop for the world," he said. "You taste delicious."

"Better than chocolate?"

A quick grin. "Why do I have to choose?"

And now I was past kidding around. "Give me more, Leo. *Please.*"

"*Fuck*, I love it when you ask nicely." He reveled in me, raining hot kisses everywhere. "Love it when you say my name, too."

Ordinarily that four-letter word would be a record scratch, a warning flash.

But then he licked inside of me, then sucked like it was summer and I was the most delicious ripe peach, and I let it go. I fell into his hunger, the silk of his hair in my hands, and the strength of his grip on my thighs, until my orgasm struck out of nowhere, sudden and sharp. I yelped and grabbed his head, kept him there as I rode it out.

The second I let him go, he was over my sated body, shoving his underwear down and kissing me like he needed to taste me, needed me to taste him. A hand reached under and tugged my hips up. "I have to fuck you now," he said, eyes like a storm. "I need to be inside you, tell me I can."

The demand in his voice made it feel like the orgasm had never happened. "Oh my God, please." I arched against him, and he notched against me.

"Fuck," he blurted, jerking away. "Condoms. You said."

Oh my God. How did I forget something so important? Leo made me feel safe, but not *that* safe. I had to take care of myself no matter how many times this man made me come.

I watched him, a little stricken, as he yanked the nightstand drawer open, dug around until foil winked in the low light.

"It's been a while since I've used one of these, hold on." But after a few seconds, he figured it out, and another second later, he'd stretched out over me, soft light from the lamp turning his olive skin gold. I trailed my fingers up his narrow chest to his sharp-edged shoulder, the bones clear under my fingertips.

He pressed a little kiss to the tip of my nose. "All right?" he whispered softly.

An unexpected wave of tenderness washed over me, a soft blanket of care. "All right."

"Good," he growled, and pushed inside me in one long glide. "*Fuck*, you feel so good. You feel so good, and you're all for me."

The pace he set was fast and hard, and not usually what would get me there, but his need spoke to mine, and I couldn't hold back, shoved my hand between us and rubbed firmly, everything almost too sensitive, but I needed the friction too much to care, bracing my feet on the mattress and pushing back as his body came down over mine.

"Yes," he praised in my ear when I moaned. "Come again, gorgeous girl. You feel like heaven." He was frantic, mindless. "Someday I'm going to fuck you forever."

Someday. Forever. I didn't like those words at all. "Just fuck me *now*," I said desperately, the edge coming faster and faster.

One last jerky thrust, and his orgasm was one long growl into my shoulder, and I followed him into pleasure seconds later, hearing him gasp my name like it was a prayer begging for an answer.

CHAPTER NINETEEN

Mari

I wasn't sure where I ended and Leo began, and even that wasn't enough right now. My greedy fingers tangled in his damp hair, my legs wrapped around his hips. After a moment he raised his head from where it had been resting on my shoulder, and his swollen mouth found mine for a slow exchange of breath and tongue. I was . . . clinging to him.

What was I doing? I tried not to cling to anyone. The tenderness was too much. "So much for being professional," I said to break the spell.

He froze, and I worried he was going to panic again, leave me alone out of some misplaced sense of responsibility. But then he rolled over and genuinely whooped with laughter, and I couldn't help but join in. It was like I'd never laughed in bed with someone before. If I'd hoped to get some distance, play it cool, Leo's laugh was like the world's catchiest pop song, impossible not to join in.

"Yes," he said with a smile once we'd relaxed into chuckling. "Definitely not part of the normal course of business." He reached out and trailed his fingers over my chest and stomach, with enough pressure this time so it didn't tickle. "It's been so long since I've done that."

I couldn't help but smile back at the wonder in his voice. "For me, too."

I closed my mouth hard at that drastic overshare, and he stared at me like I'd just said two plus two was negative thirteen. "I thought—" he started, then said with a laugh, "You just seemed so confident, the way you talked about sex. I wish I could do that."

I shook my head. "I have sex, yes, but I don't have p-in-v sex all that often." Sleeping with people with vaginas made the point moot, and with my other partners, there was always a tiny part of my brain that raised red flags at the prospect of repeating my mom's mistake.

Leo wrinkled his nose. "P-in-v?"

I wrinkled my nose back. "You think 'intercourse' is any sexier?"

He snorted. "I do, and there's a Monty Python sketch I need to show you." His face became earnest again. "So this isn't something you would do normally?"

I hesitated, not willing to bring my history of loving and leaving into this bed. "No, it's not."

He paused too, studying me, and a small, scared part of me waited for him to judge me, to turn away. "Thank you," he said quietly. "Thank you for trusting me."

I repressed a sigh of relief. Even though I shouldn't care what he thought, because he was just another partner. Right?

But I couldn't help but notice that his night-sky hair was a feathery mess, his normally tight mouth was relaxed and full, and his eyes . . . he looked blissed out. I'd made him that way.

And I was going to sink back into reverie if I didn't get practical soon. "Of course I trust you. But now I need to get cleaned up."

When I came back from the bathroom, Leo had gotten rid of the condom and was sitting up in bed looking at me. "Wait," he said, his voice a little dark.

An answering shiver went through me. "Your wish is my command," I half joked.

He crawled down to the end of the bed and sat, then reached for my hand and tugged me closer.

"I feel like I should be posing," I said. The attention, the close, close attention, felt like intense sunshine after too long in the dark.

He didn't respond, just trailed his fingers over the branch of pale pink apricot blossoms on the front of my left thigh, then turned me around and studied the vermilion tulip tattoo on my right shoulder.

"The person who did these is a tremendous artist," he said.

"She went to art school," I said. "She has these amazing paintings all over her studio."

He froze for a second, then let out a long breath and turned me around again so I faced him.

"They're all so lovely, like you." He lightly tapped the apricot flowers. "What's the story of this one?"

It had been so easy with other people to say superficial answers: *They were pretty. I liked the colors.* But Leo wanted to know me . . . and I wanted to let him in. I breathed out hard. "This was the apricot tree that grew in our backyard. Mom would spend a whole weekend making jam every summer and the house would smell like fruit and vanilla."

"And this one?" he asked, putting his palm over the tulip.

I smiled. "Mom chose the bulbs because they were the color of her favorite lipstick. In the spring the yard would turn red from them and yellow from daffodils." I flashed the daffodil on my arm. "Like nature was throwing a party, she'd say."

I swallowed hard, the next part of the story a stone in my throat. Leo waited, his hands gentle on my hips.

"She died in February, and afterward, when I missed her, I could go sit in the flowers and put my hands in the dirt. She'd always said it centered her, to do that. But Greg brought in guys who ripped out the whole backyard a few months after she died. When I came home from school, everything smelled like cut wood and chlorophyll, and the yard was just dirt."

Leo's hands tightened on me. "That's horrible."

"Then he laid down a lawn. Just grass. And having only one plant in a place is bad for the ecosystem." I sniffled a little. "There used to be noise out there, you know? The birds singing, and bees buzzing, wind in the trees. But after that, it was just silent."

"Mari." My name carried so much, sympathy and grief, gentleness and something else, something wild I didn't want to name.

Soon. Soon I'd tell him that whatever he was feeling for me, I couldn't feel back. "I'm cold," I said now.

He moved back on the mattress, reached for me. When I climbed back into bed, he pulled the comforter all the way over us, making a little world of white. From there, it was an easy slide into kissing him, touching him, taking him inside me again.

Twenty minutes later, when we were lying around getting our breath back for the second time, I looked at the stark white room, the plain furniture. It all looked so basic, almost like real people didn't live here. My hands clenched on the sheets. Wait a second . . .

"Leo? What is this place? A friend's?"

He hesitated, then smiled sheepishly. "Don't kill me. It's an Airbnb."

Indignation made me sit up. "But I told you not to spend money."

He sat up, too. "On a hotel room, yes. Which this isn't."

My fingertip found his chest and poked. "That's semantics, and you know it."

He tugged me close with a laugh. "Can you blame a poor man who's had a delicious American sex goddess drop into his lap?" He framed my face with his hands. "I wanted a place for us so much. This was the only thing I could think of. Didn't you want that, too?" His face fell. "Unless you don't want to do this again."

I couldn't imagine only having sex with Leo Ross once. Every atom of my body was pissed off about the idea. "OK, I take your point. But you have to let me pay, too. It doesn't have to be half, just something."

"It's really that important to you, to feel like you're paying your share? You won't accept this as a gift?"

I shook my head firmly. "Too big." What if I didn't please him? What if he got tired of me?

Leo sighed a little. "All right." His mouth turned up a little, and he said wryly, "Orgasms don't make you any less stubborn, do they?"

I opened my mouth to argue, but my stomach gurgled loudly instead.

"That was quite a noise," he said.

I got out of bed to find my jeans and fished out my phone. "Oh my God, it's after eight. No wonder I'm starving."

He blinked when I showed him my screen. "Oh, yeah, it's well past dinner, isn't it?"

"You're not hungry?" I asked, astonished.

A shrug of his narrow shoulders. "Not really."

Come to think of it, I didn't see him eating all that often. Besides Friday-night dinner, I'd sometimes seen him eating a few carrot sticks or nibbling on a chocolate bar, but not much else. "I'm going to go see what I can rustle up," I said.

Leo

Mari pulled on her blue pants and jumper, hiding the red tulip but leaving the daffodil and apricot blossoms. Once she'd left the room, I looked up at the ceiling and exhaled hard, trying to calm the chaos of feelings Mari's story had whipped up.

It was no good. All I wanted was to plant a garden for her. Fill it with color and scent, humming bees and birdsong, a lush little paradise where she could sit under a tree and read while I drew.

It was a mad thought on multiple levels. I had no idea how to grow anything. I didn't have a back garden. And she wasn't bloody *staying*.

We only had now, and I needed to savor every second she gave me, not piss them away with hoping and wishing.

I climbed into pants and trousers and slipped my glasses back on, Mari's tender touch resonating like the last note of a love song. When I got to the tiny kitchen and saw her rummaging around, a flash of guilt struck. "I'm so sorry, I should have run to the shops before you arrived."

"No problem. I think I've found enough to work with. The host left us some cheap white bread and butter." I watched as she dug around in the cabinets and found half a bag of sugar, an ancient jar of ground cinnamon, and some hot cocoa mix. She popped two slices of bread in the toaster on the counter, filled the kettle with water, and put it on to boil.

I shifted from foot to foot, waiting for her to ask if I wanted her to make me any food, dreading her facial expression when I'd have to tell her no. Would she be annoyed? Or worse, concerned? But she just got on with mixing sugar and cinnamon, pouring hot water and cocoa powder into mugs, buttering two slices of toast and sprinkling them with the sugar-spice mix.

"What's all this, then?" I finally asked, curious in spite of myself.

She swallowed her first bite of toast and put the slice down. "You've never had cinnamon toast?"

I shook my head.

She picked up the toast again and looked like she was about to hold it out to me, then thought better of it. "C'mere." She tugged me forward by my belt loop and put her hand on the back of my neck. Her kiss was slow and deep, intoxicatingly sweet and spiced.

She pulled back. "What do you think?" she asked with a cheeky little smile.

That she was a piece of my most vivid fantasies, come to life. "I think cinnamon toast is delicious," I half growled, crowding her into the worktop, "and that you're lucky to be upright, instead of spread out on the kitchen table with my mouth between your legs."

"Promises, promises, devil boy," she said airily.

"Devil boy?" I asked, surprised.

She reached up and tapped my lower lip twice. "You get a really evil grin on your face when you look at me. Makes me think seriously about selling my soul."

I caught her hand in mine and kissed it. "Oh, you're one to talk, wicked girl. I used to be sensible before you came along. Now all I can think about is . . ."

She wiggled her eyebrows. "Bunny, bunny, bunny."

I burst out laughing. "Not how I would have put it, but yes."

"It's mutual, trust me." She handed me one of the mugs. "But I need to eat before we can do that again, so bear with me."

I gave her space, and she leaned back against the worktop and munched her slice while I sipped cocoa. The urge to have that cinnamon taste again and fill my empty stomach warred with my fear of eating in front of other people, being judged for being slow and picky. But this was Mari, the least judgmental person in the world, who'd seen my body and wanted it. If it was safe to eat with anyone, it was her. "Can I have some toast?"

She reached for the bread bag, then paused. "Would you like me to show you how to do it?"

I narrowed my eyes. "Is this like teaching a man to fish?"

She shrugged. "More like teaching a man to push a button, but sure. How many slices would you like?"

After a moment, I stepped up next to her and followed her instructions. She told me the ratio of sugar to cinnamon to mix together, to spread the butter generously from edge to edge on the toast so all the cinnamon sugar would stick.

I took a bite, and for once my stomach didn't cramp because someone was watching me eat. "That was wonderful, by the way," I said once I'd swallowed.

She blinked. "What was?"

I took a deep breath. "Everyone has always tried to feed me because I'm scrawny. It's like people think I don't understand what food is for. But I do, I'm just . . . not hungry, a lot of the time."

She folded her arms and leaned back against the counter. "You're not scrawny," she said plainly. "You're a long, lean kind of guy. I bet you have a metabolism like a greyhound."

I found myself smiling. I knew I wasn't that tall, but I supposed to Mari I was. "And you like long, lean men?"

She grinned. "One in particular."

I leaned down and kissed her for that compliment. "But I mean it. You waited for me to tell you what I wanted, instead of forcing it on me."

She looked me in the eye. "You're a grown man, Leo. You know how hungry you are."

The words were a golden key in an old lock. When had I got so disconnected from my appetites? Not just for food, but for other kinds of pleasure?

"I had a lot of allergies until I was three or four," I admitted. "Ended up in hospital multiple times after eating the most ordinary things. Even after the allergies went, Mum would fuss over me. Practically try to jam food in my mouth like I was a baby." I took a deep breath. "It got better once I was in secondary school and uni. I would tell her I had to study all the time, then buy ready-made things and eat them in my room. But I still don't find food easy."

She paused, letting my confession settle over her. "What do you actually like to eat?" she finally asked.

I snorted involuntarily. "You know no one's ever asked me that?"

"You're allowed to like what you like," she said with a shrug.

I sighed. "I eat like a child, basically. Bread, potatoes, pasta, rice. I don't really like bits in things, except in Judith's soup. I like chicken, but without bones or skin. White fish and salmon. Cherry tomatoes, carrot sticks, cucumber slices. And I like sweets, of course."

She tilted her head. "What's your favorite sweet thing?"

You, I just barely resisted saying. "Marshmallows." Mari giggled a little, and I smiled. "I know, it's a bit silly. But I like the softness. They're like eating little clouds of sugar."

"It makes a lot of sense," she said, easing closer to me.

"Why's that?" I said, urging her forward.

She put her hand over my heart. "You're a little dusty on the outside, but you're gooey and sweet on the inside. Not to mention that you taste delicious with chocolate."

I blushed, struggled not to look down at the floor. "Is it strange that I think that's both a terribly twee and very sexy metaphor?"

She smiled up at me. "I think it's strange that you're not kissing me right now for coming up with a very sexy metaphor."

I leaned down and tasted her mouth again. I didn't know if I'd ever get tired of her kisses.

"My dentist calls me a modern miracle," I said once our lips parted. "And I'm basically impossible to go out in public with." I thought of all the times that Bex had pointed out restaurants as we walked past, or read aloud bits of reviews in the weekend papers, how she'd shaken her head when I'd suggested she go with her friends.

Mari shrugged. "Restaurants are nice, but they're not the be-all and end-all. And if your diet made you unhappy and you didn't do anything about it, then I'd be worried. But you seem to do fine."

I exhaled as a warm blanket of safety settled over me. "I do. I haven't been ill in a long time."

"And you clearly have stamina." She wiggled her eyebrows at me. "Maybe we can test that out again later. Just to be sure."

I nodded vigorously. "Oh, absolutely, any experiments you want to conduct, I'm on board with."

But then her face fell a little. "I need to give you a warning before we go back to bed."

It was like a dark shadow had slipped into the bright white room. "What kind of warning?" I asked carefully.

She reached up and touched my face, clearly trying to soften the blow. "Don't fall for me. Because I'm not going to fall for you."

A needle of disappointment pricked me. I knew that love was unlikely. We hadn't known each other long, wouldn't get to know each other much better before her time, our time, was up. But part of me wanted to kick and scream. "Am I allowed to ask why not?" I said, struggling to keep my voice neutral.

"Sure, but you won't get much of an answer."

"So you're aromantic?"

She shook her head. "No, it's not innate. I just choose not to."

There was a dissonant note to her explanation, something hollow and incomplete. It didn't make sense that someone with such a capacity for joy and delight didn't want anything more than a quick fuck. "You're trying to protect yourself from falling in love?"

"Trust me," she said firmly. "It's better this way for both of us. I'm leaving, remember? If neither of us catches big feelings, we can say goodbye and remember this fondly."

My eyebrows shot up. "'Fond' is not the word I'd use to describe how I feel about you. It's far too timid." But she was right. I'd be setting myself up for a painful fall if I let myself want forever with her. Forever wasn't for the likes of me, anyway. I'd failed at it once before. "No big feelings," I agreed. I pressed my thumb over her lush mouth. "But I don't want you to keep reminding me, all right? I just want to get lost in each other for a bit."

She hesitated, then nodded. "Let's get lost."

CHAPTER TWENTY

Mari

I was leaning on the counter of the first-floor register, contemplating the exactly three hours of sleep Leo and I had let each other have, when Catriona's astonished voice broke through my daydreaming.

"Is that Leo swaggering?"

"Huh?" I said intelligently.

"Morning!" Leo said with a huge grin, walking up to where Catriona and I were standing. I squinted. He was wearing a checkered scarf. It was black and dove gray, two non-colors repeating.

But still. *Checks.* For him, that was practically sequined tie-dye. "Hi," I said, pretending that everything was absolutely normal and he hadn't done something totally wild with his clothing. "You're chirpy."

"It's a lovely day." He sounded like he was on the verge of breaking into a Fred Astaire–style song-and-dance routine.

I couldn't help but look out the windows behind him at the wet, dreary day, but I guessed he was looking at the world through sex-colored glasses. My fingers involuntarily found the small hickey he'd left high on my shoulder during round three.

Catriona said wryly, "If you enjoy a bit of drizzle, absolutely."

Leo shrugged cheerfully. "Everything going all right here? What needs done?"

We discussed the day's work for the festival. We'd put tickets on sale day after tomorrow, so we needed to make sure everything on the website was right. All of us would meet at the end of the day to decide what books we would order, to make sure we were as stocked as possible for the whole day. It was like electricity was coursing under Leo's skin, brightening his eyes and making him just a little bit jumpy.

Once he'd left the room, whistling something jazzy, Catriona turned and looked at me, eyebrows raised.

I subtly moved the neck of my sweater, hoping it would cover Leo's love bite. "Don't know what's up with him."

She snorted. "Of course you don't know, and I live in Buckingham Palace." She glanced at my neck. "Our Leo has hidden talents, it seems."

"Aw, shut up," I said without heat. I felt loose and pliant thanks to Leo's hands and mouth, and my faint reflection in the window had pink cheeks and an extremely dopey smile.

"Well, when you've come down from whichever cloud

you're currently floating on, you were going to talk to Graham and me about how we might set up the gallery for the talks."

I shook my head to drive the sexy fog away. "Of course. I just want to check the website and social media. See you down there in ten?"

She waved an elegant pale hand at me and left the room.

I looked at myself again in the window and my brain immediately slipped back to last night. I'd woken up from a humid, formless dream with my mouth hungry on Leo's skin. He had made me come on his fingers, then pinned my wrists to the bed and fucked me so slowly that I was writhing underneath him, begging him to let me touch myself so that I could come one more time. He made me wait, and wait, and wait, until he touched me instead and I blew up into smithereens. I couldn't remember the last time I'd come more than once with a male partner, let alone had the kind of orgasms that left me shuddering and gasping for air.

I scrubbed a hand along my scalp and shook my head at my reflection. I looked loved up, Suzanne would have said. But this wasn't love, just some good old-fashioned exercise. Letting off steam. Even though I'd promised Leo we'd be exclusive, it didn't mean that sleeping with him had to take on some great significance.

"Coffee?" the man in question asked from where he'd snuck up beside me.

"Oh, my hero," I said without thinking, and he grinned while I mentally kicked myself.

"Let's not exaggerate, it's only coffee." He handed me the red-striped mug I'd silently decided was my favorite.

I took a sip. Oat milk and one sugar, just how I liked it, and the comfort of it made me sigh. "It's like I made it myself. Thank you."

He gave me the kind of look that would burn my clothes off. "I like knowing what you like, darling."

Jesus, I didn't know an old-fashioned endearment could be so suggestive. A giggle escaped my throat. "I've created a monster."

He glanced side to side, took the mug and put it down on the counter, then nudged me into a corner out of sight of the doorway. "A monster who's just discovered sex with Mari Cole," he whispered. "I can't wait until I can have you again."

The hot words flushed my skin everywhere. The idea of being *had* shouldn't have made me feel like stripping for him then and there, I was a self-respecting adult woman. No one owned me, or took me. But some part of me didn't mind when it was him. "You are such a secret alpha."

"I really need to find out what that means."

"It's your fault for not reading what I tell you to read," I said with a grin.

"Ahem," Graham coughed from the doorway, and Leo stepped back, the pull between us evaporating.

"Leo, someone's here asking for you," Graham said. "Short, skinny bloke in a designer suit?"

"Oh," Leo said, and with that one non-word my dark-eyed devil boy was gone, replaced with the burdened boss. But it wasn't just the weighed-down look. There was confusion there, too. "I'll go talk to him now."

He moved away from me, but I found myself touching his arm. "See you later?" I asked softly.

"Of course." But his smile didn't reach his eyes. I let

him go but made a note to myself to get downstairs soon and see who the short, skinny guy was.

Graham stared after Leo with a stern look on his face. "I need to have a chat with him, too."

I blinked. "What kind of chat?"

His eyes narrowed. "The kind of chat where I tell him that if he breaks your heart, I'll make him cry."

A laugh burst out of me. "No, you're not going to do that, because I don't need anybody defending my honor. It's not the Stone Age and you're not my brother." I stared at his shocked face. "You're going to catch flies like that. What did I say?"

Graham shut his wide-open mouth, and his Adam's apple bobbed, like he was choking words down. "Er, nothing. I . . . was just going to say of course you don't."

I shook my head. "I hope you don't play poker, Blondie. Anyway, Leo's not going to break my heart because I'm not that kind of person."

"I remember now. You told me when we met." A shift in the weather came over Graham's face, from stubbornness to sadness. "Should I be worried you're going to break his?"

All of a sudden, I remembered that I could count my time at Ross & Co. in weeks, but that Leo and Graham had been in the same tight little crew for years. And for the first time in a long time, I couldn't shrug off the loneliness of that feeling. "No," I answered, even though I didn't have any control over Leo's heart. I could only hope he wouldn't be reckless enough to catch feelings for me.

Graham leaned toward me and lowered his voice. "Mari, listen. You need to be careful."

I rolled my eyes as hard as I could. "I don't think what

Leo and I are doing on our own time would wreck the store."

"No, I'm not worried because of the bloody shop." He puffed out a long breath. "I'm sure he'd hate that I'm telling you this and not him."

I felt like I'd opened the door to a pitch-black room and that I'd see something I didn't want to see when the light turned on. "Tell me what?"

"Leo was married before," he blurted.

I blinked as the light turned on, fluorescent and viciously bright. Marriage was for suckers, as far as I was concerned. But it made total sense for Leo, being someone's husband. Someone so steady, so orderly, of course he'd get married if he got the chance. Out of nowhere I saw him being domestic with an anonymous someone else. Buying groceries together, going for walks, curling up together in a big bed late at night. Day after day, year after year, until his hair was all gray and his straight back stooped.

It was ridiculous, to be jealous of something I knew I wasn't suited for. Something that I'd never wanted.

But had I never wanted it? Or just thought I could never have it? Images flickered across my mind, fleeting moments of Mom and Greg kissing on the sofa, dancing in the kitchen, between screaming fights and silent treatments.

"Becca ended things a year before Alexander died," Graham said, folding his arms tight. "It gutted him. They'd known each other since they were kids and got married soon after uni. Losing them both changed him. He was always serious and a bit shy, but he's been walking around in a cold fog for ages. The fact that he wants you," he raked his fingers through his hair as he found his words, "that's *big*, Mari. It's important."

Big. Important. Those words automatically made my toes twitch in my shoes, my legs tense with the urge to walk out of the room, out of the store. How likely was it that I'd hurt Leo? I knew sweet fuck all about commitment. As far as I was concerned, love was fickle, conditional. It was Mom covering me with kisses and then running to Greg the second he walked in the room, it was her thin, pained voice begging me to think of Greg as Dad, even when he never acted like one. It was my college girlfriend Dina wanting me when I was easy, and pushing me away the second I let her see the struggle underneath.

"We're grown-ups." I willed myself to sound matter-of-fact instead of panicky. "Leo makes his own choices. If he's unhappy, he'll end it." I tilted my chin up. "I'm not sure why you're the one giving me relationship advice, here. How are things with Catriona?"

Graham clamped his mouth shut. As far as I could tell, over the last few weeks he'd still been giving her the same longing looks when she wasn't paying attention, but hadn't found the right moment to actually talk. "You don't play fair."

I shrugged. "Just saying that neither of us really knows what we're doing, here. Or has a monopoly on bravery."

He sighed. "Fair enough. Let's just try not to ruin other people's lives with our bullshit, shall we?"

"Of course I can try not to." I knew myself, and that would honestly be the best I could do.

Leo

As I raced down the steps to the main entrance, the inside of my brain was a splash painting of feelings—happiness, annoyance, and uncertainty slashing and dotting across each other. Why had Vinay come, when I'd told him I wasn't interested in giving up the shop? Why couldn't I take Mari back to bed and stay there for the rest of the day?

I took a deep breath. It wouldn't do to rush up to Vinay frantic. I let myself remember Mari's soft touch on my arm, the way she looked to me for reassurance. For all her ferocious independence, there was a tenderness at the heart of her that she'd chosen to show me, and I liked that. I liked it far too much for how short-lived this affair would be.

But now I understood what I'd been seeing between Graham and Mari. The way they talked to each other, the way he kept an eye on her and she prodded him—I could see their closeness, feel the warmth and familiarity between them, but it didn't have the electricity that surged in the air whenever my eyes met hers.

Was it possible for that electricity to be addictive, to want the heat and sizzle over my skin every second? Last night flashed like an erotic flip book, our bodies rising and falling in lines and curves. The way she'd given her pleasure over to me. How I'd made her moan and pant and beg with my hands and mouth, every sound cranking my arousal higher and higher. It had felt like flying.

It had felt *right*.

"Do you have the newest *Game of Thrones*?" a voice in a nasal, obviously fake Scouse accent asked when I got to the bottom of the stairs. "I've been waiting for it to come out for aaages."

But now I had to pay for that moment of blissful escape and remember that the real world existed. I turned, and Vinay smirked at me.

"What are you doing here?" I whispered.

"You haven't been answering your messages for the last few days," he whispered in his normal accent. "I have big news for you. Literally big."

If I kept pulling my hair like this, I'd end up bald with worry. "That's lovely, but honestly, couldn't you have sent me a text and told me to meet you at the caff?"

"Hi, can we help you find anything?" Mari suddenly said from beside me, and my stomach jumped again. Of course she wasn't going to stay where I put her, I'd been ridiculous to think she would.

My eyes zeroed in on the reddish-purple mark where her shoulder and neck met, and a shiver went through me as I remembered how she'd cried out when I'd sucked on her skin. I'd be hearing that sound in my dreams for weeks.

Now Vinay grinned widely at her. "No, just here for a natter, I'm afraid. I'm Vinay, an old friend of Leo's from uni." He snapped his fingers. "Wait. The accent. You must be Mari."

She shrugged lightly and smiled. I recognized it from her catalogue of expressions—it looked welcoming, but I knew it was just as much a shield for her. "That's me."

"Leo's told me *all* about you," he said, then dodged my attempt at subtly kicking his shin.

"Only bad things, I'm sure." She glanced back and forth between us, then raised her eyebrows. "If this isn't business, I guess I'll leave you guys to it."

I let her walk away, just barely resisting the urge to tug her back to me, to kiss her cheek, or better, her mouth. Even to hold her hand in mine. The more closeness she offered, the more I craved. After she'd shown me how to make buttery-sweet cinnamon toast and I'd eaten every bite, she'd led me back to the bed and asked me to teach her how I liked to be touched.

My face flamed at the thought of that lesson. I'd remember it until the day I died, if I didn't expire of sheer ecstasy the next time she used her mouth on me.

"If eyes were hands, she'd be naked right now," Vinay said with a quiet smile.

"Shut up," I muttered half-heartedly, rubbing my face to scrub away the utterly unprofessional memory. "Give me five minutes and we'll talk upstairs."

I got Graham to take my place on the floor with a rubbish excuse about an early lunch break, and led Vinay upstairs to my office.

He glanced around once I'd closed the door behind us and we'd sat down. "I like what you've done with the place. It's like your grandddad could walk in any minute."

I hadn't had the time or energy to care about interior design for months, but now through Vinay's eyes, I saw the state of the office for the travesty it was. I'd pinned up some of the loose photographs Judith had brought but I knew I hadn't truly made it mine. The ancient desk chair was designed for a man significantly taller and broader than me, and the carpet was a burnt-orange shag that hadn't aged well since its 1970s heyday.

But didn't that say so much about my relationship with the place before Mari arrived? That I hadn't done anything to make it nice for myself, just accepted it as it was and plowed through?

I could change things now, though. I could rip up the horrible old carpet, find a chair that didn't make my back hurt, hang up prints. I could make this a place I wanted to be, even after Mari left.

My stomach sank. I didn't know if I wanted to be here, if she were thousands of miles away.

I shook my head, letting go of futile hopes. "I don't have much time. What's your big news?"

Vinay sat forward. "My boss is really riding me to make a deal with you. They're very keen to buy the building, and they want to offer you this for it." He took a piece of paper out of his coat pocket and pushed it across the desk.

I took it, saying as I opened it, "Your boss really won't take no for an answer? She's very . . ." My train of thought went over a cliff. I'd never been skint, thanks to the money I'd inherited from Mum's parents when they'd died, but even my eyes widened at the number written in smooth blue ink. It was a number that bought houses and second houses, paid for my father's retirement, *my* retirement at age thirty-one.

The Rosses would never have to work again, if they didn't want to.

"Big, innit?" Vinay said.

"Ridiculous." I rubbed my fingers across the roughness of the paper. "It's Monopoly money," I said with a strange laugh. "I can't grasp it."

He nodded. "Me neither. It's life-changing."

I studied him. "Life-changing for you and Sonali, too. It's one percent commission for you, isn't it?"

"Right. But bidding up wasn't my idea, I promise."

I played with the scrap of paper. "You need this, though."

Vinay stared at his hands. "We've never pretended with each other, mate. Sonali really wants to stay home with the twins once they're born. Money like this would let her quit her job. And a two-bed flat was fine when we thought we'd have one child, but it's not enough for two."

We sat there silently. Vinay expectant and I . . . I wasn't sure what I was. I was so many things at once that I couldn't name them. Voices in my head talked over each other, my father's triumph, Judith's shock, Alexander's ire.

And Mari? Mari would be so disappointed with me, that I wouldn't let her see her plans through.

Overwhelmed, that's what I was.

Faced with my silence, Vinay sighed. "It's not about the money, is it, mate?"

I rubbed my left cheek as I tried to put the words together. "No." I let my fear come to the surface. "I just don't want to disappoint anyone, more than I already do."

He fiddled with one of the black buttons on his coat. "You had thirty years of Alexander telling you how to live your life, so I won't do that. I know what it's like, for families to have expectations that hurt more than help."

I nodded in recognition. Vinay was two years older than me, and he'd originally gone to Imperial to study medicine but failed his first-year exams. His father, whose only dream had been having a topflight neurosurgeon for his only son, hadn't spoken to him until he'd studied new

A-levels and gotten into LSE to study business. Even now he begrudged him any kind of approval.

"I hope that someday you feel certain enough to do what you want," Vinay said firmly, then smiled. "But now I want the goss. Tell me what's happening with Mari. You never struck me as the type for something casual."

"It's not casual," I growled.

He put his hands up with a laugh. "All right, all right, not casual. So you're mad for each other and this is forever, well done. You deserve it."

And now to explain the mess I'd gotten myself into. "She's going back to America in April," I mumbled to my desktop. "So it's not forever."

Thank God Vinay didn't die laughing at me, though I was sure I deserved it for being so foolish. Instead, he rested his head in his hand and said with a sad chuckle, "Oh, *mate*. You don't make it easy for yourself, do you?"

I laughed bitterly. "I don't think I'm capable of it."

Vinay studied me, his dark brown eyes pensive. "I never saw you look at Bex the way you look at Mari."

"Because Bex and I weren't that way," I finally confessed. "Even when we tried to be."

When we'd tried to transform best friendship into desire, it had been like trying to light a fire with soaked matches and green wood. Of course there hadn't been a spark.

Vinay nodded. "Then it's a good thing you moved on. You deserve to have the life you want, not the life someone else thought you should have." He reached out and tapped the magic number on the desk. "And you know what? This is the kind of money that means you're not tied down. You could do anything, go anywhere, for as long as you liked. Even California." He waved his hands in a "ta-da" gesture.

For a moment I let myself step into the picture he painted. Of waking up every morning in Mari's bed, making her coffee the way she liked it. Of exploring a new place, finally using the driving license that Judith had insisted I get. I'd never been outside of Europe, had only seen pictures of the Golden Gate Bridge and the Pacific Ocean, the rolling vineyards where Mari had grown up.

When I'd googled Loch Gordon one night, the photographs made me imagine going outside every day to draw, bathing in bright sunshine, breathing in the scent of dusty soil and rough-edged plants. I imagined taking time to woo Mari properly, without distractions.

But what if I made the bet, let go of my life here and followed her halfway around the world, and she got tired of me? I'd be thousands of miles from home, from Judith and my parents and my sisters, from the parks and streets and trees as familiar as my face in the mirror.

And I wasn't Mari's forever. She'd made that abundantly clear.

Don't fall for me.

A small part of me feared that it was too late.

"If I looked at a woman like that, I'd follow her wherever she wanted to go," Vinay said. He stood up and reached across the desk. "Just think about it, mate." He paused. "But not for too long, please."

I looked across at him, my friend who'd kept trying even when I'd disappeared into grief. The least I could give him was some consideration. "All right. I'll think about it," I said as I shook his hand.

CHAPTER TWENTY-ONE

Mari

There was nothing austere or withdrawn about Leo after a week and a half of sleeping together. He was all chocolate-sweet mouth and hungry hands whenever we could sneak a moment alone at the store, playing with my hair, shaping my waist, kissing my neck.

"We have a festival to plan," I whispered into his shoulder one afternoon when he'd asked me to hang back after a meeting, to smiling eye rolls from Graham and Catriona, then pulled me into his lap for a rerun of our first make-out session.

Amusement warmed his voice when he said, "Didn't you just tell us all that tickets were selling well, and that we were just waiting for one more author? Are you saying you *aren't* doing a spectacularly brilliant job?"

"Absolutely not," I retorted.

He trailed long fingers down my spine. "Then it doesn't hurt to take a break, does it?"

I sat back a little, took in the glow of his eyes behind his glasses, the high color in his cheeks and lips. The lines in his forehead weren't as deep, and the bags under his eyes had faded to shadows, even though we weren't doing a lot of sleeping. "No," I answered finally. But a small voice in the back of my brain worried that if I noticed how happy I made him, we might be heading for a different kind of hurt.

On nights when Leo and I would both work, we'd close the building together then travel the forty-five minutes to the Airbnb holding hands. I'd cook something basic like pasta with tomato sauce or baked potatoes with canned beans for me and butter and sour cream for him. As Leo got confident that I wouldn't force food on him, he was more and more willing to eat together, instead of waiting until I was busy doing something else.

Then we'd have sex. Which was all it was. Adjectives like "transcendent" and "passionate" and "all-consuming" floated through my mind, but I popped them like the bubbles they were, ephemeral and insignificant. Sex was just sex, an itch I needed to scratch, a physical requirement like food and heat and exercise. Not a religious experience.

But I would fall asleep cliffhanging like I usually did and wake up nestled in Leo's arms. I guessed unconscious me was just trying to stay warm a lot of the time. I ignored how the combination of soft sheets and his body heat wove itself around me, how the spicy herbal scent of his skin and the whisper of his breathing disarmed the part of my brain that had been wearing heavy armor for years and years. This feeling of safety, of comfort, it was all just a postcoital haze.

In those ten days, the world outside the Airbnb window had changed, too. London was still freezing, but I could see the days' shadows getting a little shorter, the light lasting a little longer before the dark took over again. I'd dared at one point to go outside without a hat pulled down over my ears and wasn't punished with full-body shivers.

"Come on, the sun's out, let's go for a walk," I said softly when I woke up with Leo on a rare day we both had off. The pale light streaming through the window and striping across the bedsheets made me want to feel it on my face.

Leo stirred against my back, and the hand that had been resting under my breasts slid slowly downward. "Let me make you come, then we can go out."

I shifted away and turned over to look into his intent face, smiling to reassure him. "It's only nine A.M. Plenty of time for that later."

His eyes darkened. "But I want to lick you," he said, his voice dropping an octave.

I didn't doubt him. He was insatiable when it came to going down on me, and I'd have to be dead to resist that kind of hunger. So I followed his urging hands, climbing up and over him until he could have his way with me, feasting while I held on to the headboard and tried not to wake up the neighbors by moaning directly into the wall.

"Again?" he whispered, fifteen minutes after he'd turned me into a messy, babbling wreck.

I burst out laughing. "Oh my God, I know you're obsessed with the fact that I can orgasm more than once, but

I think I'm closed for business. Please, please can we go outside?"

He sighed. "It just seems a waste of time now, not doing things that make you come." But after a long kiss, he let me out of bed, and he took a deep breath of rinsed air the same way I did when we stepped out the front door. We glanced at each other and smiled when we saw how people were wandering in the park, everyone's faces turned toward the watery light.

"The days are getting longer," Leo said quietly as we walked. "You can see the angle of the sunlight changing."

A small child ran screaming happily after a gamboling dog, and I couldn't help my grin. "That would explain why everybody's that little bit more cheerful."

He nodded. "The big change will come when the clocks spring forward. But it's already making a difference."

When I looked closely at Leo's face, I saw his smile didn't reach his eyes. I could guess why. Just after the clocks went forward for daylight savings, we'd have the Ross & Co. Festival. Right after that, I was going back to California.

But thinking about going home didn't fill me with relief. Despite the cold, despite the dark, despite the question mark over Ross & Co.'s future . . . I could get used to it here. Maybe it was nice not to be alone when I closed the door on the workday. To swap book recommendations with Catriona, to laugh at a stupid meme with Graham. To go home with someone special, not just for a few hours but day in, day out.

If I were being honest, there wasn't any maybe. It *was* nice. I was . . . happy. But only for now.

I rubbed my temple. In the hurry to get outside, we'd

skipped breakfast, and the lack of caffeine was starting to press on my brain.

"Let's get your coffee," Leo said warmly, taking my hand. "And a pastry? There's three different bakeries on the market, so what kind would you like?"

"Sounds wonderful. I'm definitely a croissant girl." Was this something I could have when I went back to California? Someone who wanted to know what I liked and enjoyed giving it to me? "But I'm buying," I said, unable to accept it.

His mouth opened for a second, then closed, and he just shook his head. "If it would make you happy."

Did it? Or was it just a knee-jerk reaction? But this wasn't the kind of day for deep introspection. The sun was out, I was about to eat delicious pastry, and a gorgeous man wanted to take me back to bed later. All of my favorite things.

When we got to the shopping street at the end of the park, I bought an oat latte for myself and a mocha for Leo, and after devouring two crisp, buttery croissants, we meandered down the street looking in the windows. There was a fishmonger with a man standing shucking oysters to order out front, a general store with a hodgepodge of household wares. For a second I stopped in front of a little grocery store that had pyramids of oranges and tangerines outside glowing like lanterns.

Last on the street was a forlorn-looking antique store. "Closing Down Sale," the handwritten sign in the window said.

"You want to look in there?" Leo said with an eyebrow raise when I lingered in front of the door.

"Just for a second," I said, feeling a scratch of possibility in the back of my brain.

It was a grandmother's attic of a store, flowery chintz and beige lace and walnut furniture, smelling vaguely of used-up lavender sachets and old paper. An older woman with lilac-tinged white hair sat at a desk reading a tabloid newspaper and barely looked up as Leo and I wandered the meandering path through the displays.

I picked up a single teacup, rubbed my thumb across the smooth porcelain, outlining the little painted bouquet of violets on it.

"That's not for sale on its own," the woman said. "It's one of a set of six, with the saucers." Her voice was made of cigarettes and disillusionment. "The rest are in the back. You can have them for a tenner."

I carefully put the cup down. "I'm sorry, I don't have room in my suitcase for that," I said, putting cheer in my voice.

She shrugged and turned back to her paper.

So much for customer service. "What's next for this place?" I asked, keeping my voice casual.

A grunt. "Don't know. Landlord wants to sell up, doesn't he? It'll probably be a posh shop selling thirty-quid soap and candles to all the fancy people moving in."

I studied the fixtures. "That would be a shame." I could tell the store had good bones under all the tchotchkes and fussy wallpaper. Light flooded in from the south-facing windows, and cheerful pedestrians flowed past through the glass. I pulled out my phone and googled, and saw there wasn't a bookstore anywhere in the immediate neighborhood. The nearest one was over a mile away, which wasn't much in California driving distance but was a lot in a place focused around walking.

If I looked at this place, I could see a display of beautiful new hardcovers, with a cushioned window seat for customers to enjoy. I could see setting up a coffeemaker and a teakettle behind the counter, and a cozy children's section down the narrow stairs at the back. It would be a little haven, the same kind of hideaway Suzanne had created in Orchard House, the one I'd wandered into at age eleven and never really left.

"That place could make an amazing bookstore," I said quietly to Leo when we stepped outside.

He blinked and looked in the window again. "Could it?"

"Yeah. The success story of the last few years has been little neighborhood stores like Orchard House. They don't make tons of money, but they employ a few people and stock books that their locals want to read. They're like the minnows I told you about. They swim around doing their own thing, too tiny to attract the attention of the sharks and trawlers."

Leo put his hands in his coat pockets, not exactly a picture of enthusiasm. "That sounds like it would be a lot of hard work without much payoff."

He wasn't totally raining on my parade, but I felt a little cold and damp anyway. "You wouldn't do it for the money," I said, my voice a little bewildered. "You'd do it because putting the right book in the right person's hands gives you joy, and sending them home holding a new little piece of possibility fulfills you." I hesitated at his blank face. "Isn't that why we do this? For love?"

He looked away instead of answering, and I felt like I'd opened a closet where I'd expected to find treasure and instead found cobwebs and broken furniture, chilly gloom. I'd never thought about what drove him, what kept him coming to the shop every day, putting out fires and hustling to keep things going week in, week out.

"I suppose working in the shop in Bloomsbury is all I've ever really known," he said finally. "And the building is part of what makes Ross and Co. what it is. Alexander always called it our castle. I don't think I could work anywhere else."

"I mean, you've definitely got the turrets and the gargoyles." But then I thought about what he was submerged in, all day, every day. Pictures of his ancestors watching him trying to keep the store afloat. Obligation. Duty.

Now Leo gave the little store a good hard look. "You're right," he said carefully. "This place would be amazing for someone."

But not for him, I realized with sadness. My mouth opened, to ask him what he really wanted. I thought about him with his sketchbook, about his sisters begging him for drawings. About how stuck he'd been when I'd first arrived, like he'd been dropped into a murky swamp without a compass or a clue.

Would he have stayed at the store if Alexander had given him a choice?

But that question was as loaded as an incendiary bomb and way too intimate for whatever this was between us, this bubble of sex and cinnamon toast and waking up in each other's arms that all too soon would pop.

"Too bad I already have my own place to run," I said calmly instead.

After I'd bought a few things at the grocery store to dress up instant ramen for our dinner, we walked back up the market and set out across the park. I was telling him about the latest contemporary romance I'd been reading, about a PA returning to the small Virginia town where she'd grown up and falling for the town loner, when I realized Leo wasn't listening, or even next to me. He was a few yards behind, staring straight ahead. His lips parted, his face white. What was he seeing?

I turned around to look up the path and saw a delicate woman our age who looked like the second coming of Audrey Hepburn, carrying a small bouquet of daffodils. A big man a decade older than her, with graying reddish-blond hair and haphazard features, held her other hand, a leash attached to a sheepskin rug of a dog in the other. He said something in an accent I didn't recognize that made her giggle. She shook her head, turned away from her lover, looked over my shoulder, and did a double take of astonishment. "Oh my God, Leo!"

She ran past me and hugged Leo hard, paper and flowers crunching between them. Leo's body language was board-stiff, and his eyes were closed, like he was wishing for invisibility.

"Becca," he finally forced out.

My mouth gaped. The universe must have been laughing its head off. Leo's ex-wife was now holding his upper arms, and out of nowhere I felt the urge to smack them off him.

"It's been ages since I've seen you," she blurted. "How are you?"

"Fine," he said like he was squeezing the word out of an empty toothpaste tube. "Busy."

A silence made of history fell. "I'm sorry, we're being terribly rude," she said with a big smile. "This is my husband, Paul." She raised her eyebrows at Leo. "Aren't you going to introduce me to your friend?"

"You got married," Leo said bluntly, not taking the opening, which was fine. Totally fine.

"We did," Paul said, his voice mellow. "Went to the registry office just before Christmas." He nudged his wife. "This one wanted to make an honest man out of me."

Becca smiled and rolled her eyes. "We were living together already and I didn't see the point of waiting around, or doing anything fancy. I hated all that fuss at our wedding, remember, Leo?"

Leo unstuck his jaw and said quietly, "I remember."

I stared into space, wishing for invisibility. I wasn't supposed to be here. This wasn't my place.

Paul bent and kissed Becca's crown. "As long as you let me make a fuss sometimes, I'm happy."

Well, weren't they absolutely adorable. A starburst of hurt came out of nowhere, but what was I hurt for? I'd seen plenty of couples come into Orchard House, pointing out novels they'd read and grinning at each other over piles of new books at the register.

Was this what Leo really wanted? This warm, chatty woman had been his first love. He'd planned to spend the rest of his life with her. I didn't think I had the capacity for marriage, but for the first time in my life, I felt that lack.

I *regretted* it.

A low woof woke me up, and a cold, twitching nose pressed into my hand. I smiled down at the shaggy dog, grateful for the distraction from Leo and Becca's tension. I crouched to scratch his ears, and he whined softly in pleasure.

"Looks like someone's fallen in love," Paul said above me as the dog pawed me for more affection.

I shook my head and looked up, pretending that the last word hadn't been like a static shock. "Nah, the big guy just knows a sucker when he sees one." Buoyed a little by doggy sweetness, I said, "I'm Mari, by the way."

"I'm Paul, and this is Rug," he said with a wry smile, reaching to shake my outstretched hand. "Because he looks like one."

I raised my eyebrows. "I like the literalness. Where'd you get him?"

Paul started to tell me the story of driving down a busy road near his parents' house in Belfast and seeing a matted mess of a dog limping down the shoulder, and it was really heartwarming and made both Paul and Rug impossible not to like, but I could see Leo staring at his feet, Becca looking at him imploringly. If two people ever needed space and time, it was them. "Can I play with him?" I asked abruptly.

Paul said easily, "Of course, he'd love that." He pulled a chewed-up tennis ball out of the pocket of his coat and Rug immediately leapt to attention, dancing on legs like springs. "Over here, where there's space for him to run."

I glanced over my shoulder, then jogged to keep up with Paul's long stride and Rug's trot, ignoring the pull I felt toward Leo, the urge to take his hand.

CHAPTER TWENTY-TWO

Leo

"Here we are," Becca said with false cheer as Paul and Mari walked out onto the wet grass.

I rubbed my neck, feeling like there was a blade hovering over it. "Here we are."

"How have you been?" she asked. "Vinay said at dinner last week that he'd seen you."

"I think you know the answer, then," I snapped, throwing up a wall as quick as I could against the hurt that had surged up.

She'd been my best friend, and losing her had been the beginning of the rock bottom of my life.

Just under two years ago I'd been staring at spreadsheets, trying to make the numbers add up with the Covent Garden branch and the main shop, when she'd whispered, then said, then yelled my name. When I finally looked up and snapped, "What?" she'd burst into tears and told me she wanted a divorce. We hadn't been to bed together in months, and dinner conversation had been reduced to platitudes and politeness. But she'd met someone else, this big man with his ridiculous dog and easy smile, she loved him to distraction, and it made her realize everything we'd been missing. Everything I hadn't been able to give her.

It felt like the universe had grabbed my hair and insisted on rubbing my face in every way that I was a failure.

"You told me you would be all right," she said now, accusingly. "That this was what you wanted."

"It *was*. I'm fine," I said through gritted teeth. No wonder Mari said it so often. "Fine" was easy, a quick plaster over any hurt.

Becca threw up her hands. "Then why the fuck don't you reply to my messages?"

I gawped at her. The Becca I'd known wouldn't have been that direct in a thousand years. Wouldn't have said "fuck," either.

She waved her hand at me. "Oh, don't be like that. I didn't break your heart. You loved me, of course you did, as your *friend*. But you wanted more because Alexander thought it was a good idea, not because you were really attracted to me. Tell me I'm wrong."

The blunt shock of her words surged through me. "I can't," I finally answered, the last wall of defense coming down under her sledgehammer. What had been between us wasn't great passion, or love for the ages. It was something easy, comfortable, familiar. That same warmth that I'd seen between Graham and Mari, that was Becca and me. But we'd been too young to keep it that way, I'd been too young not to listen to Alexander's prodding, and I'd ruined everything.

"You didn't ruin anything," Becca said adamantly, and I blinked, not realizing that I'd spoken those last words aloud. "Or at least, we ruined it together, because we weren't brave enough to talk about what was happening in bed." She took a step closer. "But Leo, that's the past. It's *done*. We're here now." Her face softened. "And I missed my friend. I miss you so much."

I stared at her, the wild swirl of emotions suddenly freezing to make a clear picture. Becca was as beautiful as ever, but I realized with a jolt that my pleasure in looking at her was fundamentally an aesthetic one. I appreciated how the curve of her jaw became the point of her chin, but I didn't have any urge to run my fingers along it. The line of her neck was elegant, but it didn't feel like it was made for me to kiss.

Her body had never *called* to mine the way Mari's did.

All at once, I let myself remember wild races down Parliament Hill, eating enormous cones of gelato from our favorite shop in Kentish Town, even just sitting at the kitchen table while she helped me with my maths homework.

She reminded me that I'd been light once, carefree.

Maybe I could be again, if I let her back in.

"Hi, mate," I finally said, and a little part of me relaxed that I hadn't realized was tense.

Becca's smile lit up her face. "Hi, pal," she said back.

Together, without speaking, we turned and slowly followed Paul and Mari and the dog. The monstrous animal was capering, waiting for Mari to chuck his tennis ball across the grass.

"Are you two living near the Fields, then? We've not seen you around before," Becca said, watching Mari.

I shook my head. "Oh, no. I'm still in Hampstead with my parents and the twins, and Mari's living over the shop while she's here for a few months."

She started. "In that old garret we used to play in? She must be freezing."

I snorted. "She almost did." I told her the story of Mari falling ill right after she got to England.

Becca listened closely, the way she always had. "She makes you happy, I can tell," she finally said with a laugh. "Of course you'd fall for a really stubborn woman. You're so intent on looking after everyone all the time and someone refusing would drive you around the bend. But I'm glad you've found her."

I resisted the urge to touch the smile on my lips and shook my head instead. "It's not a long-term thing. She's going home to California in April, and she's not all lovey-dovey, anyway." I hadn't meant to say the last part, but Becca's innocent face had always been truth serum.

She gasped and clapped her hands. "Not lovey-dovey? Leo Ross, are you just *shagging* her?"

My blush must have been the color of strawberries from how strong it was. "Yes."

"A regular Don Juan, you are," Becca said, resting her hand on her chest, as fake-scandalized as a Victorian matron. "I'm utterly shocked. Tell me everything."

I snorted. "Not a chance."

Becca was quiet for a moment, and I realized she was watching Mari, who was playing tug-of-war with the dog, her giggles filling the air as she struggled to keep her feet.

My ex raised an elegant brown eyebrow at me. "I'm not sure she isn't. Lovey-dovey, I mean. She's certainly a dog person, but luring Paul away so you and I could talk shows that she reads you. And one person can't read the other unless they're really paying attention."

I thought of how concentrated Mari and I were on each other when we were in bed, how she'd treated my body like a book where she wanted to memorize every page. I'd tried to have a one-night stand a few months after Becca left me, but the woman's touch, her kiss, it had felt all wrong. That was when I discovered that I wasn't capable of having sex for sex's sake. I had to make love with a person. Someone I *knew*.

I was getting to know Mari, falling for her more and more with every detail I learned . . . and I was utterly, utterly fucked. "Don't get me wrong, we like each other a lot. But it's temporary," I lied through my teeth, keeping the despair out of my voice.

Becca stopped in the middle of the path. "Why do you keep hurting yourself?"

"I don't," I responded instinctively.

"You *do*."

"I *don't*."

"Well, if you're going to be eight years old about it."

I shoved my fingers into my graying hair, which no eight-year-old would have. "I'm sorry, Bex, but I don't know what you're talking about. I'm getting my end away with a pretty woman who doesn't demand anything else from me." Though I wanted her to demand things from me. I would enjoy giving her every single one.

"I don't just mean Mari, you git. I mean your family,

and the shop, too. You don't know how to make yourself happy. You don't know how to ask for what you want, or even need."

"This is just what I have to do!" I said, the truth like a cry of pain. "Alexander's *gone*, Dad doesn't want anything to do with the place, and Judith's arthritis isn't going to get any better. It has to be me."

She took a deep breath. "I know. I'm sorry." More gently, she said, "But what about before?"

Before. I closed my eyes, remembered our silences and sadnesses. How when we were married, we'd added up to less than the sum of our parts, how the bed we'd shared might as well have been Antarctica for all the coldness and distance.

A small hand rested on my forearm. "Look," Becca said, "it wasn't all your fault. I could have spoken up. But we were just children. Barely out of uni, knew absolutely nothing about the world, had been in each other's pockets since before we could remember."

"I made you unhappy." I put layers of meaning into the word, hoping she'd heard them.

She raised her eyebrows. "We made *each other* unhappy. Your happiness *matters*, Leo, no matter what Alexander told you." Her face softened. "I forgave you ages ago. Why don't you forgive me, and forgive yourself?"

For a moment, I was lost. I'd been handed a deck of cards and told to build a house on a slippery wooden table. The uncertainty of it, the precariousness.

But the past had been certain—certain and *shit*. I needed to live in the present, to let myself feel the weak sunshine on my face, hear Mari's excited laugh at the dog's antics. "I'll try," I sighed.

"That's all I can ask for, I suppose." She nudged me lightly. "She's sexy, you know, with all that gorgeous chestnut hair and those curves. Reminds me of those paintings you used to stare at at the National."

I immediately thought of Rubens's women, soft and voluptuous and utterly unselfconscious.

"Let yourself be happy, Leo." Becca reached up and patted my shoulder. "Speaking of happiness, I'd like to see you more. Get to know each other again, as grown-ups this time."

My life was far too complicated, but maybe this one thing, right now, could be simple. "I'd like that, too."

We walked over to Paul and Mari and the big shambling dog, who was panting and staring at Mari in adoration, not that I could blame him. Her cheeks were flushed with exertion, and I wanted to tug her to me and kiss them. But I knew I needed to explain myself first. Becca and I exchanged another round of hugs, her informing me that I was going to answer her texts on pain of dismemberment, and she and Paul ambled off.

"All good?" Mari asked beside me. "That looked intense."

"It was. But it was a conversation we needed to have." My nervous fingers found the back of my neck. "I didn't mean to spring her on you like that."

Mari hesitated. "I knew about you guys already."

I blinked. "You did?"

She bit her lip, cast her eyes down. "Graham told me, when we came in the first morning looking well-fucked."

My open palm found my forehead. "Fuck. I should have been the one to tell you. I'm sorry."

She shrugged, her expression easy in a way I knew not to trust. "It's OK. We can't have that kind of relationship."

I stepped back, the words a swift slap of reality. "We can't?"

"No. This," she said, gesturing back and forth between us, "needs to be all present tense. The past, the future, they can't matter here." She shoved her hands in her pockets. When we'd first met, I'd thought it was her showing how at ease she was, how carefree. But now I knew that if she acted like she didn't care, she couldn't be hurt.

"But I want you to know me, Mari. The same way I want to know you." For a wild moment, I thought how easy it would be to say "love" instead of "know," because to me they were so close together. The way she liked her coffee, the sweet spot on her shoulder that made her tip her head to the side, how she got so lost while reading that I had to say her name ten times to get her attention. I hoarded all these pieces of knowledge, took them out and studied them in the middle of the night while Mari slept next to me.

She shook her head now. "But the more we know about each other, the harder it'll be to end it, right? As long as your secrets won't make what we're doing unsafe, I'm OK with you not telling me everything."

The rejection was a punch in the stomach, but it suddenly transformed into fear. Had she somehow overheard what Vinay and I had been discussing? No, she couldn't possibly. "What would count as an unsafe secret?" I finally asked, my voice tight.

I died by inches as she thought for several seconds. "Either of us being physical with someone else, since we've agreed to be exclusive until I leave."

"Right," I exhaled. I ignored the green-eyed monster inside me that roared at the thought of Mari in someone else's bed. Because she would be, soon enough. "Anything else?"

She examined my face for a long moment. "No. Nothing else." Then she tugged on my fingers, a little smile curling her lips again. "Can we go get cozy now?"

"Of course we can." Back to our warm little sex haven. Back to the place where I could pretend I had everything I wanted, that I wasn't starving for more from her. "I only want you," I told her, the smallest fragment of my whole truth.

She bit her lip, then nodded. "Ditto," she said softly, and I pressed a kiss to her cold cheek, ignoring the shiver it sent through me.

CHAPTER TWENTY-THREE

Mari

"Sold out," I sighed happily at my screen.

"Well done," Leo said approvingly over my shoulder, where we were both at the register, looking at my laptop on Saturday morning. "So that's it? We're all set?"

I checked the back end of the ticketing website to make sure all the little boxes next to the listings for each event had 0s in them. "The audience is, yep." Two weeks from now, Catriona's gallery downstairs would be full of people listening to what our authors had to say, and ready to hear Leo's plea to help keep the store open, to preserve the last hundred years of history and give Ross & Co. a shot at the future. The air would be full of conversation and the smell of brewing coffee, and fingers crossed, by the end of the day, the registers would be full of pounds.

I looked out the window at the shorter shadows on the sidewalks and walls. The spring equinox was tomorrow, adding to the sense of possibility in the air. I'd noticed buds on the branches of the trees of the park, and a few days ago I'd woken up not to Leo's phone alarm going off, but to the sunrise slipping in the window of the Airbnb. It felt like the store was waking up from a long winter sleep, too. Graham had taken the time to dust all the shelves, and Catriona had built tables full of bright-colored paperbacks.

"Tables by color?" I'd asked when I'd seen the rainbows.

She'd shrugged. "You can't deny that it's pretty. Figured you might want it for socials, too."

Best of all, there was a small but steady flow of undergraduates coming through the doors. Their higher voices and smiling enthusiasm felt like rays of sunshine, and they all left with a book or two.

"Marvelous," Leo said now. He glanced from side to side to check we were alone, then pressed his mouth right on the sweet spot where my shoulder and neck met. "So clever and talented."

Before I met Leo, I would have sworn I didn't have a praise kink, but there was a first time for everything. "Flattery will get you everywhere," I purred back, and felt his smile against my skin.

I'd told myself for years that I didn't like being touched outside of sex. But was that just because hugs had been few and far between when I was a kid, and nonexistent after my mom died? When Leo put his arms around me, it was a door opening, a teakettle boiling, a soft wool blanket unfolding. I wanted his touch because it felt like safety. Felt like coming home.

But he couldn't be my safety. He couldn't be my home,

because home was six thousand miles away and all of this was temporary. "We still have a lot to do. And not much time."

A little sigh. "I know," Leo said, straightening up and moving out of arm's reach. "What's on the list for today?"

We were sitting in the fiction section, comparing notes on which journalists we'd try to persuade to come along, hoping against hope the festival would end up in print at the last minute, when I noticed Graham was hovering in the doorway, looking at his phone.

"What's up, Blondie?" I called.

His shrug was more of a jerk, like someone had attached strings to his shoulders. "Er, the usual. Politicians spouting rubbish while the world burns, nothing new there."

His eyes were darting around, and his tongue flicked out of his mouth like his lips were dry.

I stood up and sidled over to him. Since when was he nervous, ever? Even when Catriona was getting under his skin, he willfully relaxed, became even more cavalier. He didn't *do* tense, as far as I could tell.

Until now.

I reached up and tapped him gently on the forehead. Instead of laughing like he should, he just looked bewildered. "Why are you poking me?"

My fingertip found his chest. "I think you've been body snatched. Who are you, and what have you done with Graham?"

"I'm fine. Nothing's wrong. Stop." He tried to grab my finger, but I was too fast. "Bloody." He failed again. "*Poking*."

"I'll stop when you stop acting weird."

He grabbed my pointer finger. "I'm *not. Stoppit.*"

"Graham," Catriona said from the doorway.

I tugged, and he gave me my hand back. "Yeah?" he answered.

Her ginger eyebrows were raised. "Your dad's here."

"*OhthankChrist,*" he exhaled. "Come meet him."

My hands found my hips. "Why?" I said, trying for humor. "Is he why you've been so ridiculously jumpy?"

He flailed at me. "Why are you being *impossible*?"

I imitated his waving arms. "Why are you being *weird*?"

"What's all this, then?" a calm voice said, like we were unruly students being called to order.

Graham stopped cold. Turned around.

A fifty-something man with graying mouse-brown hair hovered in the doorway, hands in the pockets of his black peacoat. The soft plaid scarf he wore matched his eyes, cornflower blue like Graham's.

"Mari," Graham exhaled, "this is Jamie. My dad."

"Hi." That was the only word my brain could produce, because the rest of it was frantically flipping through my memories like an infinite deck of cards, trying to work out where I'd seen this man before. This short, stocky man who was staring at me, his mouth a little agape, like I was floating in midair, and who didn't respond to my greeting.

Graham rubbed the back of his neck. "We . . . we have something we need to talk to you about."

My stomach suddenly felt like it was clinging to Half Dome, nothing but thousands of feet of air between me and the ground.

"Your mum's name was Lisa," Jamie said softly.

My mother's name in his mouth was a cold spell that made me shiver a little. "That's right." I tried to make eye contact with Graham, but he was squeezing Jamie's shoulder.

Jamie continued, "And you were born near San Francisco sometime in May just under thirty years ago."

"May twentieth," I forced out. "What does that have to do with anything?"

Jamie breathed in and out, once, twice. "I think . . ."

He trailed off, and I felt like everything I knew was a sheet of paper that was about to get ripped in two. "You think *what*?"

A hand rested lightly on my lower back. Leo rubbed gently, a little touch of reassurance that reminded me to breathe.

"I think," Jamie tried again. But the rest of the words were stuck in his throat, his mouth moving but nothing coming out.

His wide mouth, made for smiling.

His downturned eyes. His nose almost too big for his face.

For *our* faces.

Because my coloring was my mom's, but my eyes, my mouth, my nose, were all his.

"You're my father," I breathed out, the words a trapdoor into empty space.

"We'd need a DNA test to be completely sure," Graham said quickly.

"I'm sure," Jamie said, staring at me, his eyes wide. "I'm sure you're mine."

The words were a hard fist in my solar plexus, and now I understood why Jamie had struggled to speak. Why Graham had been so nervous.

Fuck, Graham was my brother. Half brother. In ten seconds, I'd transformed from an only child, an orphan, to a daughter, an oldest sister with three younger brothers.

The shock made metal in my mouth, and my hand pressed over my lips.

"How?" I finally asked stupidly. "I mean, who are you? Where have you *been*?" The last word was a cry.

Jamie's hands reached out for a second, before he balled them in his pockets. "I didn't know. Lisa didn't tell me she'd gotten pregnant, that she'd had you."

"I suspected when I compared the picture of Tim to you," Graham said, twisting his fingers. "I did some digging online, found stuff about your mum and your stepdad, and brought it to my dad."

A ball of hurt and sadness surged up my chest, desolation I hadn't felt in years. Of course he hadn't known anything about me, because he'd left her in the middle of the night. Left her to have me with another man, left me at the mercy of a so-called family who'd never love me the way I'd desperately wanted. Needed. "What the fuck am I supposed to do with that?" I snapped at Graham. "You suspected and you didn't fucking say anything?"

I was about to burst into tears, and Jamie didn't look so great, either.

Leo's hand was on my shoulder, bringing me back to earth. "This isn't the right place for this," he said to Graham sternly.

Graham's face fell. "I'm sorry, mate, of course not."

"What do you want to do, darling?" Leo asked me gently.

"Darling?" Jamie asked.

A hysterical laugh shot out of my mouth. The audacity of him, feeling the urge to be fatherly when he'd only known I existed for two whole minutes. "I think we need to talk," I forced out, in the understatement of the century.

"Angelo's, the Sicilian caff on Marchmont Street," Leo said firmly to Jamie. "You go ahead. We'll need a moment."

"Of course, I'll see you there," he said.

Graham looked between us uncertainly. "Should I go with you, Dad?"

"No, stay here." Jamie had that quiet authority in his voice again. "You did the right thing, but this next bit has to be between Mari and me."

The moment Jamie walked out the door, Leo took my hand and led me to the break room.

"That's my father," I said when he'd shut the door, tasting the strange words in my mouth.

"That's the man who *thinks* he's your father," Leo corrected.

"But he looks like me," I said flatly.

Leo nodded. "He does."

"And he knows my mom's name. When I was born."

"He does."

I bent over in half. "*Fuck*. I can't believe it. I can't believe any of it." The thing I had shoved in an iron box in the back of my brain, wrapped in chains, and locked with a dozen padlocks, the longing and the wishing and the *hoping*, had burst out and grabbed me so tight I could barely breathe.

A soft hand landed on my back, then wrapped around my waist. "Come here, come here," Leo said, and I went so easily. He tucked me into his long body, and I inhaled the spicy scent of him and felt my nerves slow down their frantic sprint. Comfort wasn't something I'd ever looked for from my partners. Pleasure, of course. Escape. But all of a sudden I felt like those feelings were candy, empty calories, and what Leo was offering was a lot more substantial. Nourishing. And right now, I wanted that. I wanted that so badly.

He kissed my jaw and forehead, letting loose some of the tension there. "Come on, darling," he coaxed softly, his touch on my shoulders and arms grounding me. "You should go hear what he has to say. I can be right there with you, if you want. And if you need to leave, you can just tell me and I'll get you out of there."

"Yes, please," I said softly. I wanted him beside me right now, I told myself, ignoring the lonely part of me that cried out that I wanted him there for a lot longer than that.

CHAPTER TWENTY-FOUR

Mari

Thirty minutes later, after I'd kissed Leo for courage, we sat across a scuffed linoleum table from Jamie, hot chocolates going cold in front of us. Leo's hand was a gentle pressure on my knee, keeping me from flying through the ceiling.

Meanwhile, Jamie's eyes were fastened to my face, his lips half an inch open. Like he was looking at a revelation.

Inside me I could feel a slow-building tidal wave of frustration and confusion, and I focused on my breathing so I wouldn't scream.

In for four, hold for four, out for four, hold for four.

"How did you two meet, then?" Jamie asked.

My eyes found Leo's, pleading. "Um, we met in the shop," he said, his smile gentle.

Jamie's laugh was high, strained. "Of course you did. Silly question. I'm not surprised that you ended up working with books. I always had my head buried in one, drove my mum mad. 'Go outside, you'll get rickets!' she'd always say. Didn't stop her from giving me a book token every year for my birthday, though." He shook his head. "I'm making her sound like she's died, but she's very much still alive. Turning seventy-five later this year." He hesitated. "She'd be delighted to meet you, Mari, if that's something you'd like."

I had a *grandmother*. A grandmother who'd be *delighted* to meet me. It was like I'd been starving for a year and presented with a box of chocolates. It was rich and sickly sweet, too much and not enough. "That's nice," I said, unable to keep the bitterness out of my voice.

A lock of hair fell out of my bun, but before I could reach for it, Leo's fingers were there, tucking it behind my ear. A careful, caring touch, a moment of respite.

"You have . . ." Jamie started.

I stared blankly as he stuttered, giving him exactly the amount of lifeline he deserved right now.

He looked down at the table and took a deep breath. "Fucking hell. I'm sorry about all this. I'm so sorry, love."

I flinched. "Don't call me love."

"Of course, I'm sorry." He swallowed hard. "If I apologize too many times, it'll be meaningless. I hope, I *hope* you know that this is as overwhelming for me as it is for you. I was going to say that you have Lisa's hair. She was always trying to push it out of her face, said it was like a living thing, had a will of its own."

Memories like camera flashes. Her long waves tickling my face as she bent down to kiss me good night. Always patting herself down for bobby pins, or digging in her purse, only for Greg to pull some out of his pockets with a knowing smile. Of her gently combing out and detangling my hair after my bath, promising she'd teach me how to take care of it myself when I was old enough.

From a mile away, Jamie said, "Graham showed me her obituary. I'm sorry you lost her so young. That wasn't fair, that you didn't get to grow up with her."

I shook my head hard. "Wait. When did she talk to you about her hair?"

"What do you mean?"

"She said it was one night. That she was blackout drunk, and barely knew who she was, let alone who you were. But you said 'always.'"

The shock on his face at my bluntness was painfully satisfying. Now he was hurt, too.

"Night?" He shook his head hard. "No. No, no, no."

Then a puzzle piece clicked into place. "And she said that you didn't know each other's names. But you definitely knew hers?" The light shifted on the cheerful, smiling image of my mom that had lived in my head for so long. What else had her smile been hiding?

Jamie reached inside his coat and pulled out a rectangle, pushed it across the table. I recognized the view of San Francisco from the Marin Headlands in the old photograph, the red spires of the Golden Gate Bridge. A summer day, thick with drifting fog. My young mother laughed at the camera in a black flowered dress and jean jacket. Jamie was wrapped around her, a man whose boyhood wasn't a distant memory. His cheek was pressed to hers, his expression utterly shocked and overwhelmed by his luck.

"I was on holiday with my best friend when she found me in a bar in the Marina," Jamie said as I studied the picture. "I was twenty-three. An immature twenty-three, so shy I could barely speak to girls. She was that bit more grown-up, and beautiful, and sparkling, and being with her was like taking three vodka shots in a row. I felt so special."

I remembered my mother's generous laughter, the intensity of her gaze as I told her about learning long division or taking care of the class guinea pig. "Like you were the only person she cared about."

"Yeah. And I thought she felt the same way about me. She wanted to know absolutely everything about England, my family." His eyes were tender, sad. He pressed his fingers into the table, like he was grounding himself in the present. "For a week, we were inseparable. She showed me all the places she liked, took me to the beach, to those hills in the picture.

"By the last day, I was off my head. Couldn't bear that I had to go home without her. I babbled out the most rubbish marriage proposal in the history of the world, told her I'd take care of everything, told her she'd love London. She laughed it off, told me it was far too soon, to ask her again later. And the next morning, she was gone."

Back to Greg, I realized. Back to her great love story. Jamie and I were just casualties. Without thinking, I wrapped my arms around myself, looking for some kind of comfort. Leo tugged me into his side, and I let myself nestle into him for a second before I pulled away.

"It was a shock, learning she'd been married," Jamie said quietly.

"She and Greg were on a break when you met," I said.

"I have a lot of memories of yelling and slamming doors, but they always made up."

"So she had you, because it was possible you were Greg's child?"

"Yeah. She even named me after Greg's mom, to tie me to him. Mari's short for Marilyn. But they knew right away I couldn't be his kid, because of my blood type."

"It's a pretty name," Jamie offered.

I shook my head. "I hate it. She was mean to me until the day she died." I swallowed back the sob I could feel pressing on my throat, kept to the facts. "Mom and Greg tried to have their own child but couldn't. They did all these fertility tests and he found out he was sterile. So I was a reminder of all the things that had gone wrong. A cuckoo in his nest, his mother said."

All of a sudden Jamie's face turned red and his shoulders got two inches wider. "That fucking... *cow*. You were a *child*."

I put my hand up to block his feelings, all that righteousness decades too late. "I don't want your anger. It's what happened to me, and it's done. I'm fine now." Though I was starting to hate the saccharine taste of "fine" in my mouth.

Jamie let out a long exhale. "All right. I may have to go to the boxing gym later, but all right. So after Lisa died, Greg looked after you?"

"Sure. I went to school, had a roof over my head, had enough to eat."

His eyes narrowed. "That's the bare minimum, Mari. Victorian orphans got that."

"No wonder I liked *David Copperfield* so much," I said coolly. "I spent as much time as I could at my local bookstore. Suzanne, the owner, she let me hang around and talked to me a lot about books I was reading. I started officially working there when I was fourteen, but I'd been learning from her for years before that. That was where I grew up, not Greg's house. He left Loch Gordon seven years ago and didn't leave a forwarding address, so he's a great big nothing, anyway."

I didn't tell him the way the house echoed when I got home from school, the way Greg's mouth had turned down when I tried to bring friends home, or when I'd had to ask him to drive me to Target because I'd had a growth spurt and my jeans and T-shirts didn't fit anymore. How he'd disappeared just before I'd graduated from college, and the emptiness had left me spinning, desperately grasping for any kind of lifeline.

Jamie buried his face in his hands. "Fuck, what a disaster." He breathed, and his face when he uncovered it was a pained mask. "But then why didn't Lisa try to track me down before she died? She knew my name. She knew we lived in Walthamstow, that I was going to be a teacher. For God's sake, I even gave her my mum's phone number."

He looked bereft, blasted, *lost*, an echo of my own bewilderment. Why would she have hidden this huge, fundamental truth? Hidden it from Greg, from Jamie, most of all from me?

Because the person she loved more than anything was Greg. Not me. Maybe she thought he could more easily forgive one night's drunk mistake than a passionate affair with someone who'd wanted to marry her. Maybe she thought Greg would take better care of me, that he would learn to love me, if there wasn't someone else in the picture.

"She didn't want to hurt my stepdad's feelings," I said finally.

But she'd been wrong. She'd lied, and it hadn't done any good. Greg saw me as an obligation with a time limit. Not a person.

The tears I'd been holding at bay for what felt like hours were a fierce pressure under my eyes. It was like sleeping with Leo had chipped away at the stone that protected me, and all my emotions were so much closer to the surface.

I was on my own, always had been, and it *hurt*.

"Mari, do you need a moment?" Leo asked next to me, his brow furrowed.

"No." The lie came out fraying, like rope pulled too tight. "I'm okay."

"If I had known about you," Jamie started.

I put my hand up again. "You didn't. I was all right on my own."

"No, you bloody weren't," he said stubbornly. "Again, you were a *child*. Your mum, Greg, even me, we failed you. Badly. But if I had known about you, I would have done whatever it took, Mari. I know it would have been complicated, expensive, getting a visa for you, or flying back and forth between England and America. But I would have done it, no questions asked."

I stared at him in disbelief. I didn't *know* this man, and hindsight was always perfect. "Because of my mom," I said flatly. My mom had been the force of nature, the charmer.

But Jamie shook his head hard. "No. She was the woman I had an affair with. Looking back, I know what I thought was love was just infatuation. But you're *my daughter*, and to be part of your life would be worth any price." Deep-blue eyes stared into mine. "*You* are worth any price."

I sat there, his kind words like knives, the story I'd been telling myself for two decades in shreds. All this loneliness, all the putting on a brave face, all the self-denial, just so my mom and Greg could preserve the myth of their great love. When I could have had a real dad, younger brothers, a grandma, *a family*.

The tears surged up, and I stared hard at my hands as I felt one traitor drop after another trickle down my cheek.

"Darling?" Leo asked.

"Mari, love, I'm sorry. I'm so sorry," Jamie said, his voice loaded with so much sadness, so much regret.

Everything inside me twisted at the apology. All of it was too little, too late. "I told you, I'm not your love," I snapped. "You don't know me. You weren't *there*."

He put his hand over mine. "I know, but let me make it up to you. *Please*."

I yanked away like his touch was poison, and started to stand. "I have to go. I have to go right now."

"Wait, *wait*." He grabbed a napkin and pulled a pen out of his pocket. "This is my mobile number." He tore the napkin in half, then held out the pen. "Give me yours." His mouth, my mouth, was firm. "I can't lose you again, Mari. I *won't*."

I paused. Something in his vow, the steadfastness, and I heard Leo's voice, gentle and sure.

I have you. You're safe with me.

I took Jamie's pen, wrote the correct number. When I was done, I threw it down and, before he could say anything else, bolted blindly out of the café.

CHAPTER TWENTY-FIVE

Leo

For a moment, we sat there stricken.

She's hurt.

The words whispered through me, and I shot out of my seat, adrenaline bunching my muscles. It had been an epic fight to stay silent as Mari's life was dismantled in front of her eyes.

She needs someone.

Jammed my chair across the tiles with a loud scrape.

I need to be her someone.

"Go, go, go," Jamie ordered unnecessarily, as I sprinted out of the café. Mari's shiny jacket was a beacon fifty meters down the street, and I heard a loud "Oi!" as she almost crashed into an older man.

"Mari! Mari, wait!" I called, heart in my throat.

She didn't stop, but she at least turned down an alleyway. When I followed, it was blessedly empty, with only a faint smell of rubbish.

She'd pressed her hands against the dirty brick and bent in half. A howl came out of her like she'd had her insides ripped out.

My palm found her shoulder. "Mari." The need to stay with her warred with the visceral urge to go back to Jamie and make him cry, too.

"She lied," she forced out through her tears. "She lied to me the whole time and she left me alone." She gasped, and sobbed, "I could have had a family and she left me all alone."

I tugged, needing to see her face, needing her close. "You're not alone, I won't let you be alone."

Mari straightened up and threw herself into my arms. Frantically pressed into me, like she'd climb inside me if she could. "Make me forget."

I tried to pull back a few inches, get a look at her face so I could have some sense of what she meant. "Hold on, you've had a huge shock."

But she buried her face in my chest. "Please make me forget," she said, her voice high and tight.

I pressed my mouth to her crown. She was so utterly lost and she needed someone to make her feel found. "All right, we'll go to the flat tonight. I'll take care of you, don't worry."

She tugged hard on my coat. "No. Now. I want you to take me back to the attic and fuck me until I don't feel anything."

That was a roller coaster of a sentence, intimacy and distance crashing into each other. A cool edge of reason cut through my longing for her, the desire to take her pain away. What she wanted was exactly the wrong thing to do. She needed to stay with the feelings she was having, not push them aside. Not to mention that my heart couldn't stand that kind of closeness without any affection to go with it.

"Now," I exhaled. "All right. We'll go to yours. But Mari?"

She looked up at me, her face red, her eyes wet. "Yeah?"

"I'll only come if you understand that I won't do exactly what you're asking." I gently pressed my fingers over her lips when she opened her mouth to object. "Yes, I know I'm being high-handed. But I can't do it."

I held my breath as she thought. Would she respect the line I'd drawn?

Her eyes softened. "I understand. I just need you, Leo."

I barely kept back a sigh of relief as I tucked her into my side. I walked her back to the shop, her hand tight in mine. Graham looked up at us when we came through the door, eyes wide with concern, phone in his hand. I nodded to him, hoping he'd understand the universal sign for *I have her*, and thankfully he nodded back.

When we'd closed the garret door behind us, I took off her coat and scarf, then nudged her into sitting on the bed and unlaced her boots, pulled off her socks, then took off my outer clothes. I piled all the blankets in the room on her bed and pulled back the covers for her. I took off my glasses and climbed in after her, wrapped my arm around her waist and buried my face in her tropical-scented hair.

"You made a nest," Mari said, easing back into me.

"You needed comfort." The low hum of arousal I felt

whenever we were close like this clicked on, but I ignored it, listening to her quieting breath, feeling how the tension in her back and shoulders dissipated slowly, slowly, until she was relaxed in my arms.

I exhaled, for once in my life knowing I was exactly where I needed to be. Where I *wanted* to be.

She turned over and snuggled into my chest. "This is a cozy sweater," she said, her voice exhausted.

She rubbed her cheek on it, such an adorable gesture that I couldn't help but smile. "I think you were a cat in a previous life. Mog loves my jumpers, too. Though she shows her love by sinking her claws into them."

Mari made a clawing motion with her fingers, and I took her hand and kissed her fingertips gently.

She pulled me in for a soft, languorous kiss, the kind where it was just our lips brushing for endless seconds. "You were right. Sex was the wrong idea." She looked up at me, her tired eyes dancing. "I'm giving you the next ten seconds to be smug, then it's over."

"How dare you. I'll need at least thirty." Then the need to say something in earnest pushed out. "I do like just holding you, Mari."

Her brow furrowed. "What do you like about it?"

I was about to jokingly accuse her of fishing for compliments, but there wasn't a hint of a tease in her eyes. She was genuinely curious about why someone wanted to show her affection, and I wanted to fly to America expressly to find her stepfather and ruin his life. Instead I answered honestly.

"Well, you're lovely to touch, but I should think that's obvious." I reached down, squeezed her delicious arse lightly, and she smiled. "When I hold you, all the things

I usually think I should be doing, that I feel guilty or anxious or generally afraid about, they don't matter." I reached up and trailed my finger down her nose absent-mindedly. "I'm just here, with you, and it's good. Being with you is good."

She stretched up and found my mouth again. We kissed softly, me trying to give her all the tenderness I had without words, knowing I was condemning myself with every brush of my lips on hers. But it was too good, the way she saw and accepted all the parts of me: the shy joker, the demanding lover she'd woken up, the gentle, steadfast supporter I could be for her.

Even after she'd left, I'd long for her like she'd taken a vital piece of me with her. But telling her that enormous feeling would destroy the little idyll we'd created in this bed.

Mari bit her full lower lip for a moment. "I hate that I miss her so much. But I can't stop thinking about her. It's like I thought it was all under scar tissue, and now it's been ripped off." She looked up at me. "What you said to Tommy, at his house. Is that how you feel about Alexander?"

Her words reached out to me and I grabbed them with relief. "At the start, I just missed him utterly. Like there'd been something torn out of me, and I wasn't whole anymore.

"I never doubted that my grandfather loved me. Not for a second. But . . . I think he might have loved me as an extension of himself. I was the person who'd inherit everything he'd made, and he wanted me to think like him, act like him."

Her hand trailed up my back. "What would he do if you didn't do what he wanted?"

"I never found out." I rubbed my forehead. "He and my dad, they'd shout at each other a lot when they disagreed. I hated that. They were like two massive bulls, always on the verge of headbutting each other over the smallest things.

"But Alexander was different with me. Affectionate, jolly. I would go to the shop after school most days, and he would set me up at the end of his desk with papers and pens, or walk me around the shop talking about all the authors he'd met. Dad was caught up in working on local campaigns, then in starting his own firm, so he wasn't around as much."

"It's easy to say and do what people want when you love them and it makes them so happy," Mari said quietly.

"Exactly. And you assume that the other person feels the same way. But then they tell you that they're doing what's best for you, when they're actually doing something selfish."

Her eyes swirled brown, murky and sad. "Sounds like we were both too trusting for our own good."

I knew she was right, but something small and lonely in me hoped that she could trust again. It was like she'd been hiding behind closed doors for so long that the locks had rusted. If she wanted to get out, she'd have to kick them down.

I asked softly, "Is that why you don't do love? What happened with Greg and your mum?"

She pulled back an inch, considering me, her mouth turned down. I wanted to take the question, shove it back in my mouth and sew my lips closed. Forget a bridge too far, I'd shoved us miles ahead of where we could be.

"It's part of it," she said, her voice distant. "But I'd always known he didn't love me, so nothing about what he did was surprising. And when I left for college, things were better. I made a few friends, dated a little bit. But then I met Dina my junior year and just got totally . . . consumed, I guess. She was the first woman I'd been with, and she was so experienced and glamorous, always made-up and put together. I was head over heels for her, but she only wanted me when things were easy, when I was her cute little small-town girlfriend. So when I panicked when Greg moved away and cut me off, she told me I was way too clingy, that I was toxic and she couldn't have me in her life anymore."

My mouth tightened. Of course, who'd want to be in a relationship when all you'd been subjected to was other people's selfishness? "What did she do then?"

"Dumped me for the girl she'd been cheating on me with. They'd met in one of her classes." She laughed, bitter as coffee without sugar. "But the other woman ghosted her after a week. I tried not to feel too much schadenfreude when I found out."

"She didn't deserve you," I said fervently. Mari deserved to be lavished with affection, garlanded with it like she'd garlanded her body with flowers.

"I realized that pretty fast," she said wistfully, "but I appreciate you saying it anyway."

I trailed my fingers through her hair and she closed her eyes and hummed. "That's so nice when you do that."

"I'm glad." The other words I wanted to say I jammed back down my throat.

Could she have loved me, I wondered, been truly vulnerable with me, if someone had shown her what was possible?

I closed my eyes and wished with all my heart that she'd let someone love her someday. Even if I wanted to snarl at the thought of that person not being me. That was my problem, and I had to find some way to live with it, because I couldn't stand to end this now.

I couldn't leave Graham on his own forever, and after ten more minutes of cuddling, I left Mari to rest for a bit, making her promise she'd text or call if she needed me again. When I got to the bottom of the steps, Judith was leaning hard on her cane, chatting to Catriona.

"Ah, there's the man I wanted to talk to," she said warmly.

I was normally beyond pleased to see my step-grandmother, but after the day of emotional revelations Mari and I had had, I was ready to ignore other people for a while. "You should have told me you were coming."

"Nonsense," she said. "I own a share in this place, I'm allowed to make surprise visits. I'd like a cup of tea and a biscuit, please."

"I'll be back in fifteen minutes," I said to Catriona. "I'm sorry I keep sticking you all with the shop."

"You're looking after people today, I understand," she said kindly. "I hope you're looking after yourself, too."

I just shook my head. I'd worry about myself some other time.

When Judith and I got to the break room and she settled herself into one of the cheap chairs, I brewed us each a cup of tea, milk and no sugar for her, milk and two sugars, no, three sugars today, for me.

Judith leaned forward and laced her fingers together on the table. "I wanted to talk to you about Alexander."

I gawped at her. "This couldn't have waited until I got home tonight? You had to get in a cab and come all this way to tell me now?"

She shook her head. "When would I have had the chance to talk to you in the last few weeks? You're almost never home."

I opened my mouth to apologize, but she said with a laugh, "I'm not saying you can't be out all hours of the night. You're a grown man, and whatever you're doing is good for you. Your color is better, and I haven't seen light in your eyes like that in years. But that's why it's even more important to talk about your grandfather."

Wariness crept up my spine. "What did you want to tell me?"

"That he didn't have the gift for happiness," she said, testing each word like it was precious.

My head shook without conscious thought. I remembered my grandfather's wide smile, his laughter, the way he made conversation flow like the wine he poured. "I don't know what you mean. He always seemed happy."

"He was good at *performing* being happy, because he knew it drew people to him. No one can ignore the life of the party. But deep down, he was restless." She looked down at her hands. "In some ways, he was empty. He needed other people to fill him up, but didn't have anything to give back."

It was like Judith had put the memories I'd excavated with Mari under a bright spotlight.

"And it made him look for affection wherever he could get it," Judith continued, hurt creeping into her voice.

I thought of how he'd looked at women, even when Judith was in the same room. How sometimes it seemed like he barely saw her when she was right next to him. "I'm sorry. That must have been hard for you."

She shrugged. "I chose life with him when I was young and naive, barely out of university. But we had some good times together, he and I. He loved me in his way, and I didn't suffer too much." Judith leaned across the table and touched my cheek. "But what I wish for you, my favorite boy, isn't the kind of loud performance that Alexander put on. I wish you *contentment*. I wish you being able to sit outside and feel the sun on your face, the soft grass under you, and to know that quiet pleasure that comes with enjoying being yourself, here and now." Her eyes were firm on mine. "And I ask you, what gives you that contentment?"

For the first time in my entire life, I muted all the noise in my head, the *should*s and *supposed to*s. I thought about sitting on a bench on a spring day with my sketchbook, drawing the world as it went by. I thought of listening to jazz and classical music with Judith in her flat, the instruments weaving a spell over me, drawing me away from all the day-to-day petty concerns. I thought of hot chocolate and custard creams, long walks on the Heath, and reading in a comfortable chair with Mog in my lap. Most of all, Mari. Mari smiling, Mari laughing, in my arms, in my bed.

I wasn't like Alexander at all, empty and seeking. One woman filled me up to the brim. I loved making her smile and making her laugh. When she nestled into my side after we made love, I felt boundless.

Pain and joy had me putting my head in my hands. I loved her. My stroppy, stubborn, mouthy ball of sunshine. And I was going to have to let her go.

"Leo? Are any of the things you're thinking of Ross and Co.?" Judith asked gently.

I hesitated. It would be like cutting a belay line, letting myself climb freely, risking that I'd fall. "No. I'm not thinking of the shop."

I opened my mouth to confess about Vinay, about the possibility of letting the shop go, but Judith put her hand up. "All right. That's all I wanted to know." She smiled at me indulgently. "Now, can my tall, dark, and handsome grandson pick me out one of those colorful romance novels downstairs and call me another taxi?"

After she left, I divided my time between following up with all our festival speakers and thinking about everything that had happened today. All families had their secrets, but some seemed to have more than most. Mari would shove away anything resembling pity, but that was what I felt for the child version of her, lies and silences stripping her of the life she was supposed to have had. I hadn't seen Jamie for long, but I hadn't been able to ignore the way he looked at Mari, the determination in his eyes.

Right before closing, Mari came downstairs, moving slowly. "Jamie texted me," she said, her voice careful.

I reached for her, and she came closer, let me take her hands in mine. "What did he say?"

"He's asking if I can come for a cup of tea at his house next weekend. It'll just be him and his wife and the three boys." She gulped. "My half brothers."

"That's a lot," I said, squeezing her hands gently. "How do you feel about it? Do you want to go?"

"I do." She shifted on her feet, then took back one of her hands and picked at a loose bit of yarn on her jumper. "Will you come with me?" she asked shyly. "I know we're not permanent, but I don't think I can do this by myself."

I understood that she just needed me to hold her hand, to feel me beside her as she confronted the life she'd missed. But I couldn't help but feel like it was a gift, her trust, something golden and glowing that I could hold on to. "Of course I will."

Her fingers moved toward her mouth, then she shoved her hand in her pocket. "I don't know what to bring," she said a little too quickly. "Or where exactly this place is. Or . . ."

"Shhh, darling, shhh." I pulled her close, tried to pet the tension out of her back, not giving a damn who saw. "You have time," I murmured into her sweet-scented hair. "We'll figure out where it is, how to get there, and I'll be with you every step of the way."

"I'm glad you can come," she said quietly into my chest, and those words felt better than winter sunlight, even though they were just as fleeting.

I would treasure them anyway.

CHAPTER TWENTY-SIX

Mari

Uniform houses in brick and stucco with black or white doors lined Jamie's street. Some had cars parked out front, others had prickly rosebushes standing sentry outside, but the lack of character made my teeth itch. I found myself tugging on the bottom of my sweater as I walked, playing with my parka zipper.

Leo finally tugged my hand away from where I was pulling on a loose thread on my cuff. "Look at me?"

He was still the skinny man with black-and-silver hair and browline glasses that I'd met on the first day, his forehead furrowed with concern. But I hadn't known there could be so much warmth in his brown eyes, how his full mouth could be gentle or devilish instead of tense or sullen.

"Remember, I have you," he said softly, and I squeezed

his hand, thanking him for that sweet protectiveness. I couldn't imagine doing this walk by myself.

Finally we reached the address Jamie had texted me, a house that looked like all the others on the street . . . except for one thing. I smiled at the door painted pumpkin orange.

"See?" Leo said. "They believe in color, too. Ready?"

It was like there wasn't enough oxygen in the world, but I was here now. "Ready."

Bark! I heard first when Leo pressed the doorbell, then the skittering of claws on wood.

Graham opened the door, a huge smile on his face. "Down, Rosie!" The yellow Labrador just barely obeyed, wriggling ecstatically. "I'm sorry, she's a bloody nuisance when she's this excited." He reached out for me, and for a split second my muscles froze with wariness. But then his face fell a little, and I remembered that he was my new favorite friend before he'd transformed into my half brother. I stepped into him, and when his arms closed around me, I felt the same quiet click, a lonely puzzle piece inside me slotting into place.

After he and Leo slapped each other's backs hello, he said, "Come through to the kitchen."

We walked down a narrow hallway to a sunlit kitchen, battered maple cabinets and navy-and-white-checked tiles. Jamie and a very tall, slim woman with light blond hair turned from laying out mugs on a tray. "Bloody hell," she blurted.

"Um, hi?" I said.

"I'm sorry, love, I have no manners," she said, her voice as quick and bright as birdsong. "I'm Annika, your . . ." She paused when Jamie looked up at her pointedly, then shook her head. "Let's say I'm Jamie's wife for now. Graham's mum, too."

They were being so careful, and I felt another layer of my armor fall away. No one was comfortable with this, and someone had to take the first step into unknown territory. "That's OK. I know this is weird. It's really nice to meet you, though."

She smiled hugely, relief written everywhere on her face. "That's good of you to say. We'll muddle through, I think." A little laugh bubbled out of her. "I don't know what Graham was playing at, being all secret squirrel. I'd have known you were Jamie's in a second." She turned to look at Jamie. "With her coloring, she looks a lot like your mum when she was young. Those pictures of her with the three of you she has in her sitting room, you know the ones with baby Keith? It's just uncanny."

Jamie nodded and smiled. It was still surreal, noticing facial expressions on someone else that I'd seen in the mirror.

"Danny and Tim went out to get some cake," Annika continued. "They're so excited to meet you."

Jamie rolled his eyes slightly. "As far as teenage boys are excited about anything."

Over my shoulder I could feel Leo was hanging back a little; all of his attention was on me. I took his hand and said, "This is my . . ." Man, we were all having trouble naming things today, weren't we? Leo was clearly holding his breath. "Boyfriend, Leo," I finished.

"Ooh, hello," Annika said, looking him up and down as she shook his hand. She glanced at me. "Well *done*."

Leo adjusted his glasses and blushed a shade of peach I wanted to eat, and I grinned and said, "Thank you."

"You two work together at the bookshop, then? Not that that's a bad way to meet someone." Annika looked at Jamie and raised her eyebrows lasciviously. "You see someone across the office and know that's the only person you'll ever want."

Leo tensed next to me, and I felt my cheeks flush. I'd been free and independent so long, but I didn't want to embarrass everyone by announcing that Leo wasn't my forever, wasn't even my next two weeks.

It was unavoidable, the stone-cold truth, and I wasn't happy about it. Not at all.

"Is that what happened to you?" I asked Annika, putting more warmth into my voice. "You saw Jamie and you knew?"

Annika smiled. "That's right. I was the new teacher, and Jamie was the one who showed me around our school. He was a proper grown-up, with his glasses and his broad shoulders and a sensible car."

"Insofar as a twenty-seven-year-old is a grown-up," Jamie said wryly.

"To a twenty-three-year-old, you were," she said with a grin. "I'd been dating boys and I was ready for a man."

"*Mum,*" Graham moaned into his hands. "They don't need to *know*."

Jamie flushed scarlet, but Annika cackled a little bit. "And he liked to play football *and* read poetry." She pressed her hand to her chest. "Poetry! Who could resist that?"

My dad looked at his feet and rubbed the back of his neck. "I was a pretentious shortarse."

Annika laughed. "You were gorgeous. Still are." She turned back to me. "So we fell into each other, and Graham came along not long after that."

"Make it stop," Graham muttered.

She reached up and ruffled his hair. "Shush, be happy your parents still fancy the pants off each other after twenty-five years."

It was like this happy scene was happening in a movie and all I could do was watch. But then I felt Leo's hand in mine, a gentle squeeze. I was here, too. I could be part of this, if I wanted.

Just when it looked like Jamie was going to die of aw-shucks, the front door opened and closed with a slam, and heavy feet tromped toward us. Two teenage boys appeared, the ones I'd seen on Graham's phone. One had his blond hair short and spiked, and the other had a sandy-brown mop that almost covered his eyes.

"Danny, Tim, this is Mari and her boyfriend, Leo," Annika said.

"Hullo," they chorused, and I smiled and said a soft "Hi."

"What did you get, lads?" Graham reached out to grab Danny's bag.

"Custard creams and a coffee and walnut cake," Tim said.

"My favorites," I said. "You guys have all these amazing baked goods that I didn't grow up with."

Graham grinned at me. "Cake's a universal language, isn't it?"

As the boys unpacked the goodies, Danny looked over his shoulder at me. "So you live in California?" he tried.

I nodded, maybe a little too enthusiastically. "I do, near San Francisco."

"I want to move there, someday," Tim suddenly said. "California."

"Tim wants to be an actor," Annika said, wrapping her arm around his shoulders. "He's been the lead in the school play for the past three years."

Tim jutted his chin out. "I'm *going* to be an actor. I want to go to RADA, not uni. And then I'll go to LA and get on a TV show."

"Manifest it," I said without thinking and he grinned at me. "See," he said to his mom. "*She* knows."

"You can study drama at uni, too," Annika said in a tone that told me this hadn't been the first or the tenth time she'd said it. "I don't know how I ended up with such a willful child."

Jamie caught my eye and rolled his, and I snorted involuntarily.

"Who do you support, then?" Danny asked. "For football?"

I blinked. "You mean soccer? I mean, Graham told me that I'm a Spurs supporter, whatever that means."

"Noooooooo," Leo groaned, while my brothers and father cheered. He wrapped his arm around my waist. "Sure I can't convince you to support Arsenal instead?"

"She's Spurs by blood, mate," Graham said with a laugh. "You can't have her."

I raised my eyebrows at the boys' possessiveness. "Don't you get divided houses here?"

Leo squeezed gently. "I'm not saying you *can't* support Spurs, but then I'd need to leave the house on North London derby days."

I sobered as I realized he meant it, that he could imagine a future where we lived in the same place, where we'd share a TV and bicker over sports, of all the ridiculous things. All of a sudden I felt like I stood on the border of an unknown country, looking through the gaps in a high fence at soft, green rolling hills under buttery, warm sunlight.

It wasn't a fence I'd ever thought about climbing before, but for a split second I wanted to try, even if the barbed wire cut me open. "You say that like I should know what any of this means," I said, trying to keep the worry out of my voice.

"You'll learn," Jamie said with a wide grin. "We'll teach you."

Except I wouldn't, and they couldn't. But I didn't want to create a cloud over the warm haven we'd created.

Annika raised her hands and shooed us out. "All right, tea's getting cold, everyone go to the sitting room and we can chat more there."

I ended up talking to my brothers about fantasy novels, telling them about Susan Cooper, Tamora Pierce, S. A. Chakraborty. I devoured a slice of coffee and walnut cake and sipped black tea. All the while, Leo silently checked on me, a hand light on my back. I felt my guard relaxing, sitting down, even letting itself slouch a little bit.

I could come back, I thought. This didn't have to be the last time I saw them. I could save up for another flight, maybe next year. I'd have somewhere to return to that made me feel as warm and safe as the stacks at Orchard House.

The doorbell rang. Jamie looked at the door, then at Annika. "We weren't expecting anyone else, were we?"

Tim put his hand up. "We saw Auntie Simi at the shops, and she asked who we were buying the cake for."

Annika groaned into her hands. "And of course she called your gran."

"Could we pretend not to be home?" Jamie asked hopefully.

She snorted. "That'll hold up about as well as a chocolate teapot and you know it." She turned to me, her face encouraging. "She's a bit of a handful, but a nice lady, your gran. And she'd love to meet you."

The doorbell rang again, and everyone was *looking* at me. It'd been a lot already. But if anything was going to exorcise the memory of my step-grandmother and her bitter lemon mouth, this was it. "The more the merrier, I guess."

Jamie hopped up and disappeared. I heard the door opening, his "Hello, Mum."

"Don't you 'Hello, Mum' me," an older woman's voice with Jamie's accent said. "Not after what you've been hiding. What did you get up to on that American adventure of yours, then?"

"I was a grown man," Jamie protested. "I didn't have to tell you everything."

An indignant sniff. "Maybe you bloody well should have. Where is she? Where's my granddaughter?"

Annika mouthed, *I'm so sorry.*

The living room door opened, and a woman with my face fast-forwarded fifty years bustled in, then stopped cold and stared at me. "Look at you!"

"Hi," I said lamely, and Leo's hand found my knee.

"I can't believe you were going to keep her from me," she said to Jamie. "She's *me.*"

"We didn't want to overwhelm her, Hazel," Annika said firmly. "She only found out Jamie existed a week ago."

Hazel reached out and squeezed my arm. "Rubbish.

You're not overwhelmed, are you, sweetheart? Not by your old gran."

Jamie and Graham broadcasted a silent apology at me, but all I could do was shrug. "No, I'm fine."

She put her hands on her hips. "Of course you are, you're a Mackay woman and we Mackay women can take whatever the world throws at us. My God, it's like looking in a mirror." She reached out and touched my cheek, her face marveling. "I want to know every little thing about you."

My mouth opened, closed, all my usual easy conversation up in smoke. I had no idea what to do with that. How much did she actually want to know anyway? Did she only want the sweet, sunshine part of me, or would she accept the darkness and the loneliness, too?

The doorbell rang again, and I heard rumbling male voices outside the window. Jamie looked at my grandmother. "Mum," he said, the word full of admonishment. "What did you do?"

She blinked at him innocently. "Don't you think your brothers deserve to meet their niece? The granddaughter I always wanted?"

I stiffened as the tiny living room filled up with men and boys. It wasn't just my uncles, Adam and Keith. It was all their sons too, a whole pack ranging in age from six to sixteen. I heard a cacophony of names, Sam-Joe-Mike-Luke-Charlie, eyes and hair in the full range of colors, but sharing my downturned eyes, my wide mouth.

"They're a bunch of monkeys, but they're already excited to have a girl cousin," my grandmother said affectionately. "You can boss them around as much as you like."

All of them wanted to talk to me, yelling over each

other to ask me questions, and Rosie started barking again. I answered as many as I could, but I could feel the claustrophobia creeping up on me again, icy fingers squeezing my throat.

Leo

The roomful of people got louder and louder, but Mari got quiet, her smile no longer reaching her eyes. If I touched her, would she shatter? Or would she bolt?

After ten minutes of watching her nod and smile and her shoulders tense around her ears, I couldn't take it anymore. "We need to get back to town," I called to Jamie over the ruckus his family was making. "We have plans tonight."

His mouth turned down, but he said, "Of course." He turned to Mari, tugged her out of the chair she'd been pinned in, and wrapped his arms gently around her. "I'll come see you at the shop. We could go for lunch, just the two of us."

"We're really busy," Mari said, not meeting his eyes. "I'm not sure I'll have the time."

Jamie looked momentarily stricken, then recovered. "Oh yes, your festival, Graham said. Listen, I'll message you later. We'll sort something out before you go." There was a thread of something desperate in his earnest voice, a desperation I'd felt when Mari pulled away.

"That would be nice," she said quietly, but the word didn't go with her downcast expression.

But then the rest of the Becketts wanted to say their goodbyes, and she endured their hugs and cheek pats and chatter for another five minutes before I could tug her out the door.

We walked silently back to the station. Mari's arms

wrapped around herself. She didn't say a word as we waited for the train, or as we found seats in an almost empty carriage, or as the train started to move.

"How was that?" I asked, trying to make eye contact with her.

"Weird," she said bleakly.

And then nothing. She turned to stare out the window, and I quietly took my phone out and refreshed my emails, then pretended to read the paper, ignoring the fact that every muscle in my body was screaming to *fix it*. To put the smile back on Mari's face, to pull her out of the cold absence she'd disappeared into. But I knew I couldn't change Mari's past, and I couldn't be part of her future.

Why not? a small, plaintive voice inside me asked for the first time. *Why can't I have what I want, for once?*

I let myself dream of summer. Of waking up with her under a sheet in a pool of sunlight, of sitting in the grass in London Fields surrounded by picnics and ball games, of kisses sticky-sweet with Pimm's and lemonade. I dreamed of a life where Mari wasn't distant, physically and emotionally, but right beside me, there for me to touch, to talk to, to learn everything about.

"How do people deal with that?" Mari asked in a rush.

"Deal with what?" I asked, slowly putting my phone back in my pocket.

She curled her fingers, knitting them in and out of each other. "Having so many people around you, wanting to talk to you and touch you and *know* you."

Love, I wanted to say. But how to explain that kind of love? It was like trying to explain a synagogue to someone who didn't even know what religion was.

"They don't know me," she continued, her voice high.

"They're only acting like that because they think they have to. How can they believe in me, just like that?"

"Because they think you're one of them. That you belong with them."

She let out a hopeless laugh. "I don't know what to do with that. I've never belonged with anybody."

That last phrase cracked my heart just a little. "Your mum loved you, for starters. I'm sure she did."

Her hands knotted together more tightly. "Maybe." The fracture grew. "But she loved Greg more. She cared more about his feelings than about telling me the truth."

Suddenly she put her head in her hands, and her back shuddered. "I have a family, and I should be happy, but I'm so *scared*. What's *wrong* with me?"

An older man was staring at Mari as she rocked in her seat, and I glared at him until his eyes found his phone again. I sat down next to her and pulled her close, letting her tears soak the front of my coat.

"I'm all messed up," she whispered shakily.

At that moment, I would have cut my chest open so she could climb inside. "You're overwhelmed, darling," I murmured into her hair. "It's been a big day. You don't have to try to make sense of it now. They're just thrilled to have you." When I'd seen how they'd embraced her with such joy, their missing daughter-sister-niece-cousin-grandchild, I'd felt so proud, that they could see what I saw. Her spark and her sweetness.

And maybe I was a little jealous, too, of that unabashed welcome.

Mari shook her head. "I'm a bad bet, Leo. I'm not lovable, and I don't know how to return it. No one showed me how."

The urge to fly to America and scream at Greg surged

back. "I know what we have is temporary, but listen to me. I . . ." My brain flailed, overwhelmed by my craving, seeking heart. What was a word I could use that wasn't the bloody l-word? "I *adore* you. If I had it my way, we wouldn't be working on the festival at all; we'd be naked in our bed and I'd be discovering all the different ways I can make you come. But I'd also be learning how to make you laugh. How to make you smile."

"That sounds nice," she said, her eyes shining through tears.

I pressed my forehead to hers, trying to communicate my feelings without saying the whole truth. "You've made me so happy. I'll never forget it. Long after you're gone, I'll still remember."

Forget the stupid unspoken rules about kissing in public. Her mouth tasted sweet from cake and salty from tears, and she kissed me back hungrily, looking for as much reassurance as I could give her.

"Let's go home," she whispered when I released her, and the words sang through me. Yes, I'd make a home for her. We'd make a small heaven that would keep cold reality away for a little longer.

I held her hand the whole way back to the flat, and she seemed a little better once we were inside the quiet blank space, especially once I'd made a nest for her on the sofa with a duvet and a mug of hot chocolate.

We ordered Thai takeaway, and I put on an episode of a silly game show Graham had told me about, savoring Mari's laughter as a hapless comedian tried to fire a rubber duck out of a trebuchet made of dry spaghetti. When the credits rolled and she nestled into me, I took her to our bed and kissed and fondled and cherished her until she sighed with pleasure.

"Sex is so much better with you," she said softly, trailing her fingers through my hair. "It's never felt like this with anyone else."

Because I've fallen in love with you. But I couldn't be certain she was anywhere close to feeling the same, not until she said the words aloud. And some dark, empty part of me knew she wouldn't before she left me. "I know," I finally said, a minuscule fragment of the truth.

She kissed my mouth with the sweetest urgency and tugged me on top of her.

Our clothes melted away and her sighs turned into moans as I slid my fingers inside her. As she begged for me, I knew I didn't want to let her go.

But she'd said she didn't do love, and any dream I had of the future was just my fantasy, not hers.

We only had this bed, this moment, and I forced myself to be present, to engrave this memory into my mind with crisp lines and deep shading.

Afterward, when our eyes had closed and our breaths had evened, sleep creeping up on us, I felt the mattress shift.

"Maybe I could love you," Mari whispered.

I tensed, suddenly full of adrenaline. My heart didn't know what to do with that. The word I prized above anything, but all the mitigation so close to it. Did I accept it as a gift, a step forward? Did I push back, ask her what it would take to forget "maybe," to transform that "could" into a "can"?

I turned over. "Mari?" I whispered. But she'd already closed her eyes, and didn't respond.

CHAPTER TWENTY-SEVEN

Mari

"How are we looking?" I asked Graham and Catriona, standing by the main registers. I had to remember not to lean against the counter now that it was bedecked with gold and silver tinsel and a poster, hand-painted by Leo, that said "Ross & Co. 100th Anniversary Festival." My nervous fingers dusted yet another gold thread off my green dress.

Catriona extended her long fingers, sparkling with gold-and-silver-striped polish. "Register's all set up for both tickets and books, sound system and mics are good, greenroom's set up with TCMF for the speakers..." she said, tapping each fingertip.

"TCMF?" I asked, suddenly confused. There seemed to be an infinite number of new acronyms and abbreviations in British English. It had felt like learning a new language for the last few months. But like when I'd learned Spanish in high school, my brain's blanks and stutters when it came to life and vocabulary in London had given way to a kind of flow. "Queuing" and "pavement" and "bin" now sat comfortably in my brain alongside "lining up," "sidewalk," and "trash can." I still had no idea who Bob was or why he was my uncle, but now I understood that the phrase was like magical punctuation at the end of an explanation. And the last time I'd taken the Tube and someone had cut me off at the ticket gates, I'd said "Excuse me" with just the right amount of contempt.

Another life shimmered in front of me like an old-time movie projected on a sheet. Powering down a crowded street on the way to work at Ross & Co. Cheering at a soccer game with Jamie and the boys. Going home every night to Leo's quiet smiles and hungry kisses, falling asleep so tangled in each other that my dreams were his, his mine.

But it was a life that would disappear the second I turned the lights on. Real life was California, real life was relying on myself, the way I'd always done.

"Tea- and coffee-making facilities," Graham filled in now with a smile.

"Cool," I said, nodding away the fantasy. "And all the speakers are on track?"

He nodded, putting his hands in the pockets of his blue dress pants and rocking back on his heels. "Yeah, I've been watching the shop email, and no one's dropped out."

"That's what I like to hear." I'd had it happen at the last

festival I ran, and the schedule shuffle had been a total nightmare.

But all the organization for the Ross & Co. hundredth anniversary had gone smoother than a jar of Skippy. Leo had warned me that there was always a possibility of sudden train strikes or Tube breakdowns or any number of snafus that happened when you had one of the most elaborate transport systems in the world.

Catriona checked a battered rose-gold watch on her wrist. "Audience should be arriving any time now." She looked at me and gave me one of her rare smiles. "We've done it. It's actually happening. Unbelievable." She shook her head. "You know, I thought you were spouting absolute rubbish when you got here. That we had no chance at all. But we needed someone from outside to see what was possible."

I smiled back at her. "You guys weren't twiddling your thumbs before I showed up. It's hard, when you're demoralized, to see a way out. But you've been amazing." I tilted my chin at her and Graham. "Both of you have."

We'd have the festival, and in two days I could fly home to California, go back to Suzanne and tell her I'd achieved what I'd come to London to achieve. That I'd successfully turned the shop around, and that I'd be a good steward for Orchard House when she retired. I'd learned all there was to learn, seen all there was to see.

Hadn't I?

A gray, empty feeling washed over me. I liked it here, and I was leaving. I liked being part of a crew, working together in the store. I liked exploring new places whenever I had a day off, submerging myself in history and culture.

I liked walking everywhere, taking in the details of the world at a slower pace.

Most of all, I liked waking up with Leo in that crappy Airbnb bed, sipping coffee and talking about books and movies and art, before he'd take my mug away, run his hands over my skin and light up every single one of my synapses until they sparked and fizzed like the city at night.

If I were being honest, the word "liked" didn't hold all the feeling I had for those moments, the sweet and the hot. Too timid, like Leo had said all those weeks ago. It didn't encompass how warm and safe I felt when he was nearby, or the tug I felt to find him in the shop when I hadn't seen him for more than an hour, if he hadn't found me first.

"Are you all right, Mari?" Graham asked. "You looked far away for a moment there."

I shook off thoughts of a very different l-word from "like." "Just distracted for a second." I looked more closely at him and Catriona, the way that they were oh-so-very-slightly leaning toward each other. "Though I have to say, I'm confused," I said innocently.

Graham's head tilted. "Confused?"

I gestured between them. "You're not arguing. It's too quiet. Is the world about to end, and no one told me?"

The result was even better than I'd hoped. Swaggering, cavalier Graham blushed so hard he looked like he'd catch fire, and quiet, shy Catriona's smile was sheer smugness. "I'm going to do one last check on things," she said, her voice relaxed. She nudged Graham's shoulder lightly as she went out of the room. His hands twitched like he wanted to reach for her, and his eyes on her retreating back were dark and hungry.

"Should I say congratulations?" I asked dryly.

"We're that obvious?" he said.

"Uh-huh. Come on, tell me what happened."

"God, you're going to be a proper pain-in-my-arse older sister, aren't you?"

I couldn't help but relish the warm feeling this new bond gave me. "Try and stop me. Spill, little brother."

He rubbed the back of his neck. "I don't know how I was so thick, but I finally understood what you'd told me at the café. That I needed to get off my arse. So when we were finishing up last night after you and Leo left, I told Catriona that she was the most beautiful woman I'd ever seen, that she was all I *could* see, and I wanted to be hers, if she'd have me."

I couldn't help myself, I clapped at the sheer poetry of it. I loved a good grovel. "Then what?"

His giggle was almost hysterical. "She told me that if I really meant it, I'd get on my knees . . ." He shut his mouth with an audible click. "And that's all I'm going to tell you, because you're my bloody *sister*."

"That's probably wise." I whistled. "But *damn*, son. Well played."

"Thanks very much." He said more seriously, "I don't know where we're going from here. We've started this way before, and it's all ended in tears. But all we can do is try again, right?"

"Of course." Not that I was qualified to say that, given that the last time I'd *tried*, I'd ended up being cheated on and lied to, with a little bit of gaslighting for good measure. But that had been seven years ago. I'd had time, and distance. And Leo had given me a taste of what it would be like to trust someone and have that trust repaid with long hugs and held hands and listening ears.

I could have that again, if I wanted. Leo Ross had given me that confidence. I just had to carry it back with me into real life.

"Is this the festival?" a young guy asked, sticking his head through Ross & Co.'s front doors.

Graham and I both grinned, and Graham said, "You're in exactly the right place, mate. Come in, come in. First event starts in thirty minutes, but feel free to have a browse while you wait."

Waves of people arrived, and the rooms filled with excited chatter and the occasional camera flash. Graham and I split up, him chatting with the audience members and directing them, me corralling our first speakers. Tommy arrived in a taxi, and I led him to the greenroom and sat him in the armchair Catriona had found on Gumtree. Leo seemed to be running late, but it'd be OK if he got here by the time the first event started. We'd slept in our respective beds for the first time in weeks, him saying he needed to spend some time with Mog and with Gabi and Sophie, that they'd been wondering where he was.

I rubbed my face a little. Without Leo's warmth I'd tossed and turned for an hour after I'd switched off the light, unable to fall asleep until I'd grabbed a pillow off the sofa and bundled myself around it.

A light touch on my arm, and I jumped a little. It was Jamie, looking shy, a canvas tote bag over his shoulder. "All right, Mari?" he asked.

"All right," I replied after a second.

He held his arms out, and I let myself trust that reach, and more quickly than before, I hugged him.

When I pulled back, he looked me up and down. "You look lovely all dressed up and with your hair like that."

I was trying a new hairstyle, half in its usual braid, half down and flowing over my shoulders. I told myself I looked a little bit like a warrior princess. "Thanks, Jamie," I said, warm with his kindness.

"And everything looks terrific." He soaked in the bustle of the festivalgoers, the decorated piles of books, the blown-up pictures of Ross & Co.'s history. "I don't know why I haven't come here more often. Got lazy with online shopping, I suppose. But there's nothing like a really good bookshop, is there?"

I smiled. "There really isn't. It's like you walk in the doors and nothing bad can happen while you're here."

"A refuge," he said simply.

A flicker of warm recognition. "Exactly."

"I like that."

Before we could slide back into shyness, I asked, my voice high, "Are Tim and Danny with you? Or Annika?"

He immediately shook his head. "No, just me today. I wanted to come by myself for this." He shoved his hands in his pockets. "I'm so sorry about the pileup at the house last week. I should have put my foot down with Mum and the others, told them that they could meet you when you were ready."

I could laugh, shrug it off, tell him it hadn't affected me. But I could sense his care, his worry, and I didn't want to just leave him with it. "Thanks. It was pretty overwhelming." I rubbed my toe on the carpet. "I just didn't have anyone for so long, and I'm going to need time to get used to people wanting me around." I hated how strained my voice was, but sometimes the truth was a scared, fragile thing.

He paused for a second. "You don't *have* to be close to everyone, Mari. You don't have to be close to me, even."

I raised my eyebrows. "Even though I'm your daughter?" Wasn't that what he wanted the most?

He shook his head. "No, that's not what I meant." He tented his hands and put his fingertips to his mouth, then said, "I'd love it if you wanted that kind of relationship with me. I'd love to chat to you about books, take you to the football. Do things a dad would do with his grown-up daughter. But you're almost thirty, and I think it's fair to say that you can decide to spend as much or as little time with me as you like. I never, ever want you to feel you *have* to." He looked me in the eye. "We should choose each other."

A wave of relief came over me, the end of stress, like I'd been running an ultramarathon, gasping and panting for air as I tried to escape from the pain and sadness chasing me, and I could finally just stop and be. "Thank you," I said, meaning it with my whole heart.

Instead of replying, Jamie reached out and squeezed my hand, and right that second I knew I would come back to London. I didn't know how, or when, but I knew I didn't want Jamie to become a footnote in my history.

My dad smiled. "Here's your man. Looking sharp, Leo."

"Thanks," my lover said. "Hello, darling." He brushed his lips over my temple.

"Hi," I blurted, lost for any other words. In his slim-cut black suit and shirt and glasses, he looked like he was about to single-handedly take down three henchmen, hack into the supervillain's computers to thwart his world domination plans, then wash it all down with a dry martini. Lethally handsome and lethally capable. He even had a pocket square ... and it was green. Not just any green, but a rich pine green like my dress. "Are you looking forward to any event in particular?" I stuttered as I turned back to Jamie.

Jamie smiled sheepishly and pulled a stack of old, battered Cliff Thomas paperbacks out of the tote bag. "I started reading Cliff as a teenager. It's rare to have an author you want to read when you're fifteen and fifty. Forgive me if I monopolize him when he's signing."

Leo put his arm around my waist. "That was all Mari's doing. We went out to his place in Somerset and she charmed him into coming."

"Of course she did, she's so clever," Jamie said, and his praise was a warm little fire I wanted to hold my hands up to. He shifted on his feet. "I should let you two get on, but I want to take you lot out for a pint tomorrow night. Graham's said how hard you all have been working, you should celebrate."

"We'd love that," Leo said with a huge smile that matched mine.

Once Jamie had ambled off to look for a seat, I turned and smoothed my hand over Leo's silky lapel. "Devil boy, if you had worn this suit when we first met, I would have done whatever you wanted me to do."

The evil grin I adored spread across his face. "And what would have been the fun in that?" He tugged me close. "Besides," he said more quietly, "I like you stubborn."

I gulped hard. The last time he'd said that adjective, I'd been writhing underneath him in the dark, half-gone from needing to come from his hand between my legs, his chest pressed to my back and his mouth hot against my ear as he told me I had to *wait*.

He brushed a finger across my pink cheek. "Lost for words, darling?"

"Mean," I finally squeezed out of my tight throat. "So mean."

He leaned in for a quick peck. "But I always take care of you, don't I?" When I nodded, still a little turned on, Leo took me in. "I do love that dress. Have ever since you wore it to charm Tommy."

I found myself craving one more compliment. "What do you love about it? Does it make you want to draw me again?" One night I'd woken up to the scratch of pen on paper, and after I pleaded, he showed me a Chagall-esque sketch of me asleep on my side, the flower tattoos on my body spilling down in cascades of blossom onto the shadowy sheets.

He smiled quietly, and trailed a gentle hand down my arm. "It's soft and touchable and lovely like you. It makes it impossible not to want to get close to you."

That gentle touch set off something wild inside me, the same wildness that had made me confess a few nights ago how I could imagine giving everything to him. If I weren't leaving, if I didn't have a life six thousand miles away. If we had world enough, and time, like the old poem said.

But we didn't. All I could do was make the most of what we had.

"Hello, children," Judith said behind us, and we both turned to greet her, Tommy standing by her side bashfully. When she pointed to her cheek, Leo leaned down and bussed it.

"Judith, I love your outfit," I said warmly.

Judith smoothed the silver velvet of her draped jacket with one hand. "Thank you, my dove. It's no poppy-red caftan with a plunge, but it's good to be dressed up again for the first time in a while."

"I remember that red dress," Tommy said with a blush.

Judith raised her eyebrows and grinned naughtily. "Do you now?"

He nodded, the ghost of the very young man he'd been rising to the surface. "I was trying to impress that old gasbag Beardsley, but I saw you in the middle of my little speech about how he'd reinvented the comedy of manners and I almost swallowed my own tongue. And then, of course, you came over and winkled out of him that he'd never read Pym, or Heyer, or any Austen whatsoever."

Judith patted his arm. "I would say I was sorry about that, but I'm absolutely not."

Tommy smiled. "I would never want you to be. I'm a better genre writer than I ever was a literary stylist, anyway."

I squeed a little inside at the electricity coursing between them. It wasn't quite matchmaking, but I was glad I'd had a part in getting these two back in the same room.

But Judith had turned back to us, her face suddenly very sober. She said to Leo, "We need to have a family meeting tonight, after everything finishes. Mari, I'd like you to be there, too."

Leo and I blinked at each other. "Dad hasn't said anything," Leo said carefully.

She shook her head. "This isn't David's idea. It's mine."

He raised his eyebrows at me, and I raised my hands palms up, so far in the dark that I didn't have a clue where the light switch was.

"Of course we can meet," he said. "Just a bit surprised."

"Of course." Judith tilted her chin at me with a small smile. "Now, I'm sure you two will want a moment alone before we begin."

We hadn't exactly been discreet, but the familiar look Judith gave the two of us, making crystal clear what she meant, made me blush anyway.

"What do you think she wants?" I asked once she'd made her way downstairs and Tommy had headed back to the greenroom.

"I'm not certain," he said, thinking aloud. "But she wouldn't ask unless it's serious." His face shifted, his mouth opened. "But we'll be there together, and that's what matters," he finally said, his voice firm, like he'd suddenly made a decision.

"Is everything OK?" I asked, a flash of panic shooting through my system.

"Come here," he said instead, and I gasped softly as he tugged my hips, molded my body to his, then kissed me like I was chocolate and marshmallows, soft lips and seeking tongue and just a hint of teeth. I couldn't hold back a moan into his mouth.

Too soon, he pulled back. "All right, we've got a festival to put on."

He turned for the stairs and I followed with my hand over my lips, feeling like something big was on the edge of happening. And despite Leo's bravado, something inside me wasn't sure if it would be good.

CHAPTER TWENTY-EIGHT

Leo

Ross & Co. had been so quiet for months I'd occasionally looked around for the invisible librarian who was shushing everyone. But now everything was an explosion of sound and color, new faces and loud voices. Hands reached out to shake mine, slap my shoulder hello, mouths moved to say "Congratulations!" and "I'd forgotten about this place!" and "This is wonderful!" Punters and authors blew around me like the spring storm buffeting the leaves outside the store, and I'd tune in for moments of two teenage girls comparing their stacks of signed YA novels, Graham listening attentively to Mr. Gissing explaining about the SOE's code-making in France during the war, Tommy telling stories about his first thriller being adapted into a terrible film, making his conversation partner Folarin laugh so hard he wheezed.

And all I could think was that Alexander would have loved every second of this, tried to speak to every single person there, would have wanted to be at the heart of it all.

But I wasn't my grandfather. Despite all his coaching and badgering, I never would be.

I was glad that other people were glad. But it wasn't the same as being happy myself.

"Hi," Mari whispered from where she'd snuck up next to me.

She'd been a green-and-brown blur with a clipboard under her arm all day, marshaling people to go to the next talk, joking with speakers, pouring coffee, crouching down to talk to a little boy with brown hair who looked up at her utterly awestruck.

I knew the feeling.

Now I brushed a quick kiss over her ruby-colored mouth that tempted me beyond belief. "You should wear lipstick more often."

She snorted. "Why, because you like getting it all over your face?" She rubbed her thumb over my bottom lip and showed me the crimson stain she'd left behind.

"You can get all over my face anytime, darling."

Her cheeks blushed a lovely complementary shade of pink. "Promises, promises."

I grinned at her. "You know I'll keep them."

A roll of applause from the gallery burst over us, and Mari looked toward the noise. "That's Tommy and Folarin. They'll sign books, and then . . . we're all done." The last words were a happy sigh.

I knew we weren't completely done. Judith had been

giving me significant looks throughout the day, and I wasn't sure what awaited us. But Mari had achieved what she'd set out to do, and a surge of pride went through me.

An hour and a half later, after Tommy and Folarin had signed everyone's books and the last punter had left, Mari closed the door and turned to us all. "We did it!" she yelled, starting to clap.

All the stress of the day broke in our claps and hoots, and Catriona let off a wolf whistle that would have woken the dead.

"Thank you so much for all your hard work over the last few weeks!" Mari continued. "Every single one of you is a superstar. Now, packing up and loading out is tomorrow morning at eleven."

"I don't want to see anyone here before half nine," I chimed in, going to stand next to her. "We all need a lie-in after today."

"And a drink!" Graham shouted, and we all laughed. "But first, three cheers for Leo and Mari, who made this whole festival happen."

As her brother led the raucous call and response, Mari's eyes found mine, shining bright as stars. I tangled my fingers with hers, wishing with every bit of me that this joy, this feeling of rightness, could last.

"Coming?" Graham said as Catriona and the others headed for the front doors.

"In a bit," I said, struggling to keep my voice even.

"I need to talk to these two," Judith said, threading her arm through mine. "Then they'll be on their way."

"All right, we'll be at the Duke when you're finished." Graham grabbed Mari and hugged her tightly. "I'm so glad you found us."

"Me too," she said into his shoulder.

Ten minutes later, we were up in my office, me in Alexander's old chair and Judith in one of the visitors' seats. Mari leaned against the wall of bookshelves, her hands in the pockets of her dress.

"Why don't you sit down, dove?" Judith asked. "It's been quite a day."

Mari shimmied a little, then folded her arms. "Too much adrenaline in my system, but thanks. What's up, Judith?"

Judith rubbed her hands across her thighs. "First, I wanted to say that it was an absolutely beautiful day. It was wonderful to see the old place full of happy readers. Alexander would have adored every minute of it." She took a deep breath. "But now I think we should consider selling."

"What?" Mari and I both blurted.

She nodded to me. "Your friend Vinay came to visit me at home. He was very apologetic. But he explained that he'd been talking to you about selling the building, and he needed an answer in the next week. That you hadn't been answering his messages."

My stomach fell through a trap door into nothingness.

"The skinny guy," Mari said to herself, her voice thin. "Of course he wasn't just your friend."

Could I crawl under my desk, the way I'd crawled under it as a child? Hide from the consequences of my own stupid indecision?

Judith's tone shifted, from bluntness to something softer, sadder. "This was never what you really wanted, Leo. Alexander decided your future for you before you had a say."

"Judith, that's not what happened," I started protesting.

Her palm smacked the table. "*No.* Remember how you wanted to go to art school? Remember how you wanted to take a year off after university to travel? How you weren't sure about courting Rebecca? Because *I* remember being in the other room as Alexander badgered you into a life that kept you close, that tied you to him. One of my greatest regrets is that I didn't stand up for you.

"Now this is your chance to be free. Unfettered, all financial worries over. And you need to seize your freedom. More than anything."

"But I love this place." My voice came out small, like I'd de-aged two decades in the space of two minutes.

Judith leaned over the desk. "I know you do, but the shop is just bricks and mortar with books in it. Do you love Ross and Co. because of what it is, or because of what it *represents*?"

History. Legacy. Alexander, all his huge smiles, his banter, his flawed charisma.

If we sold . . . I could let it go. All of it.

But *Mari*. Mari was so quiet. I looked over, and my heart climbed up my throat.

Her face was an empty sheet in my sketchbook, smooth, blank. But the tips of her fingers had gone white from how hard she was gripping her biceps, and her eyes were muddy and dull.

"I need to think," I said to Judith.

Judith looked over at Mari. "You need to do more than that, surely. We should all be on the same page." She pushed herself out of her chair. "We'll speak soon. Mari, please know it meant a lot to us, what you did. We needed an outsider to come and show us what was really important. I hope you'll listen to what Leo has to say."

Mari gave a small nod but said nothing as the door opened and shut. As Alexander's old desk clock ticked away on the shelf. As she breathed, high and thin, on the edge.

Regret had me crawling out of my chair, kneeling at her feet. I studied the scuffs on her boots, the ribs of her black tights. I'd loved trailing my fingers up those ribs, desire lines that led to my favorite places on her body. "I'm sorry, Mari. I'm so, so sorry."

"Why?" she finally exhaled now, like I'd punched her in the stomach. "Why didn't you tell me you had a serious offer?"

I rubbed the back of my neck, shame coloring my cheeks. "Because I didn't want to sell, in the beginning. Right after you'd got here, I told Vinay to fuck off."

She wrapped her arms more tightly around herself. "And then later?"

After I'd kissed her. After I'd been inside her. After I'd held her and soothed her when she cried for everything she'd lost, everything she'd never had. She didn't say the words, but I could see them written across her pale, stricken face.

I knew why I hadn't confessed. It was because I'd been happy, for the first time in forever. I'd fallen so low before she'd arrived. She hadn't been the one to drag me out of the hole, but she'd made me want to scramble up the sides, get mud on my shoes and under my fingernails and actually *live* for once. "Because you'd said that you didn't want to know, back in the park. And I didn't want what we had to end."

She shifted an inch away, an inch that felt like a mile of land, blighted and scorched. "You let me organize everything," she whispered. "You let me try so hard. And it was all going to be for nothing. It was pointless. *I* was pointless."

"It's not pointless." What I craved most sprung out of

my mouth. "Come back, and I won't sell. Come back and run the shop with me."

The laugh that escaped her was sharp, jagged. "My plane ticket has a date on it, and my three months are up."

I got up off the floor. "But you don't have to go forever."

She shook her head hard. "What do you mean? You know I'm going back to take over my own bookstore. You can't keep this place just for me."

The crevasse between us was widening, but I couldn't help but reach for her. "You could return later in the year, once there's been enough of a lag for the Home Office. Autumn here is beautiful. We could go watch the fireworks, walk on the Heath."

"I can't keep going on vacation from my real life," she snapped.

"It wouldn't be a holiday!" Exasperation filled every word, and I tried to rein myself in. "You could have a life here, if you wanted it. You have Graham, and Jamie, and the rest of the Becketts."

Mari's eyes closed, her mouth turned down. "I don't know them. They don't know me."

"They *want* to know you," I cried. "They want to love you, if you'll let them."

Mari

"What do you mean, if I *let* them?" I knew it was spring now, with green buds on the trees and blossoms everywhere, but all of a sudden I'd shot back in time, to the dark sidewalk outside Ross & Co. in early January. I rubbed my arms, feeling cold and alone and wary, even with Leo a foot away from me.

Leo started slowly. "You smile so sweetly and make jokes, but you've built a fortress around yourself, with archers and boiling oil on the parapets. And I understand why. You drew the shortest possible straw for the first twenty years of your life, and I think I'll be furious at your stepfather for another twenty." He closed his eyes, opened them. "Mari, your past made you just as much as mine made me."

I shook my head hard. "That's not true. I made my own luck, I wrote my own story. Don't you dare pity me."

He scrubbed his hand through his hair. "I have never once in the last three months *pitied* you. That's not what this is about. Stop avoiding what I'm trying to tell you."

"Fine," I snapped. "What are you trying to tell me?"

His voice came out pleading. "If you never face the past, it's just going to keep coming after you. And I'm trying to tell you that I can be beside you when you face it." He took a deep breath. "Judith kept asking me what I wanted, and I know the answer, Mari. I've known it for weeks."

"What do you want?" I felt like I was about to answer a knock on the door in the middle of the night when I would be better off hiding under the covers.

He took my clenched hands, ran his thumbs over the backs. God, I loved his long fingers, how expressive and capable they were, as they held a pen or touched my face or trailed down my body in the middle of the night. "You. More than anything, I want you."

"You can't have me," I said, my old reflex still intact. "I told you, I don't do this."

But I want to.

I smothered the naive thought before I could say it. It didn't matter what I wanted when it came to love. No one had ever put me first, and even Leo, steadfast Leo, could tell a lie to get what he wanted.

"I know what you told me, but I'm desperate." He studied my face like I was a book he could reread over and over. "You are my spring. You are soft green grass, all the flowers blooming and the sunshine on my face. If you leave me for good, it may as well be winter forever."

"You don't mean that," I interrupted, unwilling, unable to hear him.

"I do," he said, like the words were a vow. "You've changed everything for me. When I'm with you, it's like I've been suffocating my entire life and now I can *breathe*."

"But you hid the truth." God, I hated the shake in my voice.

"I hid it to keep you." He looked down. "I wanted to keep you so badly."

A ray of realization broke through the dark hurt drowning me.

Greg had treated me like a mangy stray left on his

doorstep. Dina had convinced me that she'd cheated with someone else because I was too difficult to love. Neither of them had ever knelt in front of me out of contrition. Neither of them had ever said anything resembling an apology. They'd just . . . abandoned me.

Leo wasn't abandoning me. He was staying and begging me not to leave him.

"I didn't make it easy for you to be honest," I said quietly, remembering the moment in the park when I'd blocked any confession he might have made.

He nodded at my concession, his face serious. "But I should have told you anyway. Do you think . . . do you think you can see a way forward? Toward maybe, someday, forgiving me?"

I hesitated at the shake in his last few words, remembering cinnamon toast, and silly comedians with catapults, and sweet, soft begging words in the middle of the night. "I have to go home," I finally said.

He looked at me like he knew I was hiding behind a wall made of rules and regulations. "If there weren't such a thing as visas, as borders, would you stay? Would you try?"

His voice shook on the last question, and it was all too much. The last three months, the last three weeks, the last hour—they were a riptide and I was struggling not to go under. "I don't know," I said tightly, an unwanted tear trickling down my face.

Leo's hands flexed. "I can't bear it. If you're crying, I need to hold you. Please let me?"

Without a word I stepped into him, and he wrapped his arms around me. I sank into the hug, his bay rum smell, the way he rubbed my back. It was safety like I'd never had, comfort like I'd never known.

But I needed to be brave. I tensed, and he let me go. I dashed one more tear away and pasted on one more smile. "We should go join the rest of them. Graham's going to get suspicious and come find us."

Leo's mouth opened, on the verge of one last argument. A perverse part of me wished he would get mad at me, just one more time. But he only clamped his mouth shut and nodded. "Sure, let's go for one," he said, an edge of bitterness in the words. "To wish you bon voyage."

We walked around the shop, turning out the lights. As Leo turned his keys in the door behind us, the click of the lock was a period, the end of my London story.

I told myself I'd just have to start a new one when I got back to California. But somehow, the words weren't as consoling as they'd been before.

CHAPTER TWENTY-NINE

Leo

Spring had finally come at the beginning of May, gray skies and chill giving way to warmth and light. But winter still had me in its grip.

The day Mari left for California, I went to my father and Judith and agreed to sell to the developer Vinay's firm had found. The first floor of the building would still be a retail space, and Mortons, the big chain bookseller, had already earmarked it for their next location. They'd asked if they could still call the shop Ross & Co., but the thought had felt like shackles on my wrists. I wanted my name to be my own for once, not chained to anything else.

"Thank you," Vinay had whispered when I'd bent over the contracts in the lawyers' offices. "And I'm so sorry, again."

I hadn't had any words for him, just nodded without

making eye contact as I signed. The way he'd gone to Judith behind my back was a cut that was only halfway to healing, and I wouldn't pretend. I'd done far too much of that for too long, and I'd lost the only woman I'd ever wanted because of it.

Remembering was like getting punched in the stomach every day. Every time I thought of that moment in my office, when Mari's eyes had clouded over with doubt, when her body had pulled away from mine, regret almost doubled me over.

After we'd confirmed the arrangements for the building and the money changing hands, Dad took me for an afternoon pint at an old, high-ceilinged pub near Chancery Lane.

"Here's to a new beginning," he said once he'd brought over our drinks, sitting down next to me and tapping his pint of stout against my bottle of cherry beer.

"L'chaim," I said half-heartedly, settling back into the leather-covered bench, feeling as far from cheerful as I'd ever been.

Out of nowhere, I was wealthier than I'd ever thought possible. I'd tell the bank manager to wire substantial payments to Catriona and Graham, smaller ones to the junior booksellers. Graham had already been hired on as a nonfiction buyer at Mortons, and Catriona had decided to try to get onto an MFA course for creative writing. I hoped she'd have the sense to talk to Graham first before deciding where she'd go.

"Any thoughts about what you'll do next?" Dad asked.

I shrugged, tried to smile. I couldn't deny that Dad had been much more present over the last few weeks, quicker to tell me about books he was reading, to ask me to play gin rummy with him the way we had when I was ten. He'd even taken Sophie and me to watch Arsenal Women last week. It had been like dropping bags full of boulders to lose myself in the rhythm of a football match, to join in the chants at the top of my lungs, and to jump and shout and grab Sophie in a massive hug when we scored two goals.

For two hours, I almost forgot how much I missed Mari.

Dad asked, "Have you heard anything from her? Mari, I mean."

I coughed beer as I momentarily forgot how to swallow, and he smacked me between my shoulder blades. "No," I said hoarsely. "She wouldn't want to talk to me."

She hadn't contacted me, and I hadn't tried to reach her either. Even though I thought about texting or calling every single day. One night I'd even tried to write her a letter, but the first attempt had been so polite it was asinine, while the other had been such a desperate outpouring of contrition and longing and grief that I'd torn it up and burned it in the kitchen sink. I'd hidden from her, been dishonest with her—of course she'd left me behind and gone back to where she felt safe. If she'd been afraid, I'd done nothing to soothe her fears.

"Shame," Dad said now. "When you were with her at Friday-night dinner, you looked . . ." He trailed off.

"Besotted?" I interrupted, as if being facetious would keep my regret at bay.

"Happy," he said simply, the word like white spirit on the raw wound in my chest. "You looked happy."

I pressed hard on my eyes and gulped back the sudden sob that tried to climb out of my throat. No, I couldn't burst into tears in the middle of the pub.

A big gentle hand rested on my shoulder. "I'm sorry you felt you couldn't talk to me about what was happening."

"I thought I needed to handle everything myself," I said, sounding just about as childish as I felt at that moment.

Dad sighed into his pint, and for a moment the only sound was the barman stacking glasses.

"Alexander and Natalie weren't around much when I was small," Dad said quietly.

I'd lifted my beer for a sip but carefully put it down. Natalie, Dad's mum, had always been nothing more than a hastily scribbled card on my birthday with a Melbourne postmark. Even saying her name aloud had felt like uttering a dark spell, one that made Alexander's and Dad's faces go blank and Mum titter nervously.

"I got the occasional kiss good night before they went off to another party, sometimes they'd ask if I was still being a good boy, but I was mostly raised by our housekeeper. And then they sent me away to boarding school when I was eight." He shook his head. "Bloody barbaric. All of those places should be burnt to the ground. And then Natalie ran off to Australia with her lover when I was fourteen." He pulled his hand over his face, like he was trying to rub away the hurt. "When I met your mum, I swore to myself that when we had children, I wouldn't be selfish like my parents, utterly focused on their own whims. That I would never send any of you away. But I hadn't a clue what I was meant to do *instead*. I never learned any way to be with you.

"And suddenly after decades of carousing and philandering, Alexander was behaving like Grandfather of the Year. You were always in his lap, holding his hand, looking up at him like he stood astride the world."

My mind fell backward twenty-five years, into those early, tender memories. Alexander's tobacco scent, his rich bass voice reading aloud to me, his cashmere wool jumper against my cheek. "He wasn't Grandfather of the Year once I was older. Or he was, as long as I did what he wanted."

Dad's mouth twisted. "I understand that better now. But at the time . . . I resented it. And that was horribly unfair to you. I'm sorry I wasn't better, that I didn't try harder."

"Thank you," I said. "That means a lot." Dad's words wouldn't make the tear in our fabric disappear. But we'd acknowledged the rip, how long it had been left frayed and gaping. And maybe, just maybe, we could begin to mend it.

Spring was for new beginnings, after all. Time to step out into the light, not hide in the same old dark room.

"I want to start over," I said, looking him in the eye. "Get to know each other properly. Adult to adult."

"I'd like that, too." He gave me a weak smile. "We both need to start being braver, don't we?"

I exhaled hard. "Don't I know it."

He checked his watch. "I think I'll go home to your mum. She'll want to know how it all went. Coming?"

It had been such a day. My stomach was twisted up in a million knots and my muscles were just as bad. "I think I need a little time on my own. I might go for a walk, just to digest it all."

"Of course. We'll see you when we see you." He shrugged on his suit jacket, picked up his work bag. "And Leo?"

I looked up from my beer.

"I know you could be the man for Mari, if you wanted."

My dearest wish, which felt as impossible as the sky

turning neon pink. "I don't know if she wants to hear from me," I confessed, my voice small, almost boyish.

"Oh, don't be stupid," he said, a little more London coming into his voice on the last scornful word. "The way she looked at you at Shabbos, you weren't the only smitten one. Take it from me, you have a better chance than you think. Just *try*, all right?"

After Dad left, I found myself walking north and east along the city's packed rush-hour pavements, his firm, encouraging words echoing in my head. I'd tried to fix things on my own before and made a mess of it, but I knew that doing nothing now would be like burying myself under concrete.

As I walked and thought, gleaming stone and glass gave way to scruffy, graffitied Shoreditch and then Hackney Road. The evening stretched out in front of me, winter's bite all gone, new green leaves springing on the plane trees leading toward London Fields. Pale purple fireworks of wisteria decorated the terraces, and the scent of lilac drifted through the air, sweet and delicate.

I joined Broadway Market and saw the antique shop empty and dark, remembered how Mari had seen the potential in it. Her smile, her laughter, her confident stride, they were everywhere here.

I sat on a bench in London Fields, watched families and couples walking and cycling by. Heavy black coats and bulky boots had been replaced by short sleeves and soft dresses in ice-cream shades, pistachio and strawberry and vanilla. A woman jogged past, a tattoo of lush red roses twining around her bare upper arm, and the memory of Mari pricked like thorns.

I rolled my head back and stared up at the plane trees,

tender green leaves shifting a little in the warm breeze. I had told her all the ways I needed her, everything she did for me. But what had I offered her in return? I'd begged her not to care about lies and promises and visas, and I'd acted like as long as I loved her, what she felt didn't matter.

I'd asked her to give up everything she knew, just so I could hold on to my life, a life that had driven me to lying and subterfuge to escape it. I hadn't listened when she told me how important the truth was to her. I hadn't understood that she studied and worked and focused single-mindedly on the bookshop, whether Orchard House or Ross & Co., because she loved the business and the people she met through it, and it had been the only thing truly to love her back.

I took my phone out and opened Instagram. I had my own account now, with a single picture of Mog curled up like a prawn. I was only using it to look at Mari's pictures, anyway. Fifteen minutes ago she'd posted a selfie sitting on a cloudy beach bundled in her iridescent jacket, with the caption *Can't keep a California girl away from the beach! I love my wild Pacific.* She'd studded it with multiple emojis of a blue, frozen smiley face.

Was she there alone? Not that I was jealous of some anonymous man or woman. It was more . . . I didn't want her to be lonely. She'd been so lonely, for so long.

Why wasn't I there beside her?

I sat up so quickly the world spun.

What if I asked her to keep *me*? What if I asked to be hers?

I frantically googled until I found the phone number I wanted and called Orchard House Books.

"Hello, British person who is not my dear friend Judith," a husky, nasal American voice said down the line.

I shook my head to get the cobwebs out. Judith had said Suzanne was one of a kind, but I hadn't taken that to mean mildly terrifying. "How'd you know that I was British?"

"I can see it's a UK number, kiddo. May I ask who's calling?"

I coughed. "Er, hello, Suzanne. It's Leo Ross. Judith's grandson."

"Mari's not here," she immediately said, her tone gone colder than Scotland in January. "And if you're the reason she's been looking like someone fed her teddy bear to a wood chipper, please kindly go fuck yourself."

The image punched me in the stomach. "I deserve that, I deserve all of it." I had been trying not to sound frantic, but Mari's hurt wrecked me. "Please don't hang up on me. I badly need your help."

A long pause. Had the line dropped? Then a slightly warmer "I'm listening."

Gratitude and purpose surged through me like electricity as I apologized profusely and asked her advice, and after we said our goodbyes, I hopped off the bench, heading for the train station. I had a long journey ahead of me, and I wanted to get going as soon as possible.

CHAPTER THIRTY

Mari

How had Dorothy felt the day after she'd come back from Oz?

Sure, she'd woken up that first morning in Kansas and said with a big smile, "There's no place like home!" But what about the next morning, and the next? Had she felt disoriented? Like some unseen woodworker had carved away pieces of her, glued on new ones, so that she no longer fit in her old, worn groove?

I'd been back in Loch Gordon for six weeks now, and I couldn't just blame the jet lag anymore for how off I felt. That had gone away in a few days, but the uncertainty, the discordance, had stayed.

In spite of my feelings, or maybe because of them too, I latched hard onto my old routines, the ones that had defined my days before London, before Ross & Co., before Leo. I started every morning with an hour's jog out to the Hermanos Reyes Winery and back, brilliant green vines marching tidily up the hillsides, the roses at each end that signaled the health of the soil blooming salmon pink and sunshine yellow. I'd shower and dress, then go for my oat latte with hazelnut syrup that Walker would start making when he saw me come through the café door.

But when he'd texted the first week I was back, to ask if he could come by and "hang," I'd said sorry, that I just wanted to be friends. I told myself it was because I was adjusting after a while away, that I was going through a phase where my own touch was enough.

I didn't let myself think it was Leo's touch I craved. Leo wouldn't ever kiss me again like every one was the last, wouldn't ever run his hands reverently over my skin.

Now California spring light flooded through the Orchard House windows. We had just opened, and a few locals had come in first thing to pick up books they'd ordered. The tourists wouldn't arrive for another hour or so, as they came into town looking for lunch after their first wine tastings of the day.

I rubbed my hands across the warm varnished redwood of the store counter. Life was back to normal, everything the same. The dust motes drifted, the air smelled like paper and glue and French roast, Suzanne muttered in the office about the Department of Defense spending her hard-earned money on killing machines. It was nice. Peaceful.

It was like I hadn't cried silently for four hours over Canada on the flight back.

It was like I didn't miss Leo like I would miss the blue in the sky, the pink in the roses, the sugar in my coffee. I could go on without them, I could survive, but something fundamental was missing.

My phone buzzed, and I forgot the missing piece of me for a moment as I smiled at the new WhatsApp message. Jamie had texted me a picture of Danny plastered in mud after a rugby game. My dad wasn't all up in my business, which I appreciated, but he texted me every week to tell me what he'd read and ask what books I loved, and we'd scheduled a Zoom for this weekend.

I'd go back to London someday, to get to know him and Annika better, to spend quality time with Graham and Danny and Tim. Not for a while, though. I needed to let everything settle, let the memories of the past three months get farther away in my rearview mirror.

"An end of an era in bookselling," *The Guardian* had blared in the article I'd seen a few days ago, announcing the closure of Ross & Co., the building's sale to commercial developers. It had the usual odes to Alexander, his prowess, his charisma. But nothing about the Ross family now. What their future would be.

From the record player, Billie Holiday cried into the empty bookstore, "In my solitude, you haunt me."

Her voice, full of warmth and smoke and winter light, dragged my mind back to that bookstore basement in January, a siren song of stillborn dreams, lost love.

Why had I ever thought this song was cozy? It was the saddest fucking thing I'd ever heard.

I rubbed my face hard. Being on my own wasn't safe anymore. I was unarmed against everything the world had to throw at me. There was a gaping hole in the wall I'd put up, the one Leo had smashed open, and I couldn't rebuild it. I didn't even know if I wanted to.

Enough. I stalked around the corner to the record player, shoving the cover up.

"If you break that record, I'll make you pay for it," Suzanne said behind me, her many-ringed hands on her hips.

I yanked my hand back from the needle. "Sorry."

She stomped to the front door and shut it with a jingle. The "Closed" sign made a firm snap against the glass as she turned it. "I'm tired of you apologizing. Honestly, what happened to you?"

A reasonable part of me knew she was right to be frustrated. I'd told her a little about what happened with the shop, and a lot about meeting Jamie, but I'd kept everything about Leo to myself, like I was pressing a hand over a cut and refusing to look at how bad the damage was. I automatically shook my head. "Nothing. Don't worry about me."

"Bullshit. You've been walking around with a storm cloud over your head since you got back from London. I'm tired of pussyfooting. Tell me what's going on."

"I'm fine," I said, keeping my voice bland.

She raised her thin eyebrows. "Don't kid yourself, chickie. That crappy old mask of yours does the trick with other people, but it's never worked on me."

As I continued my stubborn silence, choosing to die on this particular hill, Suzanne stared down at the counter. "I made a mistake," she finally said.

I straightened. "What kind of mistake?" I asked carefully. "With the tax forms?"

She snorted for a second. "No. I made a mistake telling you I was going to give you the store."

A spike of panic made me blurt, "But I love it here. You can't give it to someone else."

She put her hand up. "When I promised this to you,

it meant you didn't have to take any risks." She said more gently, "And you won't jump unless you're pushed, chickie. It's not in your nature."

"But this is the life I want," I begged. "I want to be like you, more than anything."

She reached out and pressed her purple-manicured hands to my cheeks. "But I chose this after I ran a marathon. I have had a glorious life, and while there are days I look back on and cringe a little bit, I wouldn't trade a single one. You, Mari? You're giving up before you've even jogged a mile. What are you so afraid of?"

The ground was crumbling underneath me. "I'm not afraid of anything. I like it here. I like . . ." The tears started falling down my face. I wasn't even sure what I *liked* anymore, I just knew I wouldn't be secure anywhere else.

Suzanne tugged me into her arms for a hard hug, and I buried my face in her velvet-covered shoulder. "Oh, sweetheart," she said softly. "I made a safe place for you when you needed it the most, when you were just a kid. Your shithead stepfather didn't take care of you, even though he was all you had. He was frozen from the inside out, and you needed warmth and affection."

I nodded. "And you gave that to me. This is home. This is what I wanted to come back to."

She shook her head. "But that doesn't mean you can't take risks. That doesn't mean you can't love someone else, and let them love you."

The truth was written across her face. "You know about Leo," I realized aloud.

She smiled a little. "The Rosses and I have never had secrets from each other." She raised her hand when I protested. "I know, Leo hid the truth from you, the way your mom hid the truth about your real father. But did you tell him how hurt you were, what you needed?"

Ice formed in my stomach. "No. I didn't. I just . . . shut down." Because when things got hard, all I knew how to do was run and hide.

"Maybe you should let him talk to you. Then decide. From everything I know about him, he's a good boy and he wants to do right by you."

I gulped. "Why didn't he just say what he'd done?" I asked plaintively.

"Because I didn't know what I wanted at first," a totally-out-of-context voice said behind me. I whipped around, and Leo was standing in the bookstore doorway, hands in his pockets like it was a normal thing for him to be six thousand miles from home. "I'd been sleepwalking for so long, and I had none of your confidence," he continued, ignoring my agape mouth. "And then later, when I was awake, because I'd fallen in love with you, I was terrified you'd end things if you knew."

"What are you doing here?" I blurted, stunned.

"Trying very, very hard not to be a coward," he said, all seriousness.

"Did you arrange this?" I asked my boss.

Suzanne shook her head, smiling. "No."

"But you knew," I accused.

She shrugged lightly. "So what if I did? Is that really what matters to you right now?"

I looked again at Leo, my eyes and heart ravenous for him. He was still allergic to color, in his black jeans, T-shirt, and Converse. His hair was a total mess, a spray of raven feathers streaked silver. Skinny and intense, dark sunglasses covering his whiskey eyes, his mouth a firm line.

He carefully took off the sunglasses and put his browline glasses on. "How is it so bright outside? It's like you have ten times as much sun as anywhere else in the world."

"That's California for you," Suzanne said with abundant cheerfulness. "Speaking of California, I feel a pressing need for an avocado sandwich and green juice from that place in Healdsburg. I think I'll say hello at Copperfield's, too. Mari, you're in charge for the rest of the day."

"Thanks, Suzanne," Leo said. "Judith sends her love."

She patted his arm as she passed him, shouldering her battered woven purse. "Just be good to my chickie, huh? That's all the gratitude I need."

The bell rang brightly, then silence settled over us. My hands were fluttering helplessly, and I clamped them on the edge of the counter so I wouldn't fly away. "Welcome to Orchard House," I said, my voice cracking on the last word. "Can I help you find something today?"

He hesitated for a second, then decided to play along, sauntering up to me. He leaned against the counter and wrapped his hands around his elbows, a smile turning up one corner of his mouth. "I'm looking for a romance, actually. I read one a few weeks ago, then immediately went to a bookshop and bought three more."

A hysterical giggle jumped out of my mouth. "I mean, we have so many different ones. Is there any particular trope you like?"

Instead of answering right away, he leaned over the counter and rested his hand gently on top of mine, a question in his eyes. When I let go of the counter, he turned my hand palm up and placed a soft little kiss right in the center. Then his index finger found a daffodil petal and traced its edges, and he said softly, "Second chances. I love those."

I'd like one with a dark-haired alpha who drives away the love of his life and spends the rest of the book trying to get her back."

"But what if she doesn't deserve him?" I said, my voice suddenly thick with held-back tears. "What if she loves him too, but she's just as much of an alpha and runs away instead of talking things out?"

Long fingers touched my chin and tilted it up. "Then they'll fix it together." He wiped away the salt water on my cheek with his thumb. "Some days they'll think they're losing their minds, but they'll still love each other forever. I mean, he will if she'll let him. And he hopes with every bit of him that she'll love him, too." He sobered. "But this isn't a story, this is both our lives and it's all very real." He took a deep breath. "I'm so sorry, Mari. I'm sorry I didn't confide in you. You deserved my honesty and I wasn't brave enough to give it to you." He looked down. "I'm not expecting anything from you. I know I was a selfish arse, begging you to stay even after I'd hurt you, and that the distance makes everything horrendously complicated.

"But I need you to know that if you want to try again, I'll do my best every single day to be your partner, not just your lover. Because nothing is more precious to me than *your* trust. Nothing."

The relief of his words was so intense I could feel my hands shaking. "I want to try again," I finally said. "I want to do better for *you*, too. Because I held you at arm's length the whole time, even though my heart wanted you more than anything." I sighed. "I don't know how the hell this will work, but I love you, and I've missed you so much. It was like everything had gone dark, no color, no warmth."

"Perhaps that's a little dramatic? We can live without

each other, darling. I know we can. But it's like we can live when it's gray and cold outside. Sunlight makes everything better, though, doesn't it?"

I smiled at him. "It does. Though I've got to say, I think winter has new charms for me."

He grinned back. "For me, too. Now," he said, tapping the redwood, "any chance you might want to come around so I can kiss you properly?"

He reached for me as I came to him, and after one long, claiming kiss, he slowed down, gentled, but still stayed with me, his hands dallying on my waist, stroking up and down my back. I matched him, sank into warmth and tenderness. We didn't have to kiss like each one would be the last. We could love each other slowly. Deliberately.

But something was missing.

I pulled away slightly, our lips coming apart reluctantly. "I need to get you some hot chocolate."

"Cocoa sounds wonderful, even in this heat," he whispered back, "but I suppose that's not what you meant?"

I brushed my lips over his. "I miss the way you taste."

He buried his face in my neck and growled softly.

"I'm so sorry, baby. I'm sorry I chickened out," I told him, needing to atone more before I could let myself enjoy him.

He straightened a little and kissed my forehead. "Don't be. I needed to realize just how far up my arse my head had been. I'd been buried in my own rut for so long, and you leaving made me realize that I'd been holding on to things I should have let go of ages ago."

"How did it feel, to sell?" I asked.

"Right," he said simply. "It still hurt, though. But that's why I'm talking to a therapist about it."

I sighed. "Speaking of talking, I'm seeing someone to

go through all the history with Mom and Greg and Jamie. It's going to take a while for everything to make sense, and I might try to push you away in the meantime because of my stupid avoidant brain."

He shrugged. "Push all you like, I won't move. I'm going to be very stubborn when it comes to you."

"What if I hurt you?" I asked timidly.

He leaned in and rubbed his nose with mine. "You'll make it up to me. And I'll make it up to you, starting now."

He was close, and smelled so good, and all of a sudden all I wanted was his skin on mine. "Am I right in thinking you've been busy pining for me? That there hasn't been . . ." *anyone else?* I asked silently.

His eyebrows rose. "When I wasn't working on getting the shop ready for sale, I only dreamed of you. The same way you've only wanted to work here and listen to sad lady singers and long for me?" *No one else.*

"Exactly."

His eyes went dark. "Good," he said, and his approval sent goose bumps across my skin despite the heat. "I'm glad."

"Then I think there's a desk in the back office with our names on it," I teased.

A perfect devilish grin. "Lead the way."

I took his hand and led him through the back door into the lean-to of the office. He closed the door behind us and gently turned me around so that I was sitting on the edge of the desk. "No bending over. I want to see your beautiful face react to everything I do to you." He trailed his hands up under my dress and gently pushed my underwear to the side. "You are the loveliest thing, you know that? Every time I touch you, I think I'm dreaming." And then his lips were on my neck in an open-mouthed kiss, and his fingertips started drawing gentle little circles exactly where I needed them. As he stroked between my thighs, he trailed his mouth up to my ear, told me with a voice like dark chocolate and smoke that I was everything he'd ever wished for, so perfectly soft and hot and slick on his fingers, how he'd tortured himself in his lonely bed thinking of my sexy little sounds, how hard he was going to fuck me once he made me scream.

"Oh God, Leo, *please*," I begged as I pushed my hips into his hand.

He groaned. "*Yes*, that's right. Let me make you feel good, love. Let me give this to you."

His fingers pushed, thrust, beckoned, and with one hard press of his thumb and one little bite where my neck and shoulder met, I fell into my pleasure, jerking against his hand and crying out his name.

I was about to collapse back onto the desk, but then he jammed his fingers into his mouth, sucked, moaned, and my need for him, all of him, overrode anything else.

"Fuck me now, please, now," I chanted, opening up for him, until he'd fished out a condom from his wallet, unbuckled, unzipped, and I moaned with pleasure and relief as he pushed inside me.

"I missed your skin," I whispered as I ran my hands under his T-shirt, up his back. "It feels so good against mine."

A gasp cut off my words when he thrust. "This won't be pretty," he half laughed. "I missed you too much."

"I don't want pretty, I want *you*." I kissed him. "I love you."

His smile was pure sunlight. "I love you, too."

And then there was a lot of snarling and gasping, papers

and books sliding to the floor every which way, Leo's loose belt buckle pressing into my thigh, my fingernails digging into his back as he ground against me, chasing his pleasure until he yanked my hips tight to his and groaned into my shoulder.

It wasn't pretty, but it was us, and it was blissful. He buried his face in my neck and I tangled my fingers in his damp night-sky hair.

"My Mari," he sighed as he pulled out. "Let me clean you up."

Once we were zipped up and smoothed out, I moved toward the office door, but Leo gently tugged me back. "I need to hold you. It's been so long and I missed you so much."

He sat on the edge of the desk, and I nestled in his arms. "This feels so good," I said softly, inhaling his spicy scent and rubbing my cheek against the soft cotton of his shirt.

"Because it's where you live, darling. I thought that from the very beginning." He pressed his lips to my smile.

We were quiet together for a few minutes, wrapped up in love and safety. "How long are you here for? A few days?" I finally asked.

He pulled back a little so he could see my face. "I booked to stay until August."

I blinked. "Three months?" I said, my voice high with shock. "What the hell were you going to do if I said I couldn't do this?"

He smiled. "I had more certainty than that, thanks to Suzanne." He dotted a kiss on my nose. "But I figured if this didn't work out, I'd go traveling around America. I have the summer off before my course starts in September."

I wanted Leo to have as many adventures as he could, after the claustrophobic life he'd been living. But wait. "What course?"

"A short course in illustration at Central Saint Martins. If I do that and I love it, I'll apply in the spring for their graduate diploma."

I couldn't help myself, I squeezed him, pride making my hug tight. "You'll love it, I know it."

He smiled. "But that's later. For now, Suzanne has said I can help out around the shop a little, but I don't want to be underfoot all the time. I'll go exploring around here, too. There are so many places I want to draw already, the mountains and the vineyards and the buildings." He stroked my hair gently. "But I want to go to sleep with you every night, darling, and wake up with you. I want to try being together without holding anything back from each other." He brushed his lips over mine. "That's what would make me happy. Would that make you happy?"

I let the fear out, instead of shoving it in a small box and ignoring it. "What happens to us when your vacation is over? When you have to leave?"

He sighed. "I won't stop loving you just because you're not in the next room. I think I'd keep loving you even if you got on a spaceship to bloody Mars." He put his hand on my cheek. "In all honesty, I don't know what will happen after. But I want us to decide what to do *together*, when the time comes. Do you want that, too?"

The rush of rightness I felt was like a creek in spring. The fresh knowledge that we'd care for each other, that we'd support each other, coursed through me. "Yes," I said, my heart flying in my chest. "Let's do that."

CHAPTER THIRTY-ONE

TWO YEARS LATER

Mari

I stood in front of the floor-length bedroom mirror in Leo's flat in London Fields—no, my flat too now—loving the feel of the June sunlight on my skin as I brushed out my hair. I had been awake since before six because of the midsummer dawn creeping through the bedroom windows. Ordinarily I might be mad about the early wake-up call, but excitement and anticipation were better than caffeine for tiredness. I'd gone into the kitchen, brewed coffee and made cinnamon toast for the both of us, then carried it back to the bedroom just to see the look of surprise and pleasure on Leo's face. He made me feel so cared-for every single day, and I loved knowing that I could show him the same kind of care.

Now, a few hours later, Leo wandered in, studying

his tablet, and my hands paused as I watched his reflection. His navy suit pants sat low on his narrow hips, and his navy-and-white flowered shirt hung open, showing golden skin leftover from his last trip to California. After some persuading and cat-calling from me, he'd spent a lot of time sitting by the pool at Suzanne's house reading Dorothy Sayers mysteries wearing just a pair of swim trunks and sunglasses, and it turned out the sun glanced at him and he tanned like an Italian movie star, the jerk.

But if I watched him for too long, we'd end up back in bed. "How much longer do we have?"

"Fifteen minutes until Graham and Catriona come get us," he said, marking something on the tablet with a stylus.

I smiled to myself. He'd become a little bit dreamy over the last year, coming home from the college studio full of ideas, his hands always moving on his tablet or his sketchbook. He'd even gotten his first commission, making pen-and-ink drawings of London street scenes for a new travel website. I loved that he had something that gave him so much joy, that he was letting his creativity run free instead of shoving it in a too-small box.

But we had places to be. I swept my hair over my shoulder, the opal in my vintage engagement ring flashing rainbows in the sunlight. "Zip me up?" I asked with a purr.

My love looked up to meet my eyes in the mirror and smiled. "With pleasure." He put his tablet on top of the bureau, then his bare feet padded across the wooden floor to stand behind me. He zipped the bottle-green silk up my back, then he placed a tender little kiss on my neck, then another next to it, then another . . .

I couldn't help but close my eyes from how good it felt.

"You look really handsome in navy, but it must be thirteen minutes now."

He growled softly and ran his hands down my sides, teased his fingertips at the hem of the short dress. "I can be quick, if you want me to."

I bit back a moan. I had extremely fond memories of being yanked into a random janitor's closet on a vineyard tour in Napa and Leo's mouth and fingers sending me to heaven in three minutes flat. "I want you to take your time with me tonight. When we're at the hotel."

"No, I wasn't planning to very thoroughly consummate our marriage. I was thinking we'd watch telly and fall asleep without touching. But I suppose your idea is better."

I loved how he could go from turning me on to cracking me up so easily. "Devil boy."

"All yours, darling," he said with a smirk.

"But now—" I held up a bottle of tinted moisturizer, and with one last peck on my cheek, he waved his hand and turned around to finish getting dressed while I did my makeup.

Yes, we were a little cheesy, I thought as I smoothed on the moisturizer. But it just felt . . . right. Right to wake up in the morning and wrap myself around him. Right to feel that little lightning bolt of excitement when he walked into the room. Right to go to the pub with Graham and Catriona and hold hands under the table. It had taken a year of dating long-distance, crisscrossing the Atlantic when it was a particularly quiet time at Orchard House or when he had a break from studying.

I painted on pale eyeshadow and curled my eyelashes as I remembered how last June, I'd gotten to the arrivals area at the international terminal at SFO ridiculously late at night. Leo's flight had been delayed, the turbulence over Canada had been unusually terrible, and my poor boyfriend was ragged and exhausted. When he'd gotten down on his knees, I thought he was so tired he didn't know what he was doing. It was only when he held out a ring, a sparkling opal flanked by two tiny diamonds, the jewels emerging from gold scrolling leaves, that my brain turned from fear into amazement. I was so grateful for every conversation we'd had, every love letter Leo had written in messy blue script and sent across the ocean, every kiss and touch we'd claimed when we were together in person. But this moment was more than I'd ever dreamed of in all my lonely life.

"I love you. I love you, I love you," I'd blurted, kneeling on the cold airport floor.

He'd smiled tiredly. "I had a whole proposal planned, but I suppose I only have to say please?"

He was so funny and so smart and he wanted to be mine forever. "Yes. Yes to all of it."

Of course, it hadn't been that easy. We'd had to decide where we would live and, when we'd finally agreed that we'd live in London for the first few years, securing a fiancée visa for me had taken many more months than it was supposed to. I'd finally landed at Heathrow at the beginning of March, and Leo greeted me at the airport with endless kisses and an armful of daffodils, an explosion of spring just for me.

Leo stood behind me again in the mirror, tying a plain navy tie as I stained my lips watermelon pink. He was already wearing a navy jacket over the shirt, and dark brown brogues so well polished I could have done my makeup in them instead of the mirror.

When I finished blotting, he put light hands on my hips and admired our reflection. "So pretty," he said softly.

I leaned back against him a little bit, getting a hit of his bay rum shower gel. "You're the artist, you would know."

He reached over and grabbed his phone.

"We need to go?" I asked.

"Two minutes. Plenty of time." He tugged on my arm so that I'd turn around.

"For what? One hundred twenty seconds aren't..." I stopped, because Leo's mouth was on mine, slow and loving and thoroughly ravishing. I lost myself to his chocolate taste, to his grasping hands, to the attraction that burned between us hotter and hotter all the time.

After a moment, he pulled back, his mouth stained pink and turned up in his most evil grin. "I would say I'm sorry..."

"Yeah, yeah, yeah," I joked, handing him my trusty jar of makeup-remover gel.

Ten seconds after I finished repainting my mouth, the flat buzzer rang. That would be Catriona and Graham coming to walk us to Hackney Town Hall. Neither of us had wanted a big, flashy ceremony—just our closest people around us: Suzanne, Judith and Tommy, Jamie and Annika and the boys, Elaine and David and the twins. But tonight, at the old antique shop space Leo had bought with his Ross & Co. money, we'd have a party with his friends from his course, Bex and Paul, Vinay and Sonali, and, of course, the whole Beckett gang. There'd be champagne and chocolate cake, hugs and cheers and toasts, and I couldn't wait to be surrounded by all that sweetness, all that love.

And then? Then I'd build a new bookstore. It'd be small, with soft cushions in the bay window and a cozy children's section downstairs at the back. It would be a store, but it would also be a gathering place, a refuge for anyone who needed it.

I slipped on my yellow kitten heels, checked my vintage clutch to make sure I had my lipstick, phone, and keys, then headed for the door. But Leo's gentle hand on my forearm stopped me.

He looked down at me, his whiskey eyes bright. "I know it's about to get really busy," he said, his voice warm and velvety, "so I wanted to tell you that I love you, and I think this is going to be the best day of my life."

"Oh, so it's all downhill from here?" I wrapped my arm around his waist. "I love you, too. So much. And how about it's the best first day of our lives?" Because before we'd met, we'd both thought in our own ways that our lives were over just as they'd begun, that we were stuck doing the same things forever. It had taken meeting each other, pushing each other, giving ourselves away to each other, to make us realize that our lives were what we made them. We were each other's spring, each other's new beginning.

He nodded, his cheeks pink. "I like that. I like that very much." He leaned down and kissed the tip of my nose. "Now, let's get started."

ACKNOWLEDGMENTS

Sometimes if you want something to exist, you have to make it yourself.

For the last fifteen years, I've been carrying around an Arts Emergency badge with these words on them. It's a good principle for embarking on big adventures, reaching out to new friends, forming a community, building a life thousands of miles from where I grew up. And of course, writing another book! But I didn't make anything alone, so here's a great big tribute to everyone who helped bring Mari and Leo's love story to life.

In case you missed it, *Love Walked In* is a book-length love letter to indie bookstores! First and foremost, thank you to The Broadway Bookshop, my local indie and refuge. Particular thanks to Tom for his idiosyncratic recommendations, his genuine curiosity about romance (even though he hasn't read any, *yet*), and for being an all-around kind and thoughtful human being. Back in California, Brad Johnson and the team at East Bay Booksellers in Oakland were part of what kept me sane and well-read during the worst of the pandemic. Thank you for being your stubborn, nerdy selves, and may you rise from the literal ashes even better than before. Shoutouts as well to the indies who generously hosted events for *The Slowest Burn*: Omnivore Books (with The Ruby) in San Francisco, Smitten Bookstore in Ventura, and The Ripped Bodice in Culver City and Brooklyn.

Thank you so much to the wonderful friends and family who came out to support me in London and across the US, and the amazing authors who partnered with me at events: Kate Leahy, Elissa Sussman, and Sarah MacLean.

Thank you as well to all of the talented and generous writers who read and said lovely things about *The Slowest Burn*: Emma Barry, Mia Hopkins, Emma Hughes, Laura Kay, Erin La Rosa, Lily Lindon, Cressida McLaughlin, Annabel Monaghan, Cecilia Rabess, Bethany Rutter, and Laura Wood.

Speaking of saying nice things, thank you so much to *The Slowest Burn* readers who have emailed and posted about the book! I'm so glad Kieran and Ellie resonated with you, and it means a lot to me that you took the time to get in touch.

I'm grateful for the work of the following writers, whose words inspired *Love Walked In*: Anne Fadiman (*Ex-Libris: Confessions of a Common Reader*), Lewis Buzbee (*The Yellow-Lighted Bookshop*), Jeff Deutsch (*In Praise of*

Good Bookstores), and of course, Helene Hanff (*84, Charing Cross Road*).

Thank you to the London borough of Hackney for maintaining warm, comfortable, and free libraries I could escape to when I needed to write and edit away from my house. Thank you as well to the Arvon Foundation for their self-guided retreats at the Clockhouse in Shropshire. Six days of solitude in the countryside was exactly what I needed to finish the first draft of *Love Walked In*.

To Heather Jackson—I tell everyone I have the best agent in the entire world, and that's no exaggeration. Thank you for being so incredibly supportive and generous with your time and energy, and I can't wait to meet up for another lychee martini soon.

To Alex Sehulster and the rest of the dream team at SMP—I'm so glad I got to collaborate with you all on another book! It wouldn't be nearly as good without your hard work. Thank you for everything you do.

To the author friends I've met virtually and in real life in the last few years—writing and publishing a novel is strange and difficult as well as hugely exciting, and I appreciate you being there to talk about all the ups and downs. Thank you particularly to Martha Waters for London writing dates, Emma Hughes for your kind words and encouragement after reading the roughest beginnings of *Love Walked In*, and Anna Bliss for hashing out plot points with me in long transatlantic phone calls, and for the flurry of excited emails you sent me while reading the first draft.

To Nicola Swift—thank you for going on retreat in the Kent countryside with me, cooking delicious food, and being the accountability buddy I desperately needed for several brutal days of developmental edits.

To Julie Coryell—thank you for sharing your invaluable bookstore knowledge, and for being such an energetic cheerleader for my work from the very beginning.

To my parents—thank you for making me think a house literally packed with books is completely normal and desirable. And thank you to my mom in particular, because I wouldn't be writing novels now, especially ones about bookstores, if you hadn't always been happy to drive me to A Clean, Well-Lighted Place for Books (RIP) and Barnes & Noble.

To my beloved husband—thank you for loving books and reading as much as I do, for supporting me and looking after me as I draft and redraft and swear and draft some more, and for being the absolute best thing to come out of moving to the UK all those years ago.

And to my British friends, from the earliest days in Edinburgh (Super Robot Monkey Team Hyperforce Go!) to this exact moment—you make me laugh, you make me think, you comfort me when things get hard and celebrate with me when times are good. Above all, you make this place home. I am profoundly lucky and so, so grateful for all of you. (And I'm sorry for embarrassing you with this deeply earnest public display of affection. You know I can't help it.)

ABOUT THE AUTHOR

Andria Lo

Sarah Chamberlain is a writer, editor, and cookbook translator whose articles have appeared in *The Guardian* (UK), *Food52*, and *McSweeney's Internet Tendency*. When she's not writing witty, sexy contemporary romance, she enjoys making dinner for her friends and family, watching Cary Grant movies, and setting records as an amateur competitive powerlifter. Originally from Northern California, she lives in London.